Unwritten

Unspoken Series Book 1

M.C. DECKER

*Brynn,
your future is
always unwritten!
xxoo
M.C. Decker*

UNWRITTEN
Copyright ©2014 M.C. Decker
All rights reserved. No part of this publication may be reproduced, distributed or transmitted in any form or by any means including electronic, mechanical, photocopying, recording, or otherwise, without the prior written consent of the author.

This book is a work of fiction. Names, characters, places and incidents either are products of the author's imagination or are used fictitiously. Any resemblance to actual events, locales or persons, living or dead, is entirely coincidental and beyond the intent of the author or publishers.

Cover Design: Kari Ayasha, Cover to Cover Designs
Interior Formatting and Design: Christine Borgford, Perfectly Publishable
Cover photos: Mandy Hollis, MHPhotography stock and custom photos

Connect with M.C. Decker

Facebook:
https://www.facebook.com/authormcdecker

Goodreads:
https://www.goodreads.com/book/show/21847053-unwritten?from_search=true

E-mail:
author.mcdecker@yahoo.com

Twitter: @AuthorMCDecker

About the Author

M.C. Decker is the author of the upcoming, debut novel, *Unwritten*. She lives in a suburb of Flint, Michigan with her husband, Brian, and spoiled-rotten Siamese cat, Simon. For the last decade, she has worked as a journalist for several community newspapers in Michigan's Thumb region. She enjoys all things '80s and '90s pop culture: movies, boy bands, music and especially the color, hot pink. She also strictly lives by the motto, "Life is better in flip flops," and is a diehard Detroit Tigers fan. You can e-mail her at author.mcdecker@yahoo.com. She would love to hear from you.

To my mom; my role model; and my best friend:

While writing this book, I often wondered what your words of encouragement would be, but I know you would have told me to push through and that you believe in me, always. Thank you for being the greatest mom a girl could ever have. And, thank you for introducing me to the boxes of Harlequin Romance Novels that would come in the mail each week. That is how I know that you would approve of your daughter writing a "smutty" book without even blushing. I just wish more than anything that you could have had the opportunity to read it. Love you and miss you, always.

Prologue

October 2011

There was a limousine waiting for me when I exited the terminal at Dulles International Airport, just a little after daybreak. I'd only ridden in a limo once before and it had been with *him*. I never imagined a potential employer going to such extremes for an interviewee. First, I received first-class boarding passes and now a stretch Hummer with my very own driver. This was certainly a few hundred steps above my current, small-town, reporting gig.

Even while riding in the lap of luxury, I couldn't shake the butterflies fighting in my stomach, or the incredibly sweaty palms that I kept wiping on my navy, pinstriped, pencil skirt. Thankfully, I decided to forgo breakfast before catching the red-eye out of Detroit. That would've made the butterfly situation a whole lot worse.

I could do this. I should have researched the editor, Davis, a bit more. Why didn't I think of doing it two days earlier? Where was the brown paper bag when you needed it? They were always so readily available to the broken heroines in the kinky romance novels that I enjoyed reading.

After what seemed to be a short drive, the limo began to slow down in front of a large building with oversized, tinted glass windows. Both an American flag and the flag of Washington D.C. flanked the entrance of my destination, the home of the *Washington Post*. Before the car came to a stop, I wiped my sweaty palms one final time, pulled my compact from my purse, applied a light pink lip gloss and took a deep breath. *Showtime!*

My driver came around and escorted me from the car. For that I was thankful, as I'm not sure my nervous, wobbly legs could have survived my new ankle-strap, cream leather Louboutins that I purchased just for this interview. Sure, they may have cost me half an entire paycheck, but I wanted to look the part of an up-and-coming Washington reporter. My new shoes paired nicely with the vintage Valentino suit jacket that I found on clearance at my favorite consignment store and with my favorite go-to, pencil skirt.

I made my way up the front stairs, opened the heavy doors and headed toward the receptionist's desk. There sat a young blonde with what appeared to be a fake rack and an even faker tan.

"Hi, I'm Brooke … Brooke Anderson. I'm here for an interview with Mr. Davis."

The much-too-perky female handed me a visitor's badge and directed me to the twelfth floor where I was to ask for Mr. Davis's secretary, Caroline. I waited at the elevators for what seemed like an eternity before the doors opened and a group of people pressed forward.

A few suits exited the elevator on the sixth floor before the doors, pinging open on the twelfth floor, snapped me out of my nervous trance. I straightened my skirt and began to exit the elevator when I collided with all solid muscle and six feet three inches of him. And, that smell – why did this man smell so familiar? ... I hadn't smelled that perfect scent since ... it's then that I looked up and was greeted by those teal eyes. I'd never forget those eyes – those eyes that I never believed I would gaze into again. It was immediate déjà vu. I'd met him like this once before, only eleven years earlier. I had been a young and naïve student with so much to learn about life, love and heartache. I felt my heart begin to race and I feared that it might actually leap from my chest.

I thought it was too late for us. I thought our story had already been written. ...

PART ONE:

September 2000

I remember the first time I saw him, stepping off the elevator, on my way to journalism class, chatting with my best friend Cassidy and not paying too much attention; that's when I collided with all six feet three inches of all solid-man muscle. Against my tiny, five feet three inch frame, it felt like I had hit a solid brick wall.

Standing against his chest, I couldn't help but breathe in his intoxicating scent – a mix between Giorgio Armani's Acqua Di Gio and Irish Spring Body Wash. What can I say? I know my fragrances. I worked at a drugstore the previous summer and all my male friends from high school wanted my advice on the cologne that would be sure to "get them laid." I would always tell them Acqua Di Gio. After all, it was almost a sure thing. In fact, just this man's heady scent alone was making my lady parts pool with desire.

I remember peeling myself back and looking up into his striking, tealish blue eyes which reminded me of the deepest depths of the ocean. Those eyes alone stopped me dead in my tracks. And, let's not forget his perfectly chiseled jaw and Hollywood smile and that shaggy, messed-up, yet perfectly styled, chocolate brown hair. He was my ideal man ... until he opened his mouth.

"Hey, can you watch where you're going? You're going to make me late for my class."

"Ugh, underclassmen, never paying attention," he continued under his breath.

I stood just inches away from him, utterly speechless. I wasn't sure if it was because of my awe over his perfect male beauty, or because he was such a dickface. Probably a combination of both, I would guess.

"Wow, you don't have to be a complete jackass," Cassidy yelled back in my defense.

I made a mental note to thank her later before finally talking, "Shhh, Cass, it's not worth it. He's not worth it."

Well, so much for that. Dream over and let the nightmare begin! I went from feeling an instant, butterflies-in-my-tummy attraction to an instant sense of dreaded annoyance. To make matters worse – much worse – I followed him right into room 208 and straight into my Journalism 101 course.

"You have got to be freakin' kidding me," I muttered under my breath.

I soon learned that Mr. Gorgeous Asshole's name was Rich Davis. He was a year my senior and thought he knew everything! Every time he opened his mouth it was to suck up to Professor Markley, or to correct another student. Ugh, he really just made my skin crawl.

When I found out that I was paired up with him for a writing assignment during the third week of class, I just wanted to vomit right then and there. Maybe then I could get out of it and pass it off as the latest stomach bug making its way around campus. Who cares if it would be a little embarrassing? I was known as Brooke the Klutz during my high school days, so what would a little vomit-and-dash incident really matter? Besides, I was already spoken for and completely in love with Jason James so I really couldn't have cared less what other male students in the class thought about me. And the girls would just feel bad for me and give thanks that it hadn't happened to them.

Oh, it would never work. With my coordination, I'd somehow slip and fall in my own puke.

"Miss Anderson, please move your seat over to where Mr. Davis is sitting so you can start on your assignment," Professor Markley said with an annoyed tone.

Crap, I'd been in my own vomit- induced stupor so I totally zoned out. Way to go, Brooke. Give Davis even more of a reason to be a complete douche monkey.

I quickly scooted over to sit in the empty chair next to Rich; that's when I was once again infiltrated with that most delicious scent – one that I can only describe as "man" ... I know. Cliché, right? But, oh, so true! It was almost as if he bathed in the Irish Sea and then spritzed himself with fresh pears and melons. *Seriously, again, Brooke? Snap the fuck out of it! He's gonna think you're an alien sucking in its very last breath. You despise this man, remember?*

"Soooo, you're Brooke, right? I don't think we've been formally introduced. I'm Rich Davis, third year. I'm an English major, but I decided to add this new journalism minor. So, that's why I'm here in this intro course. What about you?"

"Right, I'm Brooke … Brooke Anderson. I'm a sophomore majoring in political science. I worked on my high school newspaper and really liked it, so I thought I would give this new minor a whirl, too. I figure maybe I can mix the two, you know, work for the *Washington Post* one day."

"Cool," he replied apathetically.

I swear I saw the jackass roll his sexy eyes at me. You just watch, Mister, I WILL work for the Post someday!

"So have you read over the assignment? I guess we're each supposed to write an article of our choosing for the *Eagle* and then we need to critique each other's work. Markley is giving us two days to finish, but it seems pretty easy to me. I'm thinking we could get this knocked out by tomorrow," he added so flippantly.

"Uh, OK. I have an obligation this evening and have a few other assignments, but I guess I could move this to the top and shoot for tomorrow."

And now I had completely forgotten about that most amazing scent and those cerulean eyes. How the eff was I going to get this assignment done by tomorrow? Ugh, this brownnosing jackass is just infuriating. I couldn't wait for class to end just so I could get on with my day and forget all about Hotty McAsshole.

I ran back to my dorm, which was only slightly bigger than my bedroom at home, but jammed with double the stuff, to quickly change before heading to my sorority's recruitment-mixer event co-hosted with Chi Omega. I threw on a black camisole and layered it with an off-white, crocheted sweater. I decided to stick with the flared-leg jeans I was already wearing and slid on a pair of black flip-flops that were hiding out behind my clothes hamper. I ran a brush through my thick, wavy hair, ran some gloss over my lips and checked myself in the mirror. Pleased with my reflection, I headed out the door for a night of mingling and obnoxious sorority cheers. Really, I love my sorority sisters, but the constant clapping, bopping up and down and loud screaming could really get annoying especially after a long day dealing with gorgeous, yet super-irritating, upperclassmen. I heard the familiar chant of one of our famous recruitment cheers as I headed to the Chi house on the west end of campus.

"Hey Brookie, how was Markley's class today?" my roomie and bestie, Cassidy, asked as I walked over to grab a slice of pepperoni pizza.

Cassidy Carpenter and I had been best friends almost since birth – literally; we were born just a day apart. I always harassed her for being a day older, too. It usually worked out to my advantage except when she turned sixteen and was able to drive a day before I could, or when she turned eighteen and bought a lotto ticket to wave in my face. I'm sure she would use it to her advantage in a few years when she would be able to legally down a beer a day before me, too. Not that it really mattered anyways, because we were already drinking every weekend.

Cassidy and I have pretty much been inseparable our entire lives. Since we were both only children, we shared everything with each other – from our secret crushes to our annoying problems with pimples. I remember acting out plays in her living room and making candy out of snow and pancake syrup in my kitchen. We would sit on the phone for hours each night until our moms would literally have to pry the receivers out of our hands. She was my breath of fresh air and I was her stable rock. Of the two of us, I was definitely the more focused one, but she always taught me to have a little fun, too.

We both attended the same Catholic school before going our separate ways in high school, but still remained close and decided to go to college together at Western Michigan University, just as we had planned as girls in pigtails, swinging on the jungle gym. We always knew we were going to be Broncos, pretty much since birth, because both of our dads played on the football team and were also best friends, or "bros," as they called each other in "man code."

Anyways, that's how Cassidy and I met – through our dads. The two of them had us wearing Western Michigan Broncos onesies straight out of the womb. So, we were both ecstatic when we were accepted into Western, not only because it would thrill our dads but also because it was close to the Lake Michigan shore and only about a two-hour drive to Chicago. We both loved spending time at the lake in the summer and who doesn't love a shopping expedition in Chicago? My bestie was also a fashionista of sorts and now that we lived together, I loved to raid her closet.

"Ugh, don't even get me started," I responded to her question, trying not to get pizza sauce all over my sweater. "What the heck happened to you? Did you decide flirting with Sean over Instant Messenger was more important than class, or what?" I asked, giving her the eye roll.

Cassidy was absolutely gorgeous with her strawberry blonde hair and big brown eyes. I swear the girl could eat anything in sight and not gain an ounce. Unlike me, who hit the gym every morning, she hardly had to lift a finger to keep her petite frame. In fact, I think she had already consumed an entire pizza by herself. She really made me sick most days. Practically every guy on campus wanted Cassidy Carpenter, yet she was obsessed with the already-taken, Sean Thompson.

"Shut your face, bi-atch," she responded. "And, how the h-e-double-l do you know me so well? He kept telling me how cute I looked in astronomy this afternoon. I couldn't ditch him after that. I think we might actually have something going."

"Gag me," I shot back. … "He has a girlfriend at home, ding-a-ling. Or, did you forget that?"

"Different zip code, doesn't count," she explained with a wink.

"Does, too, count. I would bust a Lorena Bobbitt on Jay's ass if I ever found out he tried to pull that 'different zip code' bullshit," I hissed back at her, using air quotes.

"Calm down, Brookie, you know I wouldn't really do anything with Sean anyways. Just wishing he would dump the blonde Barbie at home, that's all."

"Oh, Cass, I love you. I pray that one day you find a single boy to Internet flirt with," I said, before bursting into hysterical laughter while, at the same time, dodging her flying fists. "P.S. - you know you are a blonde Barbie, too, right?" I added as I fled to the opposite side of the room.

I spent the next few hours plastering on my fakest smile and chitchatting with half the freshmen class. I kept thinking about what a long night it would be trying to research and write an article for Markley's class. Maybe I could write about egotistical juniors and just interview the most conceited one I knew.

"So, you never did tell me how Markley's class went today. Did I miss anything?" Cass asked, as we finally made our way home after the mixer.

"Other than Rich getting under my skin for the billionth time and Markley pairing us together for a writing assignment ... um, no, not much," I answered, as nonchalantly as possible.

"Whaaaaat? You have to work with the most beautiful jackass to ever grace this campus? Glad it's you and not me, friend. I would be sent to the dean for either molesting that boy, or kicking him in the nuts - depending on my mood."

"Right," I responded with a chuckle. "Our assignment isn't due until Wednesday, but Rich wants to finish it by tomorrow. So, I guess I need to get my ass to the library."

"All right, I'm gonna put my sweats and bunny slippers on and wait for Sean to get back from his night class. ... At least that's where his Away Message status tells me where he's at."

"Stalking and bunny slippers? Sexy, Cass … real sexy."

With that, I felt one of her bunnies hit the back of my head as I walked toward the bathroom that we shared with an adjoining room. I quickly changed into a more comfortable pair of black yoga pants and threw on my favorite Michigan State Spartans' sweatshirt before heading out the door in pursuit of the quiet stacks of the campus library.

As I walked through the library's dimly lit entrance, I noticed Mr. Brownnoser himself. I considered acting as if I didn't see him, but I must have been thinking too hard because as I began digging in my purse, as if to make a phone call, he started yelling at me across the room.

"Brooke, I'm working on our assignment. Come join me?"

"Hey, Rich … sure."

I walked over to where he was sitting and dropped my heavy shoulder bag onto the round table. What a relief! I really needed to invest in something lighter and less cumbersome. Sure, my sorority letters attached to the side were cute, but it wasn't worth the pain in my neck, literally. I took a seat next to Rich and was rummaging through my bag looking for my notepad when he broke my concentration.

"I decided to write my article on the recurring injuries on the varsity football team," he began. "I'm just researching some physical therapy books now. I already scheduled an interview with the athletic director, football coach and head trainer for first thing in the morning."

Of course he did. Ugh, who was this guy? He can't possibly have any social life which is so weird considering how GORGEOUS he is.

"Hey, are you there?"

"Uh, yeah, sorry. It's been a really long day and I'm beat, but I told you I'd have this done by tomorrow. ... So, here I am."

"Right, so, Brooke, what is the subject of your article?" he asked.

"Well, I decided to go with an opinion piece," I replied. (Mainly because I didn't think about scheduling interviews and I certainly didn't have time for that now. But, I thought I would leave Rich out of that little secret). "Since the election is coming up, I thought I would write about the pros and cons of the Electoral College and how the candidate with more popular votes can sometimes lose the election."

I must admit, for thinking of a topic on the fly, I was pretty proud of myself. I think I'll give myself a proverbial pat on the back. Way to go, Brooke.

"Riiiiight. ... You know, that would NEVER actually happen?"

"ACTUALLY, it's happened three times in history. Did you know Benjamin Harrison actually received more popular votes than Grover Cleveland?"

"Hmmph, I meant in like today's era. That was, what, like 1884," he said, as more of a statement than a question.

"Whoa ... Mr. Smarty Pants got one wrong. It was actually 1888," I spat back, feeling slightly superior.

"Whatever, it will still never happen again. Your article is going to be a waste of time. I thought you said your dream was to write for the *Washington*

Post? They would never publish such farfetched, political propaganda."

"Well, I believe it could very well happen again this year. And that, Davis, is why they call it an opinion piece, and when it does happen … you can kiss my ass."

He paused for a moment and I could briefly see a spark in those sexy blues of his. Then – in barely a whisper – he said, "I wish, Brooke. I wish."

What the hell? I must be really tired or really delusional or both because I didn't just hear him say that. You're imaging shit now, Brooke Christine Anderson. Get a grip.

After that, we worked in silence for what seemed like forever. I got up a few times to grab some reference books from the shelves and he prepared his interview questions. I completed a fairly good outline and decided I would wake up before class to finish my writing.

It was approaching eleven o'clock and I wanted to be home before Jay called. We'd had a standing phone date each night at that time since he moved "Up North" to Michigan's Upper Peninsula two years ago to attend Michigan Tech. After packing my bag and heaving it over my shoulder, I muttered goodnight over my shoulder to Rich. I swear I heard him say, "Goodnight, beautiful girl," as I headed toward the door. *Seriously, I either need to make an appointment with the school nurse to get my hearing tested, or with the counselor to get my head examined.*

Jason James or Jay, as he was known by everyone around our town, and I were high school sweethearts. I met him my first day of my freshman year. He was the stud sophomore, baseball player and I was the new girl who transferred to the public school after spending nine years becoming educated by the nuns at St. Mary's Catholic School.

If there was such a thing as "love at first sight," I think that's what Jay and I had. We had that instantaneous spark of chemistry people often talk about. He asked me to have lunch with him that day and we were inseparable for three years.

All of my high school memories involved Jay. We swayed as one at both of our proms. I watched as he was crowned prom king his senior year and he returned the favor the following year by watching as I was named homecoming queen.

I was his personal cheerleader during every baseball game and he held my hand in the emergency room after I slipped on some ice a few winters back and broke my wrist. (Remember, I said I was known as Brooke the Klutz).

It was one of the hardest days of my life watching my Jay-Jay Bear pack up his Chevy Blazer before making the four hundred mile, seven-hour drive to his new home and away from my everyday existence.

But, even with the distance, we had already made it work for two years. He called me every night at eleven o'clock. I think in those two years we have only missed a handful of telephone dates. Really, those twenty to thirty minutes were the highlight of my day. I couldn't wait to hear his voice each night before falling asleep.

I was relieved when I got back to the room and Cassidy told me I hadn't missed my call from Jay. I figured I still had a few minutes to take care of my nightly routine before he called, so I padded off to the bathroom. I was in the middle of applying my face scrub when I heard the phone ring.

"Hey Jay-Jay Bear," I heard Cassidy say as she answered the phone from the other room. "Hang on a sec. She's getting herself all pretty for your nightly phone sex ... I mean date."

"CASSIDY! Shut up and hand me the phone. You ARE crazy!" I screamed at her as I grabbed the phone and plopped down onto my plush comforter.

Jay and I talked for about half an hour before he had to end our conversation to finish some mechanical engineering homework. I told him about my day, the sorority mixer and studying in the library; I didn't mention Rich at all. Not because I was trying to hide anything ... after all, I did loathe the guy, but I just didn't see any reason to get Jay jealous about me talking, or studying with other guys.

He talked for at least ten minutes about the Yankees game. Evidently one of the players, a Derek Jeter or something like that, hit a grand slam against the Texas Rangers to clinch a playoff spot for his beloved team. I really couldn't have cared less. I never understood why he loved the damn Yankees so much anyways. We both grew up just an hour or so from Detroit and I had always rooted for the Tigers. Well, honestly, I didn't really care all that much for baseball in general, but if someone asked I would cheer for the "Old English D." I guess Jay just liked to be different and since he had a number of relatives living in the Bronx, he had adored the Yankees since he was pretty much still in Pampers.

After hanging up, I decided to grab the latest issue of *US Weekly* before calling it a night. (Don't judge me. ... I enjoy my latest celebrity gossip). Cassidy was still over at her desk bopping her head to the beat of whatever bubblegum, boy band she was listening to and giggling at everything Sean Thompson tossed her way. I swear she was worse than a puppy about to get a Milk-Bone. If I listened closely enough I could probably hear her panting.

I think I fell asleep somewhere between reading about Jennifer Aniston and Brad Pitt's honeymoon and the recent star athletes of the Sydney Olympics. I woke up the next morning with the crinkly magazine pages off to the side and my glasses still fixed on my face. *Fuck what time is it?* I looked at my clock and the red digits glared back that it was nine-fifty in the morning. *NO! NO! NO! Class starts in ten minutes and I didn't finish writing my article.*

I quickly ran to the bathroom: brushed my teeth, washed my face and tried to run a comb through my thick brown, tangled tresses. Since that didn't seem to be working too well, I grabbed a scrunchie off the counter and twisted my hair into a half-knot on top of my head. Once I was finished in the bathroom, I ran to my wardrobe, grabbed a sports bra and cotton panties, threw on a faded pair of jeans and one of Jay's baseball T-shirts, and slipped on the same flip-flops as the previous night, before rushing out the door.

I got to class right as Markley was taking roll call for the day. *Good thing our classes all start at ten past the hour. It never really made any sense to me until today.* I slipped into the empty seat next to Rich right before I heard Markley say, "Miss Anderson?"

"Present," I called out. *Phew.*

"Here's my article. Want to read it? We can trade," Rich said, as he shoved some papers in my face.

Fuck, I was so busy worrying about making it to class on time I forgot about the damn article. Think ... you need an excuse Brooke. ...

"Sorry, Rich, I need until tomorrow. I want to head back to the library to do some more research before I let you see my draft. I want to make sure this is such a brilliant opinion that I even have you bowing down before me." *Ha! Eat that, jackass.*

"So, you flaked out and didn't finish, huh? It's OK, I figured you for the slacker-type anyways," he harrumphed.

"Whatever, don't be an ass, it's not due until tomorrow, anyways," I shot back. "Take a chill pill, will ya? Where do you get off anyways? ... What the fuck is your problem?" I couldn't help spewing off a series of insults ... He really did know how to get under my skin.

"My problem is that I don't have time for people who don't take their work seriously, always so wrapped up in college drama. I came here to study and earn my degree so I can get a good job. People like you just waste my time."

"Talk to the hand," I said in my best Alicia Silverstone impression. I know it was stupid and immature, but I was so exasperated with this guy that I didn't have any snappy comeback for him. "I'll have my assignment when it's due – tomorrow."

I didn't talk to him for the rest of the period; I just sat in the chair and stewed. I probably could have used the hour to write my damn opinion piece but this cocksucker really pissed me off. I wanted to smack him upside the head, but what I really didn't want was for him to see the tears beginning to pool in my eyes. This guy would not get the satisfaction of seeing me cry. Finally, the clock above the door read eleven o'clock and I couldn't get myself out of there fast enough.

October 2001

The following year, Rich and I began seeing eye-to-eye a bit more frequently. After that disastrous first writing assignment, we started working together more often on articles and even had some joint bylines run in our campus newspaper, the *Eagle*, during the spring semester. I still thought he could be a brownnosing cocksucker and he still thought I was a high-maintenance bitch, but our writing style suited each other's so well. In fact, he even had to eat crow when my electoral vote theory did, in fact, hold true in the November 2000 presidential election.

I think it might have been that incident that really changed the course of our friendship, or at the very least, our working relationship. Indeed, he even admitted that I had a knack for governmental reporting and that he could see me making it at the *Washington Post* – someday.

I also realized, through my time spent with Rich, that he wasn't necessarily trying to be an arrogant asshole. He was just intense and when he wanted something, he wanted it done right and he gave it 110 percent. I learned to embrace that quality in Rich instead of loathing it.

I was still with Jay and still very much in love. But, let's face it. He was four hundred and fifty miles away with no firm timetable for us being together in the same zip code. Rich was fun and I enjoyed spending time with him – most of the time anyways. You might actually say, we even often flirted back and forth. He knew my relationship status though, and never tried to cross over that line.

We were both taking Professor Markley's advanced journalism course that fall and had both been hired to work for the *Eagle*. He was in charge of the sports' desk and I had taken over the duties as editor-in-chief. Each Monday and Tuesday night, after our classes and other obligations had ended for the evening, we would head over to the *Eagle's* office, which was located on the top floor of the student union, and crank out that week's edition.

I remember one night, in particular, the office was buzzing with all the editors and reporters trying to get their final assignments completed before deadline. Rich kept eyeing me from his station, as I was talking with each editor about their pages. The radio was tuned to a pop rock station and Puddle of Mudd's "Blurry" began playing over the speakers.

"Hey Brooke, could you turn the radio up a notch? I really like this song," Rich asked. "And, it's message," he added in an undertone, just loud enough for me to hear.

It's message. What is he talking about? I guess I had never really paid much attention to the lyrics before. It was then that I started to listen and I felt my entire world shift. *Does Rich have feelings for me? Do I have feelings for Rich? Not possible, I love Jay. Focus Brooke, you have a paper to produce and it's a deadline night.*

As hard as I tried to focus, it just didn't seem possible. Rich kept sending me messages with those ocean-blue eyes of his. *Damn those eyes.* I just needed to get out of there and call Jay. Once I heard his sweet voice, I would forget all about Mr. Blue Eyes. *Yep, keep telling yourself that, Brooke.*

"Earth to Brooke," Rich said as he waved his hands in my face. "I need to snap a quick photo of the intramural basketball game before we send this puppy off to press. Want to walk down to the rec center with me?"

"Uh, um, sure, yeah," I stuttered out. "Sorry, I was focusing on this article. You surprised me."

Ugh, I really hope he buys that. Shit, Brooke, what the eff is your problem all of a sudden?

Since it was a cool October evening, we both grabbed our sweatshirts (he sporting the University of Michigan and I wearing Michigan State University) and headed down to the lobby of the student union.

"Spartan fan, huh? I always knew you seemed a bit off, Brooke."

"Whatever, you're just worried that we're gonna kick your Wolverine bootie next week!"

"Hah, don't count on it, sweetheart."

Sweetheart, did he just call me sweetheart?

I remember riding down in the elevator at what seemed like a snail's pace. "Seriously, could this thing move any slower? It must know we are on a deadline, or something," I snickered, trying to break the tension that had quickly formed between us.

We finally made it to ground level and began our walk down to the basketball game. We were both quiet for awhile just enjoying each other's company.

"Nice night, isn't it?" Rich said, breaking the silence first.

"Mmmhmmm," I whispered.

I swear he moved closer to me and brushed his arm against mine. I felt a chill rush up and down my spine. How did this guy do this to me? It was only a year ago that I wanted him to fall and drown in a sewer somewhere.

"Do you want to play a game?" he asked.

"A game?" I questioned. "Sure, what do you have in mind, Rich?"

"Truth, Dare, Double-Dare, Promise, or Repeat."

"You're kidding, right?" I said between giggles. "Are we at a fourth-grade, slumber party now? How do you even know about that game?" I asked curiously.

"My sister, Jennifer ... she's a few years older than I and her friends always wanted me to play with them at her sleepovers. I was like their little mascot, or something," he said, smiling at the memory.

In that moment, my heart softened a bit more where Rich Davis was concerned.

"Sure, let's play. I'll start with a truth. Give it to me," I dared.

"Do you love your boyfriend?"

Whoa, that is not what I was expecting. I was expecting something more like – Is your favorite color purple? These questions were a lot less serious when my girlfriends asked them nearly a decade ago. Why did he care if I loved Jay? Most importantly, why was I hesitating?

"Did you hear me, Brooke?" he asked in a louder voice.

"Yes, I heard you ... and, yes, I love Jay."

"OK, repeat," he said, trying to hide the disappointment in his voice.

"Ooooh, OK, let me think. I need to make this a good one. ... How about ... Brooke Anderson is the most beautiful, brilliant and bodacious girl I've ever had the privilege of knowing."

His Hollywood smile appearing, Rich erupted in a hysterical fit of laughter. "Bodacious?"

"What? I was going for alliteration," I shrugged. "Now repeat!"

"That's the best B-word you could come up with. How about bad ass, or babbling ... because we all know that you sure do babble a lot," he teased.

"Whatever, just say it already, would you! Unless you're giving up already," I insisted.

"Fine," he said with a sigh. "Brooke Anderson is the most beautiful, brilliant and bodacious girl I've ever had the privilege of knowing," he repeated, stifling his laughter.

"Damn straight! Now hit me with a dare."

"Kiss me," he challenged.

"Wh—What?"

"You heard me. Kiss me," he repeated.

I couldn't let Rich win. We were only in the second round. What kind of loser goes out in the second round of Truth, Dare, Double-Dare, Promise, or Repeat? I needed to think and think quickly – got it!

I leaned over and gave Rich a quick, chaste peck on the cheek. *After all, he didn't specify where he wanted that kiss.*

"Nice one, you got me there. Now hit me with a dare," he shot back.

"Hmmm, OK. You know my feet are killing me. I think you should carry me the rest of the way to the rec center."

Before I knew it, Rich scooped me up in his arms and began carrying me down the steep hill that led to the college's gymnasium.

"That's all you got, Beautiful? You're making this way too easy on me."

"Whatever, I choose truth again," I said, without missing a beat.

"What's your idea of a perfect date?" he asked.

"That's an easy one! An afternoon at the beach; maybe a picnic, or some stargazing. Ohhh, fireworks over the water. … Yes, now that would be perfection." I always envisioned Jay proposing to me in that exact setting, but in that moment, it was Rich I envisioned lying next to me in the sand.

"That does sound perfect … I'll go with a promise," Rich said this time.

"Yes!" I exclaimed. "I was waiting for you to choose promise. When you become the editor of a big-time newspaper – because we both know you will someday – you need to hire me. Got it, Mister!" I said, poking at his chest.

Chuckling, he answered, "Yes, Brooke, I promise that when I'm the editor of some big-time newspaper you will be my second-in-command."

"Wow, I just asked for a job and now I'm second-in-command – score," I joked.

"I don't have the job yet, sweetheart."

"I know, I know. OK, give me another dare," I requested.

"Brooke, I, uh, dare you to grab dinner with me tomorrow night?"

Crap, crap, crap, I can't do this. I LOVE Jason. Jay-Jay is your forever, Brooke. Well, at least I made it to the fourth round. "I don't think that's a good idea, Rich. I'm sorry if I have been giving you the wrong idea, but you know I am spoken for ... not to mention, I'm kind of your boss," I tried to tell him as convincingly as possible. The question remained as to whom I was trying to convince.

"Yeah, yeah, I know. I just thought ... never mind," Rich said, with a hint of regret in his voice.

Game over. The light, carefree banter from earlier was gone. Rich still held me in his arms, but they were now cold and stiff. We continued on to the rec center in silence and I watched as he took a few photos of the team.

He really did have a flare for everything he did. He took some fantastic shots and could write a very captivating article. I was convinced the guy was bound for a great future. I would never admit this to him, but I was extremely envious of his writing. He would probably be the one sitting behind a desk at the *Washington Post* someday. Heck, as I admitted to him during our little game, he was probably even good enough to be the editor.

We didn't say another word to each other the entire night. It was as if that spark between us that seemed so real earlier had been completely extinguished. I couldn't shake the feeling that I had ruined something that might have been good. *Why was I thinking that way when I had a completely happy relationship with Jay? Sure, something had seemed a bit off about us lately and we'd been missing more of our "phone dates," but he was still my forever.*

Gone was the easy banter once we returned to the office that night. There was a definite tension in the air between us now; he didn't offer to take me back to my room, after we finished the paper, as he had in the past several months. I had definitely succeeded in putting a strain on our newly formed relationship. I pouted a bit as I walked back to my room … alone.

Heaving my shoulder bag onto the bed, I lazily sauntered into my room after sending the paper off to the printer that night. It was approaching one in the morning and I was exhausted.

"Get the paper sent?" Cassidy asked from across the room. She was up either working on a research paper, or chatting with her next boy toy on AIM – probably the latter of the two.

"Yep, thank God. It seems like everything that could go wrong, went wrong tonight."

"You wanna run over to the Campus Diner and grab a bite before crashing?" she asked.

"What are you drunk? That greasy stuff only sounds good mixed with alcohol and lots of it!"

"No, but for some reason a greasy omelet with lots of Swiss cheese and bacon sounds delicious right now. And, before you say it – NO, I'm not preggo," she added, as she lightly shoved me in the arm.

"I think I'm falling for Rich Davis," I told her, without taking a breath, from the corner booth of the restaurant.

"I'm sorry ... WHAT?!? I could have sworn you just said you were falling for Douche Monkey Davis."

"I did," I admitted sheepishly.

"What about Jay? I mean sure he can be a tool sometimes, but he loves you Brooke."

"Does he, Cass? We haven't talked for three days. It's like we don't even make time for our phone dates anymore. I know we're both busy with school and our other activities, but we always used to make time, even if it was just for five minutes. I'm starting to think he just loves the old Brooke; maybe we don't even know each other anymore."

It was true; Jay and I had started drifting apart earlier that spring. He didn't even come home that summer. He decided to take an internship with the college's mechanical engineering department and I completely supported his decision. It was good for his future ... our future, I thought at the time, but maybe it wasn't such a good idea after all. Since he'd decided to stay in Marquette all summer, I told him that I wanted to visit and spend some time on the beaches of Lake Superior, but he even told me that was a bad idea because he'd be working all day and studying at night since he'd also added on a few summer courses. It was just strange.

Then one night, during one of our phone dates, he hit me with the bombshell that he thought we should take a break. I completely freaked out on him. I remember my stomach sank and I began to sob uncontrollably. I started hyperventilating before rushing to the bathroom and losing the entire contents of my stomach. Sitting there on the cold tiles of the bathroom floor for what felt like hours sobbing into the phone, I begged Jay not to break up with me. I guess I finally broke him down to the point where he decided it was just the stress of the internship and his missing me that made him finally realize he'd made a mistake. Things seemed to go better after that and I continued to be hopeful for our future.

"You two will work it out," Cass tried to reassure me, while slurping on her chocolate shake. "You always do. Remember when you thought you loved Tommy Jenson our sophomore year in high school? I had to snap you out of it then and I will snap you out of it again. You and Jay are just in a rut right now. Maybe you should get all sexy tomorrow night before you call him. You know – throw on a sexy nightie, forget the panties and let him hear the hum of your B-O-B (battery-operated-boyfriend)."

"Oh my god. I am not having phone sex with Jay in our dorm room. What if our suitemates overheard, or better yet, where the hell will you be going? Plus, even if that was a good idea, I don't have anything sexy here. What's the point when my boyfriend is over four hundred miles away?"

"That's it!" Cassidy blurted out.

"Oh gawd, that face scares me, Cass."

"We're going shopping. You need something lacy and definitely some new batteries."

I had no words for Cassidy and all I could do was shake my head at my best friend as we finished our greasy late-night omelets, hashbrowns and buttered toast. *I would really need to spend a few extra hours in the gym tomorrow.*

The next day, after a little more convincing from my best friend, I decided that maybe Cassidy was right. We skipped classes and spent the entire day shopping for my phone date with Jay. Honestly, I was glad to skip class that day. I couldn't stand the thought of spending the afternoon with Rich after what had happened between the two of us the night before. Plus, I wanted to focus my attention solely on Jay – the love of my life.

After a day of shopping, I came home to prepare myself for some sexy time. I bought myself a new nightie which I planned to photograph and e-mail to Jay. If that didn't get him in the mood for some fun, I wasn't sure what would. I flipped the switch on the battery-operated candles, slipped into my new outfit, put the new container of lube on the bedside table, and inserted some fresh batteries into B-O-B (just like Cassidy had suggested). I mean, after all, we do want maximum pleasure and performance. We'd hate for B-O-B to go limp right before the fireworks show. I called Jay exactly at eleven o'clock and got the voice of his roommate, Mark, on their answering machine. *I'm sure he'll call me soon.*

I woke up during the middle of the night, hearing a light knocking on the door. I realized then that it was after three in the morning. I was freezing, wearing only a lacy negligee, and my boyfriend had blown me off, instead of getting me off, yet again. I threw on my bathrobe and padded to the door to let in Cassidy. She had spent the majority of the evening studying in the library in order to give me plenty of alone time for my "heated" conversation with Jay. I think she could tell by the look on my face, or maybe the sleep cruds in my eyes, that it hadn't gone according to our plan.

"No luck, huh?"

"I don't want to talk about it," I huffed, as I crashed back into bed and pulled the covers over my head. I cried myself back to sleep that night.

The following day, Jay surprised me with a call in the middle of the afternoon. He explained that he had been invited to watch a Yankees playoff game with some of his buddies at one of the frat houses. He had contemplated pledging this particular fraternity this fall and he didn't want to turn them down.

"So, what you are saying is that smelly boys are a priority over your hot girlfriend now?"

"No, Brookie, what I'm saying is the Yankees were on. You know how much I love the Yankees. They clinched a spot in the World Series last night. I really wish I could get you to like watching the games."

"Whatever, Jay, it was a stupid baseball game. I even went out and bought some lingerie thinking we could ... just nevermind."

"Wait ... Are you saying you wanted to phone fuck?"

"Yes, that's what I'm saying, but you blew that chance. ... instead of your load."

"Baby, why don't we start what should have happened last night?"

"It's too late, Jason. I have class in twenty and Cass is sitting right next to me."

"Oh crap, you just Jasoned me. I need to make it up to you, Brookie. Hey, I just thought of something.

Baby, would you watch the Yankees with me if we had something big riding on it?"

"The Yankees – are you fucking kidding me right now? Your big plan on making it up to me is the goddamn Yankees?"

"Calm down, baby. Let me explain my idea."

"What? Like phone sex? Is it always about those damn Yankees with you?"

"No baby, I was thinking more like … we could get engaged if the Yankees win the World Series."

"Wait, hold the phone. … Did you just fucking say that you want to marry me if the Yankees win the fucking World Series? Like seriously? Have you lost your fucking mind?"

"Wow, I thought you'd be a little more excited than that."

"You can't be serious, Jay."

"I'm serious, baby. The Yankees are a sure thing. They have great Vegas odds. I want you to be interested in the things that I love. And, I love you, baby. I want you to be my wife."

Lord knows that I had waited for years to hear him say that. Sure, we had always talked about our future, but we had never discussed marriage. At least when he was sober, anyways. I mean granted; it wasn't the most romantic of proposals, but once they won, he would get a ring and get down on bended knee for real, right? "Uh, this is so crazy. But, of course, yes. I want to be your wife, Jay, more than anything. If it takes the Yankees winning the World Series for that to happen then go Bronx Bombers!"

For the next two weeks, I watched every Yankees' game while sitting on pins and needles. When they weren't playing and I wasn't at class, I spent the majority of my free time searching for the perfect engagement ring online.

The Yankees lost the first two games of the series and I was crushed, but I was ecstatic when they came back to win the next three. I think I annoyed Cassidy because I wouldn't give up the television to let her watch her reality bullshit. It was probably just some show about some douche trying to find love amongst twenty-five bimbo Barbies, anyways. Like that would ever work! Besides, I had my own version of reality to live. It would be much more entertaining for her to watch it play out live. And, boy, did she ever like telling me that I was acting ridiculous. She yelled at me numerous times for accepting such an "absurd proposal" as she called it.

The big game was finally here – game seven of the World Series. I made sure to clear my schedule that night so I could watch my happily-ever-after play out.

"You are so absurd," Cass called out from the bathroom, where she was prepping for a date with lord-only-knows-who.

"I know … You have mentioned that like two hundred times in the past three weeks. But, thanks for clarifying once again," I shouted back.

"I just don't get it, Brookie. If he loves you like he says he does then he shouldn't need some stupid baseball game to determine your future."

"He's going to propose anyways. I know he will. By Christmas, I'll have a huge rock on my finger. He just wants me to cheer with him for his team. It's kind of cute, really, when you think about it."

"Yeah, OK. Whatever makes you sleep better at night," Cass quipped, while adding in her signature eye roll.

After Cassidy left for her date, I relaxed on my bed with a huge bowl of microwave popcorn to watch game seven of the World Series. I anxiously sat on the edge of my bed, unable to eat much of the popcorn. The game was a true pitchers' duel. Neither team scored a run until the sixth inning when Arizona scored first. When that runner came across home plate, I felt my heart sink. The Yankees, however, came back to score two runs during the next two innings to lead the game, 2-1.

As I watched the eighth inning, I envisioned Jay's face as I walked down the church aisle toward him on our wedding day. His smile brought out his perfect dimples and there was even a tear rolling down his cheek. I was wearing a white, satin gown with a sweetheart neckline, embellished with tiny crystals. My dad was at my side wearing a perfectly tailored, black penguin suit, as I liked to call tuxedos. My mom was sitting in the front pew, blotting her damp eyes with tissues.

The Yankees maintained the lead going into the ninth inning with their amazing closing pitcher coming out to the mound for the second consecutive inning. This was it ... I was going to get my engagement ring, my husband and my happily-ever-after.

Waiting for the closer to toss some warm-up pitches, I envisioned welcoming our first child into this world – a girl. She would have her father's eyes and my little, upturned nose.

Well, that perfect closing pitcher ... turns out that he wasn't so perfect, after all. He ended up blowing the game and the Yankees lost to the Arizona Diamondbacks, 3-2. I broke down in tears, spilling the uneaten popcorn all over my bed and Jay never called that night. All of my hopes and fantasies slowly began to fade away that night.

I figured Jay was just upset about the game. He had been so excited about our upcoming proposal. I was convinced that he would go ahead with it anyways. After all, he just wanted me to watch and love the Yankees, too, right? Mission accomplished. I knew he would call me the next day, and with Christmas just around the corner I could anticipate a sparkly diamond on my finger. Just as I had already explained to Cassidy – why was I suddenly not so sure?

A few days went by after the Yankees' loss and I still hadn't heard from Jay. I mean I could understand how he may have initially been upset, but this was ridiculous. It was just a game, after all, and if he still wanted to marry me then all he had to do was ask. I still watched and tried to enjoy the baseball games. He still had me interested in his team, and if it was that important to him in the future, I would learn to love the Yankees. After all, if I loved him, I should embrace his hobbies and other interests, I reasoned to myself.

It was a Thursday afternoon and I was finished with my classes for the day. Having no sorority obligations that night, Cassidy and I had made plans to meet in the library at eight o'clock for a study session. Checking my watch, I realized I had about two hours to spare. It was time to call Jay and see where his head was at.

I waited through three rings before I heard Mark's voice on the other end. Mark had been Jay's best friend since high school. They were both on the baseball team and earned scholarships to play at Michigan Tech. After being accepted, they decided it only made sense to rent an apartment together near campus.

"Hello," Mark answered.

"Hey Marky, long time, no talk. I feel like the only time I hear your voice anymore is on that silly, answering-machine message."

It was something along the lines of "You've reached Jason and Mark. We're not around right now ... Hopefully, we're out scoring some home runs, if you know what I mean. Anyways, you know what to do after the beep."

"Brookie! How've you been, baby girl?" he asked.

"Oh, pretty good. I keep quite busy down here between school, sorority activities and the student paper."

"Yeah, Jay filled me in on all your stuff. Hey, any cute sorority sisters you could hook an old friend up with?"

I couldn't help but chuckle at his request. "Um, not that I can think of, Marky. But, I'll keep you in mind, OK?"

We both knew I wouldn't actually give it a second thought, but he agreed anyways, probably in the hopes that I was telling him the truth.

"Is Jay around?" There was a long pause and some chatter in the background ... "Marky, you there?" I asked a bit confused.

"Uh, yeah, Brooke. Sorry, Jay's not here right now. I think he said he was going to go lift weights before dinner," he replied.

"Then why did I just hear him talking to you? And, is that a girl I hear whispering in the background? What the fuck is going on? I know he's there. … Hand him the damn phone."

I could feel myself begin to shake as I was yelling at Mark. It wasn't his fault that Jay was being an ass, but he was covering for him. Fuck the "bro code." I'm supposed to be his friend, too, and Jason was being a jackass.

"Calm down, Brooke. Here's Jay." Before I had the chance to tell Mark goodbye, Jay grabbed the phone.

"Hey, Brooke, what's up?"

"Seriously, you haven't talked to me … your girlfriend, might I add, for four fucking days and I get a 'hey, what's up?' I'll tell you what's up, Jason: one, what the fuck is your problem and two, who the hell is your lady friend, whispering in the background?"

"Calm down, Brooke. I don't have a problem. I've just been busy the last few days, that's all. I was pretty upset after the Yanks lost and I had to hash over a few things."

"Hash over what, exactly? And, you still didn't answer my second question." I barked back.

"Uh, um, that's just a friend of Mark's," Jay said with hesitation.

"Yeah, OK, whatever, what did you need to think about? Does it involve us?" I asked, already knowing the answer.

"Yeah, um, Brooke ... I think we need to take a break. And, before you go all crazy, or start crying on me, just hear me out, OK?"

I was silent for a minute ... waiting for the tears to brim around my eyes, but they never came – not right away, anyways. "Sure, talk."

"Well, for a few months I've been wondering where our relationship was headed. I mean, after all this time, we should be talking marriage, right? I just wasn't sure that's what I wanted ... or, maybe, what you wanted. We never really talked about it, until I came up with the World Series plan. I figured if the Yankees won the Series, then it was meant to be. You were meant to be my wife. But, they lost, Brooke. Don't you think that is fate's way of stepping in and telling us not to get married?"

"I'm sorry, are you fucking kidding me? Are you breaking up with me because of some lame-ass fate, excuse? Why can't you just use your brain for once, Jason? Do you love me? I mean you've told me you love me for the last five years. Has it all been a lie?" I questioned accusingly.

"No, it wasn't a lie, Brooke. I did love you ... maybe I still do. I just need a break. I don't know that it has to be permanent, but we need to cut all ties for awhile, anyways. I just need some time to figure things out," Jay replied pathetically.

"There's someone else. Isn't there? Just tell me the truth, Jay."

He hesitated a minute before answering in the faintest whisper ... "Yes."

With his declaration, the tears that didn't originally come poured out in a flood. I couldn't help the loud sob that escaped my lips. "Ho-w, cou-could yo-you do –thi-this to me"? I managed to squeak out in between sobs.

"It just happened, Brookie. I do love you. I guess I'm just not in love with you anymore. I need to spend some time with someone else. You're the only girl I've ever been with and I'm just not sure if I'm ready to commit to one person for the rest of my life. Maybe this break is what we need right now to know if we're meant to be together."

My tears had subsided for the time being, and now all I felt was rage building up inside. "Let me tell you something, Jason. I had the opportunity to cheat on you, too. But, I didn't because I LOVE you. I turned down a great guy and maybe we could have been good together, but now I will probably never know. Your selfishness most likely ruined that chance for me. So, thanks for that," I sarcastically spat out.

"And, no, this break isn't for us to determine if we're meant to be together. If you choose her over me, then I already know we aren't meant to be together. If you choose her over me, then we are done, Jason … forever. So, here's my ultimatum; do you want her, or me? You can't have us both."

He was silent for what could have been just a few seconds, but, after my ultimatum, it seemed like minutes, or even hours – it was so deafening.

"Never mind, don't answer. Your hesitation tells me everything I already need to know. Goodbye, Jason. Thank you for the memories. I hope you have a nice life."

Before letting him get another word in, I hung up the phone and wrote the final chapter of that portion of the book that was my life.

Chapter Three

Was I a horrible person for seeking out Rich, just minutes after breaking up with Jay? After spending the last five years of my life loving one person and even wanting to be his wife, you'd think I would be a little more torn up about this. Instead, I was about to walk out of my dorm room to find Rich and accept that dinner invitation that I should have accepted weeks ago.

I quickly ran to the bathroom to blot my red eyes and tear-stained face. I patted on some concealer and added a dab of lip gloss before quickly tossing on my favorite Spartan sweatshirt – the same one I was wearing when Rich asked me out the first time. Unfortunately, the weather had turned cold as it was nearing late October in Michigan and I couldn't just step into my go-to flip-flops. I sat down to pull on my socks and running shoes before heading out the door to find Rich.

I took the chance that he might be working on his weekly sports column as I made my way to the student union. I didn't want to wait for the elevator, so I ran up the four flights of stairs to the top floor of the building. I was slightly winded as I entered the *Eagle's* office.

At first, I didn't notice him as the lights were dimmed, but on scanning the room, I noticed him sitting on the couch with his long legs up and his laptop resting on his knees. He had a small radio playing '80s classic rock set up in the corner. He looked relaxed with his wire rims covering my favorite pair of eyes, and wearing faded, denim jeans and a Detroit Tigers sweatshirt. *Great – another baseball fan,* I thought to myself.

He was humming along to Poison's "Every Rose Has Its Thorn," as I cleared my throat to gain his attention. He looked slightly startled by my sudden presence, but flashed me a smile anyways.

"Hey, Brooke. You OK? I didn't expect to see anyone else up here this evening. What's going on?" he asked.

"Yeah, I'm fine. It's just been a really long night and I was hoping I would find you up here, actually."

"Yeah? What's up?"

"I, uh … I just broke up with my boyfriend, or rather he broke up with me."

"Oh, Brooke, sweetheart, I'm so sorry. Come here and sit down."

He quickly swung his legs off the couch and sat his laptop on the side table as he patted the couch and gestured for me to take a seat next to him.

I went and nestled into the cushion next to Rich. His perfect scent overcame me; I so badly wanted to plant my lips on his. Rich moved in and wrapped his arm around me, pulling me even closer to him. Snuggling into the crook of his arm, I rested my head on his shoulder. He leaned and pulled me back, as I lifted my feet onto the couch.

"Do you want to talk about it?" he asked, while beginning to stroke my hair.

"He's just a jackass. He was going to propose to me if the Yankees won the World Series; as you probably already know, they lost. So, instead of proposing to me, my boyfriend of over five years dumped me."

"Fuckin' Yankees."

I broke into hysterical laughter. "Thanks, Rich. I needed to laugh. You always seem to know what to say to bring a smile to my face. ... This may seem too soon, but do you want to grab that dinner sometime," I asked.

"Brooke, you know I'd love to, but I don't want to be your rebound, sweetheart. Take some time for yourself and then decide if it's really me that you want. I'll wait."

I couldn't argue with him because, truth be told, he was probably right. I did need some time – time to find Brooke. I hadn't been single since before high school and I needed to find my place in the world – a place without Jay and, unfortunately for right now, a place without Rich Davis.

I cuddled with Rich for awhile on the couch while we listened to several '80s power ballads. We laughed at the memories of the big hair and brightly colored spandex.

"Hey, how about we watch a movie? It might help take your mind off a certain 'jackass,'" Rich suggested with a laugh.

The staff had purchased a TV and VCR for the *Eagle's* office the previous year. We kept a collection of movies, mostly featuring journalists, to watch during our downtime.

"Sure, that sounds like a great idea. What do we have over there?"

Rich walked over to the cabinet and pulled out *The Pelican Brief*, but I had another movie in mind.

"How about *Up Close & Personal*," I asked with a pouty face.

"Fine, you're the one who's had the rough night. I'll let you pick, but only this once," he replied. "Besides, I can't really complain about watching Michelle Pfeiffer for two hours," he added with a wink.

I lightly punched him in the arm before we sat back down on the couch. I quickly snuggled myself into his body once again and we watched the movie without saying too much.

"Maybe journalism isn't such a safe career choice," I remarked, as I watched Michelle Pfeiffer's character fight for her freedom.

"Any profession has its risks, Brooke, besides, not all outlets cover such hazardous assignments."

"I know. It's just a movie, anyways. Not like this kind of stuff actually happens in real life," I responded.

As the movie ended, I couldn't see past my tears as the credits scrolled down the screen.

"Wh – Why did Robert Redford have to die – die at the end," I said between sobs.

Rich pulled me closer into his side, "Don't cry, Brooke – remember what you said, 'it's just a movie.'"

"I –I know, but it's so – so sad," I said, trying to catch my breath. "Promise me that you will never become a foreign correspondent. I can't stand the thought of losing you that way."

"Brooke, don't take offense to this, but I think you are just overly emotional right now. But, if it makes you feel better, sweetheart, I promise I won't become a foreign correspondent," he reassured me.

It was getting late and I had an early morning class the next day, so I reluctantly pulled myself from Rich's hold.

"What time is it? I didn't wear my watch and I forgot the clock here needs a new battery."

"About eleven," he answered, looking down at his watch.

"Crap, I was supposed to meet Cassidy in the library three hours ago. I didn't realize I'd been up here that long. I'm sorry for taking up so much of your time. You probably had work to finish. Anyways, I should get back to my room before Cass sends a search party out for me."

"I'll walk you." He didn't mean it as a question. He was walking me back to my room whether I wanted him to, or not. In this case, though, I very much wanted him to.

After just a short distance, we made it back to my door and Rich scooped me into his arms once again. I could tell that he wanted to taste my lips against his as much as I did, but neither of us made the move toward each other. We both knew we needed to wait, if there were to be any future for us.

Rich and I didn't see much of each other outside of class and our duties with the *Eagle*. Several months passed and the holidays came and went. I spent the month-long winter break back home with my parents. My mom was pleased to know that I had broken up with Jay. While most of my friends loved Jay, my mom was never his biggest advocate. Other than Cassidy, my mom was my best friend and her opinion mattered, but I just couldn't understand her problem with Jay … until now. I suppose a mother's intuition is always right. I appreciated the time I spent at home. Ever since I moved to Kalamazoo, I hadn't been able to spend much time with my folks. We had always been close, probably because I had been their spoiled-rotten , only child.

This Christmas hadn't been any different. My mom took me shopping before the big day and bought me a bunch of new clothes and even threw in a few "toys." I was so excited to take my new DVD player back to campus to show Cass.

After the holidays, the winter seemed to drag along as it always did. Rich and I hung out casually a lot, once we returned to campus following the winter break. Although I was disappointed that our relationship seemed to be going nowhere, I had hopes that things would soon change.

We would often spend hours writing articles, studying and preparing research papers, while locked away in the Eagle's office together. We talked about everything from our classes to our families to the conflict in the Middle East. We would laugh and sometimes even cry together. OK, I was the one usually crying on his shoulder, but I tried to avoid scaring him away with too much personal drama. In a way, Rich Davis had become one of my best friends in just a matter of a few short months. I often wondered if he would become anything more than just that.

My mid-March birthday finally arrived. Cassidy had big plans to help me celebrate my twenty-first in style. She had invited a group of our closest friends and sorority sisters out to celebrate at Monaco Bay, the hottest bar near campus. I decided to send Rich a message over Instant Messenger to invite him to, what would probably end up being, my first legal, drinking marathon.

> *Hey, Rich ... The girls and I are about to head out to Monaco Bay to celebrate my roommate's and my twenty-first. You want to tag along?*
>
> *Rich: Sure thing, Babbling Brooke. I wouldn't miss watching you make a drunken fool of yourself. ;) I'll meet you lovely ladies there in twenty.*
>
> *Ugh! You know I hate it when you call me that!! It's my birthday and you have to be NICE to me! ;) See you soon. Smooches.*
>
> *Rich: Fine, no Babbling Brooke comments – tonight! But, I am entitled to give you 21 birthday spankings, pretty lady! ;)*

For some reason, I suddenly felt my nerves begin to tingle over my entire body. My brow and hands began to sweat and butterflies began taking up residence in my tummy. The thought of Rich spanking me was really getting me worked up inside. *Why was I getting nervous about Rich? Was I ready? It had been over four months since the breakup with Jay. I think my nervousness was my body telling me that I was really ready for this … whatever "this" was between Rich and me.*

Cassidy helped me rummage through my closet to find the perfect outfit to celebrate my twenty-first.

"Sophisticated, yet flirty," she said, as she handed me the emerald green tank top and skin-tight, black pants.

I paired this ensemble with a jean jacket and black boots since it was still a chilly March evening. I then straightened my hair and put on some light makeup before going back into our room. Cassidy was just finishing up getting herself ready for the evening.

"Oooh la la. Look at you, birthday girl … you are gonna get laid tonight," she declared with a wink.

"Shut up, Cass. I haven't even kissed Rich yet. I very much doubt we're going to have sex … tonight."

"Whatever you say, Brookie. Now let's go get you drunk."

"Thanks for waiting a night to celebrate your twenty-first. I'm glad we can do this together. Although, I must say, I'm a bit surprised you didn't bring a beer home last night to rub it in my face."

"Oh, don't kid yourself, Brookie. I stopped at the bar and downed a few shots while you were working on the *Eagle,* last night."

"Oh, I see … So much for waiting to party with your best friend," I replied sarcastically.

She linked her arm with mine as we walked out the door and the few blocks to Monaco Bay.

I bellied up to the bar with a bunch of my closest girlfriends as the bartender mixed me my first cocktail on the house. I don't remember what name he gave it – some house special. It had been nearly twenty minutes when Rich strolled in with one of his buddies – always punctual that Rich Davis.

"Hey there, birthday girl. Can I buy you your next drink? I know, how about a shot?" As Rich was talking, I felt him slide up behind me and place his arm around my shoulder while his buddy took the open seat next to mine.

"Sure Rich, I'm kind of new at this ... a shot ... virgin. I guess you could say. Surprise me with something."

"Oooh, I get to pop your cherry, do I?"

I couldn't help but contain my giggle at his innuendo.

"Can I get four tequila shots over here," Rich yelled to the bartender.

"Comin' right up."

"Tequila? Are you trying to get me drunk, Davis?"

"Brooke, it's your twenty-first birthday. Of course, I'm trying to get you drunk, sweetheart."

The bartender slid us our four tequila shots and Rich grabbed the salt, poured some on his wrist and licked it before passing me the shaker. I followed his lead and did the same before he handed me the small shot glass filled to the rim with Jose Cuervo.

I closed my eyes and plugged my nose before I put the glass to my lips and took a small sip. Even that one small sip left me gagging and gasping for air. I heard Rich laughing hysterically at my troubles in between my frantic gasps.

"What the hell are you doing, Brooke? Let me show you how it's done."

He brought the glass to his lips and with one quick movement swallowed the entire contents of the glass before slamming it back down onto the bar. He then quickly picked up one of the lemons that accompanied the shots and sucked it between his lips. *Oh how I wish I was that lemon.*

"Now … you do it – just like that."

"I can't chug it like that … It'd kill me!"

"Stop being a pussy, Brooke. Take the damn tequila shot like the feisty woman that I know you are."

"Fine." *There he goes infuriating me again. I couldn't let Rich Davis call me a pussy … not unless he's referring to sinking his rock-hard cock into it.*

I tilted my head back and dumped the warm liquid into my mouth. I didn't gag this time and felt it slide down the back of my throat as heat radiated throughout my body.

"Thata girl," Rich cheered, as he slammed back his second shot and slid mine, along with the rest of the lemons, across the bar in my direction.

Just as I was finishing two more tequila shots that Rich had shoved in front of me, I heard Cass sneak up behind us.

"Be careful with that tequilllllllla," she slurred. "It's a sneaky bitch. One minute you're dancing like a sexy mutha and the next you're on the ground pantless and making out with a shoe. And, let's just hope in your case the shoe's name is Rich effin' Davis."

"Oh my gawd, you are SO wasted! What are you even talking about? Go get some water, hooker!" I shouted over the booming music.

I was laughing hysterically by the time my best friend sauntered off to go flirt with some freshman who had probably sneaked in with a fake.

I was feeling the effects after several drinks that evening. It seemed like every time I turned around someone else was buying me a Sex on the Beach, Slippery Nipple, Screaming Orgasm, and even a Leg Spreader. *Seriously, who thought of these names? ... Obviously, a horny man!*

After what I believed to be my eighth or ninth drink, I realized that Rich had gone missing. I looked around the bar and that's when I saw him and he wasn't alone. He was sitting at the other end of the bar, looking rather cozy with Aubrey Sullivan.

Aubrey Sullivan was the *Eagle's* feature editor. She had the perfect sun-kissed blonde hair, large green eyes and the perfect body ... legs that went on for miles, narrow waist and huge boobs. Word on the street was they weren't even real. *I wasn't quite sure how a twenty-one-year-old paid for a boob job, but then again, what did I know?* And, tonight they were perfectly on display in a tight black, v-neck sweater.

I felt a surge of jealousy run through my drunken veins. I didn't want Rich anywhere near Aubrey. He promised me that he would wait for me. Why was he not waiting for me? And, not only did he appear not to be waiting for me, but he was with her ... with freaking Aubrey Sullivan!

I decided that I needed to take action. I stepped down from my bar stool and onto my very wobbly legs. The alcohol was making my head spin, but I made it my mission to make it somehow down to the end of that bar to claim my Rich. *My Rich? Wow, I really was plastered.*

Suddenly, I was facedown on the cold, barroom floor. *Uck, I think I just landed in someone's spilled beer. Brooke the Klutz strikes again.* I heard Cassidy run up on my right, as she asked me if I was OK.

"Yes, just help me get up before anyone else notices. Oh god, this is so humiliating. Why did you let me drink so much? You were supposed to cut me off, remember?"

That's when I heard Rich come up from the other direction and ask me if I was all right.

"Yes, Rich. I'm fine ... thanks for asking. I just need to get home. I reek of stale beer now."

"I'll walk you," he offered.

"It's fine. I saw you were cheat ... umm, chatting with Aubrey, anyways. I wouldn't want you to leave her here alone." *Like hell, I didn't. Of course, I wanted him to leave her, to walk ME home.*

"Aubrey will wait. I'm not letting you walk home alone like this, Brooke."

Rich extended his hand to help me up from the floor. The minute I felt his warm flesh against mine, that infamous shiver I'd grown accustomed to ran down my spine. After regaining my balance, Rich took his other hand and tucked the loose hair behind my ear that had fallen in my eyes. As he did this, I couldn't pass up the opportunity to look deeply into his eyes ... I could tell there was a story written there, but was unsure of the ending. Rich was still nothing but a mystery to me. There was something that I had wanted to ask Rich for a few weeks, and since I wasn't really thinking clearly, it was probably now, or never. After all, I had made it my mission before my little slip-and-fall to claim Rich for myself.

"Rich … will you … … never mind."

"Will I, what, Brooke? Spit it out."

"Well, my sorority is having a spring formal at the end of April and I was wondering … if you'd be my date." My nerves had taken up residence in my body again, and the last part of my question to Rich flew out of my mouth.

"Did you just ask me to go to your sorority formal?"

"Um, y--es, but it's OK. Forget I asked …"

"I'd love to go with you, Brooke. You can fill me in on the details later, but first we need to get you home and tucked into bed."

Rich grabbed my denim jacket off the bar stool where I'd been sitting. I'd taken it off earlier in the evening when I got too hot, probably from the excessive amount of alcohol now coursing through my veins. Rich stepped behind me and helped me get into my jacket, pulling it up to my shoulders. As he did this, his hand grazed the area between my neck and shoulder, near the strap of my tank top.

I wanted badly to turn my neck in his direction so he could softly plant a kiss in that sensitive area near the crook of my neck. I could almost feel his breath on my skin when he pulled away and propped me up against the bar for a minute, while he walked back to where he had been sitting with Aubrey, just minutes before.

I couldn't tell what they were saying, but was hoping it was just a simple goodbye. … And, then he kissed her. He fuckin' kissed her … kissed Aubrey fuckin' Sullivan. Why had he just agreed to go to the sorority formal with me if he was going to go over there and kiss her?

I felt tears welling in my eyes and I sure as hell wasn't going to let Rich see me upset. I wiped my eyes on the sleeve of my jacket before Rich made his way back to me. I then let him grab my hand and walk me out of the bar and back to campus. He saw me back to my dorm like a true gentleman and stood behind me as I unlocked the door.

After opening the door and turning to Rich, he pulled me into his hard chest. I felt his hands rubbing circles on my back and I wanted to remain locked in his warm embrace forever. Rich finally pulled away and leaned over to give me a peck on the cheek.

"Thanks for inviting me out tonight, Brooke. Get back with me about the dance. Oh, and happy birthday, sweetheart," Rich whispered in my ear, before hopping off my porch and into the moonlight.

It was the second time in just a matter of months that Rich had left me at my doorstep, yearning for his lips to assault my own in a heated kiss.

Chapter Four

I woke up the next morning, or maybe afternoon, with a severe hangover. I wasn't sure what hurt the most: my pounding headache from all the booze I had poured down my throat the night before, or the sting in my chest every time I envisioned Rich's lush lips smacking down on Aubrey's lips and not on my own. I swear my lips ached for his touch. *Oh, that definitely hurt worse.* I could take an aspirin to lessen the pain in my head, but there wouldn't be any relief for the ache in my chest until Rich was mine.

I dragged myself out of bed and into the bathroom to freshen myself up as best I could. Luckily, it was a Friday and my academic schedule didn't include any Friday classes this semester – the perks of being an upperclassman, I suppose.

All I wanted to do was crawl back into bed and sleep for two days, but I knew that wasn't possible. There were some articles I had to write for the *Eagle* and the deadline was quickly approaching. I brushed my teeth, spritzed on some perfume in hopes of masking the stale bar odor in my hair, and lathered on my go-to, mango, lip balm. I also threw on a pair of stretchy yoga pants and hooded sweatshirt. The gym would have to wait today as I was just not up to exercise at that moment. Since the snow was fast disappearing, I figured it was safe to throw on my flip-flops, my footwear of choice, if weather permitted, and go about my business.

Since most students had class on Friday afternoon, I was hoping I would have the *Eagle* office to myself, at least until evening. Still not feeling well, I wasn't in the mood to fraternize with anyone. Grabbing the key to the office from the front desk, I made my way to the elevator. Before the doors closed, I heard Rich's sexy baritone calling out for me.

"Brooke, hold the door, please?"

Ugh, not the person I wanted to deal with at the moment ... ah, fuck ... to make matters worse ... as Rich rounded the corner and into the elevator, who should appear from behind him, clutching his hand, but none other than Aubrey Sullivan. *Gag me with a spoon.*

"Hey Brooke, I hope you had a happy birthday. How are you feeling this morning?" Aubrey asked, in the most sickeningly cheerful voice imaginable.

"Thanks, I did." *Until you stole Rich out from under me anyways, you bitch.* "And, I'm doing all right, I suppose. Thank you for your concern."

The three of us walked into the dark office. I watched as Rich and Aubrey cuddled up together on the same couch that we had shared on the night that Jay broke my heart. The sight of them together hurt worse than the memory of the breakup. He told me that night on that same couch that he would wait for me.

I remember his exact words, *"Take some time for yourself and then decide if it's me that you want. ... I'll wait."*

I'm ready, Rich. It's you that I want. You! But, evidently, you don't know the meaning of wait because you are getting awfully cozy over on our couch with Aubrey effin' Sullivan.

"Hey Brooke, are you feeling OK? You're looking a bit green," Rich said, with his brows furrowed and upper lip raised. He was obviously terrified that I was going to lose it on the carpet.

"Yeah, I'm fine. I just need to keep myself busy," I answered, as I walked to a chair on the opposite side of the room. "You two just pretend I'm not even here." Unfortunately, they took my statement a little too literally as I could hear them making out and giggling right behind me. *Really, where is that spoon?*

Rich told me the following week that he and Aubrey were officially a couple. *Well, no shit, Sherlock.* He wanted to reassure me that he still planned to escort me to my sorority formal, though. He talked it over with Aubrey and she completely agreed that he needed to take his friend. I mean, after all, they both assumed that I had only asked him as a friend.

I was somewhat relieved that I could still spend the evening with Rich, but also disappointed because I knew there wasn't a chance for us to be together – really together. I caught myself, on more than one occasion, thinking about the way Rich's lips would taste and feel against my own; I knew they would taste of cinnamon. He was always popping cinnamon gum into his mouth during class. I wasn't really a fan of the flavor, but was convinced Rich would soon change my mind. I could easily learn to love the cinnamon flavor of Rich Davis's lips and tongue entwined with my own. Suddenly, I was in the mood for a Red Hot candy.

Cassidy and I spent the Saturday before our formal, searching for the perfect dresses. We took the two-hour drive into Chicago to shop at some of the boutiques on Michigan Avenue and tried on what seemed like dozens of dresses in all colors, fabrics and styles, but neither of us seemed to have any luck. Everything seemed too frilly or ruffly and in the wrong colors for my skin tone.

"I found it!" I heard Cassidy finally exclaim from the dressing room next to mine.

Pulling on my T-shirt and khaki shorts that I'd worn on this unseasonably warm, April afternoon, I ran out to the sitting area to watch as Cassidy appeared from her closed-curtain dressing room. I gasped, as she floated out wearing the most beautiful, turquoise-lace chiffon gown. The cap sleeves fit perfectly over her toned arms.

"That's the one, Cass. You look absolutely stunning. … Is Prince William available because you look like a princess."

"I know. I think I'm in love! Now, let's go find one for you," she squealed.

I was starting to give up hope when we stumbled into what appeared to be a bridal salon. I saw it hanging on the display rack and knew instantly it was what I'd been dreaming of since the moment Rich agreed to escort me to the formal. After trying on the most perfect dress, I made my purchase and we headed back to campus. I couldn't wait to see the look on Rich's face when he would see me next weekend.

After what seemed like a never-ending week, Friday finally arrived. Cassidy and I had made appointments to get our nails done before the big event the next day. We spent the evening sipping on wine and enjoying some girl-time in the local salon.

I had talked to Rich earlier in the week just to give him some simple details about my dress. I wanted his tie and tuxedo vest to match its deep purple hues. After all, it would have clashed something horrible, if he'd shown up in a chartreuse vest.

He also discussed our dinner plans, saying he would pick up Cassidy and me early and take care of the arrangements. He wanted to surprise the two of us.

Other than that brief chat about our wardrobe and meal, I hadn't really seen or spoken with Rich in weeks. I guess he was too busy with his new girlfriend to pay much attention to his old friends. Oh well, tomorrow I would have him all to myself. Even if nothing would happen between us, I couldn't wait to feel the same warm embrace that had cuddled me the night Jay broke my heart.

"You're simply stunning in that dress, Brooke. But, I would do anything to see how stunning you look out of it, sweetheart." Rich said, as he was grinding up to my midsection while we danced to R. Kelly's "Bump N' Grind." *Convenient, isn't it.*

I felt his lips nuzzle into my neck near the faux diamond and amethyst choker I was wearing and move up toward my ear. He nipped on my earlobe while moving his hands down from my waist, to grip my ass through the thick fabric of my dress.

"There's too much between us. I need you now, Brooke. I have waited far too long for this … for us."

"But, what about Aubrey?"

"I never wanted Aubrey, Brooke," he assured me, as he moved from my ear to nip on my lower lip. "It's always been you. Only you …"

Before I could react, he slowly began parting my lips with his tongue, as if he were asking for permission to enter.

His confession and assault on my lips made my insides quiver in anticipation. I opened my mouth wider, telling him without words that he was what I wanted, too. I immediately tasted the cinnamon on my lips that I had always imagined. It was pure perfection. Rich pulled away from me and looked me straight in the eyes.

"I can tell that you want me as badly as I want you, sweetheart. Your eyes turn that magnificent shade of deep green when they're filled with heated desire, as they turned the same shade on your birthday. I just didn't want to take you after you'd had so much to drink. I wanted you to remember this … to remember us, together."

He pulled me off the dance floor and into a dimly lit and empty hallway off the main ballroom.

"No one will find us here," he whispered as he began to fondle my breasts through the thick fabric of my corseted top. I wasn't wearing a bra with my strapless dress and I instantly felt my nipples begin to harden under Rich's stimulating hands. He pressed me back against the wall and stood flush against me so no one else would see my naked, lower half as he hiked the front of my floor-length dress up off the ground to rest at my hips. He parted my already slickened cleft with two of his fingers and I whimpered at the sudden and very much desired contact.

"You're already so wet for me, Brooke. Just like I always imagined you would be, just as ready for me as I am for you."

Rich kept working me with his fingers until I felt my temperature rise and my legs begin to wobble. He placed his other arm around my waist to help hold me up as I began to seek my release. As he continued to fuck me harder with his fingers, he gently brought his thumb to my clit where he rubbed small circles on the trembling nerve.

"Oh my god," I panted. "I'm gonna come, Rich."

"Come for me, sweetheart. Look me in the eyes and come for me."

I opened my eyes and saw Rich's deep blues staring deeply into my soul. I came undone with the fiercest orgasm, right up against that wall. Then I heard the sound of Rich's zipper ... and an alarm clock? ... What the hell?

I slowly came to, as my own hands were rubbing my nipples through my thin camisole. I could tell my panties and sheets were soaked from my self-induced orgasmic experience. *I just had my very first wet dream.* I quickly glanced over at Cassidy's bed and heard her snoring away. Thank God she was such a heavy sleeper. It was a bitch trying to wake her up during mock fire alarms, but, in this case, it really worked to my advantage.

"It all seemed so real. I swear I can even taste cinnamon on my lips," I mumbled out loud to myself, as I shook my head in disbelief and stumbled to the bathroom. After changing the sheets, I made it to the shower to begin readying myself for my real date with Rich later that evening.

I heard Cassidy answer the door for Rich as I was applying the finishing touches to my makeup. I checked myself once more in the full-length mirror and admired the beauty that was staring back at me. Walking out of the small bathroom, I found Rich in his perfectly tailored tuxedo, sitting on our futon. I saw him mouth WOW as I made my way toward him in my sweetheart-design, strapless, ball gown. The deep purple, organza dress was accented with a sheer layer of black tulle and beading on the corset bodice.

I wore my hair partially pinned up while a layer of mahogany curls swept over my bare back. I paired the gown with the same faux diamond and amethyst choker from my dream and matching, dangly earrings. It was just enough sparkle to really make my best features pop.

"You are stunning tonight, Brooke. Really, breathtaking … a pure beauty."

I just smiled as Rich led me to the door where I slipped on my silver, glittery stilettos and sheer, purple wrap. It was a warm, yet windy, April evening and since the formal was taking place on a riverboat,

I didn't want to go without something to cover my shoulders.

Rich led the three of us outside where an elegant, stretch limo waited at the curb. Cassidy had decided to go solo to the formal. Since it was a co-hosted event with the Lambdas, she thought she could snag one of the single frat boys.

"Rich, you got us a limo? That really wasn't necessary, but it's gorgeous. Thank you," I said.

"Yeah, thanks." Cassidy said, with a stunned look on her face. She must have loved it because it took a lot to leave that girl stunned and nearly speechless.

"After you, my ladies," said Rich graciously.

We ducked into the limo with Cassidy leading the way. She quickly took up the large, leather sofa seat all for herself, kicking her legs up to make sure Rich and I shared a more intimate seat on the opposite side of the limo. She proved my theory correct when I saw her slyly wink as Rich stepped into the vehicle. I just rolled my eyes and scrunched my nose in her direction. Secretly, though, I was thanking her for her devious ways.

The interior of the limo featured a TV, VCR, and stereo system and also its very own wet bar with beautiful crystal decanters, filled with a variety of amber-colored liquors. Next to the decanters sat an ice bucket with a chilled bottle of champagne and three flutes resting inside. It didn't take long for Cassidy to take note of the champagne.

"Champagne," she squealed with excitement, as she clapped her hands together. "Let's pop this baby and get this par-tay started."

Rich grabbed the bottle and pointed it away from us, as he popped the cork and let a bit of the foam spray from the bottle's top. He poured us each a glass of bubbly and asked the chauffeur to turn on the stereo to his best dance station. "Love Shack" piped through the speakers and we all laughed, before breaking out into our best B-52s impression.

After some time had passed, the limo began to slow as it pulled up to a somewhat dilapidated building.

"Uh, we're eating here? I think we're a little overdressed," I said to Rich, with hesitation clearly in my voice.

"Hmph, you ladies just stay here. I'll be right back with our entrée," he replied.

Rich had been gone for about five minutes, when he returned with pizzas that had an aroma to die for.

"My ladies, dinner is served." He opened the boxes and the cheese was so hot and gooey that it partially stuck to the box lids. Every topping imaginable was piled onto the deep-dish pies. I couldn't help but lick my lips in anticipation.

"Oh, Rich. This is absolutely perfect – a limo, champagne and pizza."

"I'm glad you like it. This is the best pizza on the planet, I'm pretty sure. When you told me the riverboat cruise was in Lansing, I immediately knew what we were having for dinner. You can't come within twenty miles of Lansing and not stop to savor the deliciousness that is Giuseppe's. Really, I think it should be on the list of deadliest sins."

None of us said another word as we enjoyed the pizza and champagne. I think I ate three huge slices all by myself when I felt the bodice of my dress begin to tighten.

"Oh, I'm stuffed. That was heavenly."

"I hope you saved room for dessert. I may have snuck some chocolate-covered strawberries into the mini-fridge before I came to pick you two up."

Rich reached over to open the fridge and pulled out the ripest, most enormous strawberries I had ever seen. They were covered in creamy, milky smooth chocolate and I couldn't resist the urge to shriek with pure delight.

Rich grabbed two from the tray before passing it over to Cassidy. He set one down on the plate he had used for his pizza and brought the other one close to my mouth. I leaned forward and felt the cool chocolate graze my lips. I lightly bit down, being careful not to bite Rich's fingers. The creaminess of the chocolate, married to the sweetness of the berry, was the perfect blend for my taste buds.

"Mmmmmm," I groaned, as I closed my eyes with pleasure.

Rich pulled back the other half of the strawberry and lightly brushed the lingering juices from my lips. I opened my eyes just in time to watch him lick the juice off his fingers that he had just wiped from my lips. He leaned into me, just inches from my face. I thought he was going to lean in further for a kiss when I heard Cassidy shout from above us, "Hey, you two, did you see this thing has a moon roof? We can stand up and see the stars. It's such a beautiful night. Come on Brookie, come lookie with me!"

Leave it to Cass to ruin what I thought was going to be my first kiss with Rich.

"You should go and join her, Brooke. We wouldn't want her to tip over from all the champagne she's already consumed."

It was true. Cassidy had already drunk an entire bottle of bubbly all by herself. I sighed and shook my head in disbelief as I stood and shimmied my body out of the moon roof and put an arm around Cassidy. It would be only a matter of minutes before we made it to the riverboat launch. I wanted to take a minute to enjoy this beautiful spring night.

After we boarded the riverboat, Rich immediately grabbed my hand and pulled me to the dance floor. Just as we stepped onto the smooth surface, the DJ began playing Enrique Iglesias' new ballad, "Hero." Rich pulled me tightly into his chest as I wrapped my arms around his broad shoulders. We swayed to the haunting melody for several minutes with only the fabric of our clothes separating us. The sweet smell of his Acqua di Gio infiltrated my senses and further ignited my desires.

"You really do look gorgeous tonight, Brooke," Rich breathed in my ear.

"You can take my breath away," he added, whispering along to the lyrics of the chorus.

"Thank you," I mumbled into his crisp shirt. "You're looking very fine yourself."

Just as the last note played, Rich leaned into me and placed a soft, lingering kiss on my forehead. The sweet and romantic gesture left me weak in the knees and hoping for more, but just as I was about to take the risk and place my lips on his, he pulled away and suggested we step away from the dance floor and grab a drink before dinner.

"Want a shot of tequila? You know for old time's sake," he said with a wink.

"First, it was like a month ago. Second, no I'd just like a white wine tonight, please," I replied. "After all, I need to keep an eye out for her. She did already consume an entire bottle of champagne before we even stepped foot on this boat," I added, as I pointed toward an already inebriated Cassidy.

Rich just laughed and shook his head before ordering a beer and Chardonnay from the bartender.

After dinner, I spent a few more rounds out on the dance floor with Cass and the rest of my sorority sisters. We always brought the house down with our special rendition of Sister Sledge's "We are family." After, at least, a dozen party songs, Cassidy had found some Lambda to finally entertain her. I hadn't seen my best friend for at least an hour and I was finally able to spend some time with Rich – alone.

As the evening was winding down, we made our way to the boat deck where we stopped to take in the clear night sky. I started to shiver a bit as a cool breeze came up off the water. I probably should've grabbed my shawl from the coat check area.

"Here, take my coat. You must be freezing," Rich said, as I felt the sleeves of his tuxedo touch my arms.

"Thank you. I didn't realize how chilly it would be up here. It is beautiful, though. Isn't it?"

"You can say that again," he said as he gazed into my eyes. He didn't say anything else; he didn't need to. It was what he didn't say that heated my core even more than the jacket he'd just placed over my shoulders.

We could hear the music rising from the dance floor below as Rich stood behind me with his arms around my waist, moving us in time to the music. A giggle erupted from my throat when I recognized the song playing below. Rich was grinding up to my backside to Next's "Too Close."

I could tell by the hard length pressing against the small of my back that I was indeed making it hard for him. I felt a sense of victory with that sudden realization and leaned my head back to rest it on Rich's shoulder. I didn't want this evening to ever end and certainly didn't want Rich to go back to Aubrey. I wanted us to stay entwined forever.

My thoughts of Rich and I together were suddenly interrupted by the ringing coming from Rich's pants pocket. He grabbed his cell and checked the caller ID.

"Sorry, it's Aubrey. I better take it." Before I knew it, Rich had removed his arms from my waist and was walking to the other end of the boat deck for some privacy.

"Hey, babe ..." I heard him say as he walked away from me.

There was a monumental shift in his behavior after that call from Aubrey. He hardly spoke two words after he returned to me on the deck. The heat we had generated had been replaced with an icy, cold shoulder when he returned.

I couldn't wait to get off that boat and into the bus where I could talk to other people besides Rich. It didn't really work out in my favor, though; Cassidy was too busy flirting with what appeared to be three single Lambdas in the back of the bus and my other girlfriends were all busy making out with their boyfriends. I sat pinned between the window and Rich during the ride.

"Well this is awkward," I thought to myself.

"What's that?" Rich asked.

Crap, I didn't mean to say that out loud ... "Oh, nothing. It's not important," I said, as I leaned my head against the cool, glass window.

I must have dozed off on the way home because I was suddenly woken by the sound of Rich's voice and his hand rubbing against my shoulder.

"Hey, Brooke, we're back, Sleeping Beauty. Let's get you off this bus and back to your room."

Rich walked me the few blocks back to my room and an eerie sense of déjà vu overcame me. Just like the two other times when Rich walked me to my door, he wrapped his arms around me. This time felt different though; I didn't feel the same intimacy as before when his arms were wrapped around my waist on the deck of the boat. He seemed more distant this time. His mind must be on Aubrey because it certainly wasn't with me.

Rich gave me a quick, chaste peck on the cheek and thanked me for inviting him. I smiled and told him goodnight before I stepped into my room and shut the door behind me. The third time would not be the charm for Rich and me.

Rich was to graduate summa cum laude from the Western Michigan University class of 2002, just a few weeks following the sorority formal. I didn't see him much in those weeks, as we'd wrapped up production for the *Eagle* in early April due to student finals and the impending graduation.

I found myself daydreaming a lot about what could have been had I dumped Jay when he first expressed his absurd proposal ultimatum. Rich wouldn't be with Aubrey Sullivan right now and he would probably be waking up with me in his bed on the morning of graduation. I would lick all the cinnamon goodness from his mouth before helping him get ready for his big commencement ceremony.

As usual, Cassidy snapped me back to reality when she returned with, at least, a dozen boxes in tow. She'd stopped by the local grocery store to pick up some empty shipping boxes so we could pack our stuff, before heading back to our hometown for the summer months.

I decided to attend the graduation ceremony that next morning. I wanted to congratulate many of my sorority sisters as well as see Rich one final time. I had convinced myself that this was it for Rich and me. Our hometowns weren't really all that close and I had no particular reason to see him outside of school.

Cassidy sat next to me and whistled annoyingly as each one of our sorority sisters walked across the stage to claim her diploma. The loudest catcall I'd ever heard, erupted from her throat, as Rich strutted across the stage, shaking the hands of the academic hierarchy. He looked amazing with his perfectly ironed, black robe. The knot on his cobalt tie and collar of his white shirt peeked through the top zipper of his gown. What I would do to get him out of that gown and every layer underneath it.

After the diplomas had been distributed and the class of 2002 had been announced, the graduates were released to the embraces of their families. I congratulated several of my sorority sisters and other friends before I noticed Rich with whom, I assumed, were his parents and sister. I slowly made my way toward him and our eyes locked, as I continued across the spacious quad area that had been set up for the commencement ceremony.

A smile widened on his face as I walked into his extended arms. He held me tight against his chest for a minute before I forced myself to step away. Feeling tears welling up in my eyes, I attempted to tell him goodbye.

"Well, I guess congratulations are in order, huh," I said. "Seems like just yesterday you were driving me bat-shit crazy in Markley's class and now you're graduating. I just can't believe it's time to say goodbye." I blinked back the tears as best I could before I felt one escape down my cheek.

"Hey, don't cry, Brooke. We'll keep in touch. This isn't goodbye, I promise. Besides, you'll be such a hot shot senior next year, I'm sure you'll forget all about Rich Davis."

"I'll never forget about Rich Davis," I told him, as I gave him my most forced smile. "Is this ... is this your family?" I managed to ask between sniffles.

"Yes, how rude of me. This is my mom, Brenda; my dad, Michael; my sister, Jennifer; my brother-in-law, Connor; and this precious angel is my niece

Leila," he said, as he rubbed the infant's soft, blonde head. "Guys, this is my friend, Brooke."

I made small talk with his family for a few minutes before noticing Aubrey come up and hug Rich from behind. He quickly turned around and pulled her off her feet before giving her a chaste kiss on the lips. I decided it was my cue to leave and placed my hand on Rich's shoulder as he put Aubrey back on her feet and turned around to face me.

"Well, I guess it's time for me to head out. Keep in touch, Rich," I said.

"I'll miss you, Brooke. But, remember, this isn't goodbye." He used his fingers to wipe the tears that were now falling from my eyes and gave me a quick peck on the cheek before I turned around and quickly walked back toward Cassidy who was standing with a group of our friends.

The next year went by in a blur. Before I knew it, I was the one walking across the stage, shaking the hands of the academic hierarchy. Rich was right about one thing he had said a year earlier: I may have become a hot shot senior, but I would never forget him. He didn't keep his promise either, though. I hadn't talked to him since that day a year earlier in this exact same location. I wasn't sure what he was doing, where he was, or if he was seeing anyone.

I asked Aubrey about him when we began our senior year, but she informed me that the two of them had ended their relationship shortly after his graduation. She didn't go into much detail, but I didn't really expect her to, as we never had been very friendly toward each other.

As I turned my tassel from the right side over to the left with the rest of Western Michigan University's class of 2003, I decided it was finally time to end the Rich chapter of my life. I was moving to East Lansing in just a few months to begin graduate studies in journalism at Michigan State University, and it was time to start fresh.

As I made my way toward my parents who were sitting next to Cassidy's mom and dad, I knew my story with Rich Davis had probably come to an end. Perhaps, it wasn't the greatest love story ever written, and maybe, it wasn't a love story at all, but, at least, it was our story.

Part Two:

Fall 2011

I just wasn't feeling myself lately. Ever since Cassidy had Kaitlyn, we hadn't been able to go out much. Sure, I loved my goddaughter to pieces, but hanging out watching every Disney princess movie wasn't my idea of an entertaining Friday night. In fact, ever since she turned two, it had gotten to be a bit much since Aunt Brookie had to dress in her tiara and princess tutu before watching said movies.

Oh, I was only kidding myself. That little girl, her mom and I dressed in tutus, eating popcorn mixed with Junior Mints and singing at the top of our lungs to "Under the Sea" was the highlight of my life. Oh, and don't forget the wine. Cassidy and I even invested in special wine, sippy cups so that Kaitlyn would think we were just drinking apple juice right along with her. Hopefully, she would be twenty-one before she realized our dirty little secret.

Cassidy's short relationship with Steve What's-His-Name only lasted about two months, but those two months produced the most beautiful baby girl. Steve What's-His-Name wasn't in the picture for obvious reasons. He did nothing but bail on my best friend when she informed him she was pregnant, a little over three years ago. I believe he mumbled something about her "getting fat" before he left her in tears, just a few weeks pregnant. Of course, I was the first one she called when he left her a blubbering mess. I could barely understand her through her hiccupping sobs, but I rushed to her little apartment and spent nearly the entire pregnancy at her side.

I moved in with her during those nine months to help hold her hair back through the morning sickness and spoon with her at night when she couldn't sleep. Not only was I best friend, I had also become Lamaze coach, surrogate dad and Aunt Brookie. I loved both of them like my family. And, besides my dad, they were the only family I had. I suppose all three of them were the reasons I put my dreams on hold. At least, that's what I always told myself.

After my mom died nearly six years ago, I wanted to stay at home so my dad wouldn't be alone. I completed my master's degree at Michigan State University, but I didn't use it much to further my career. Sure, I was writing and editing for a local paper, but I wasn't soaring high at the big-city paper like I had always envisioned. Instead of covering presidential campaigns and the latest scandal on Capitol Hill, I was covering small-town politics and stories like the latest membership drive for the Red Hat Society.

UNWRITTEN

My most fascinating story was when the water installation project turned sour in one of the rural townships. I suppose I could credit myself with, at least, reporting hard news instead of writing about the latest fashion trend, or diet fad, like all the reporters I read about it my favorite romance novels.

I did consider myself a real reporter even if it wasn't at the *Washington Post*. I had given up on my dreams of moving to Washington D.C. several years ago. Most journalists aim for a position at the *New York Times, Los Angeles Times* or *Chicago Tribune*. But, with my focus in college on both political science and journalism, it was the vision of working at the *Post* that stayed with me for so many years. I remember working on a research assignment for one of my political science courses and using an article for my outline. "One day this will be my byline," I remember telling Cassidy, as I ran my thumb across the inky paper.

For the last six years, I kept making excuses for why I never applied to positions in the larger cities. I kept telling myself that I probably wasn't cut out for an urban assignment. After all, what if my dad needed me? What if Cassidy and Kaitlyn needed me? I was starting to think that it might not be the case after all.

I was really more afraid of me needing them and I needed to get past my fears and insecurities. Maybe the big city is just what the doctor ordered to help get me out of this rut and this funk. Come to think of it maybe the funk is just because I haven't showered in two days ... *maybe that's why I haven't gotten laid in six months.*

Besides my career being somewhat of a mess, my love life was even worse. It was a joke, really. I hadn't been out on a date in over six months. I swear cobwebs had taken up residence down below. B-O-B wasn't even getting action lately. Cassidy had tried to set me up on several blind dates, but each one of them ended up in the "epic failure" category.

My most recent, failed blind date was with Matt. Matt was Cassidy's accountant for her bridal boutique business and she insisted that he was an attractive, normal guy. I hadn't been out with someone in several months so I figured it wouldn't hurt to give Matt a whirl. What's the worst that can happen, right? Matt and I had talked on the phone for several nights before we finally decided to go to dinner. He seemed down to earth during our phone conversations and we seemed to really hit it off. For the first time in several years, I was looking forward to spending quality time with a man.

When Matt picked me up at my apartment for dinner, I was a little surprised when I answered the door and he was wearing a black polo shirt that was entirely covered in cat hair. I guess I was hoping for a man who was a little more kept.

I was even more shocked when I got outside and Matt opened the back door for me to slide in. He wouldn't let me sit in the front seat because it was already taken by "Princess Sophia," his feline companion. *Seriously, this is a true story; I couldn't make this shit up if I tried. I really thought "Krull the Warrior King" was going to emerge from the back seat.* I remember thinking that this date was over before it even began, but I smiled and scooted into the back seat, trying not to get white cat fur all over my black mini-dress.

All through dinner, Matt kept talking about Princess Sophia and showed me at least a dozen photos and six film clips from his iPhone. He even ordered a takeout of the salmon filet special for her to eat. Might I add, that he paid for Princess Sophia's dinner, but did not pick up my tab.

Before taking me home, Matt also made a trip to the pet store to pick up some kitty kibble. Let's just say that I didn't even allow Matt to walk me to the door when he finally dropped me off at my apartment.

I yelled at Cassidy for weeks about "Cat Matt," as we dubbed him. She did apologize profusely when she realized the ten photos of his cat on his desk should have been a telltale sign. I haven't allowed her to set me up on a blind date in the last six months because of my horrible feline-induced nightmares.

I decided one Saturday evening, as I was feeling sorry for myself, that if I couldn't do anything for my social life then it was, at least, time to put my skills and degrees to work. I still owed far too much to the government in student loans to remain at a crappy-paying job. I had plenty of experience now and I knew I had the ability to make a decent living still doing what I loved. My dad would understand. Maybe in time he would even want to move out East with me.

The three of us had visited the Mid-Atlantic region during my childhood on several occasions. My dad's ancestors had settled in the Maryland and Pennsylvania areas in the 1800s and my mom always enjoyed working on his family tree. She had already completed her genealogical lineage and made it her mission to complete his, as well.

I remember taking two trips to Maryland when I was about twelve. We spent our vacation among dusty books in the basement of area historical societies, libraries and even walking around cemeteries looking for century-old gravestones. At the time, I remember wishing I could be riding the tea cups at Disney World like all the other kids at school, but I wouldn't trade that time helping my mom for anything now.

I had to start putting myself first again. After Jay dumped me all those years ago and after losing my shot at love with Rich Davis, I had put my efforts into my education and later my career. My mom was my rock through those first years and when we lost her unexpectedly, it was the hardest time of my life. I remember walking around zombielike for days, or even weeks. Heck, maybe that was still me. Maybe that's why I never took the leap and moved to D.C.

I used my poor father as my excuse and my crutch, but maybe the truth was that I didn't want to leave home and the memories. Sure, I didn't live in their house anymore, but I visited at least every other day. I would often cook dinner for dad and even helped him with laundry from time to time. I knew deep down that he was self-sufficient, but it gave me a reason to stay and to feel needed.

My mom died unexpectedly from what doctor's originally thought was a simple infection. I could still hear her voice as she talked to me in the hospital just a few days before she died. My dad and my uncle (her brother) were there visiting, but had gone down to the cafeteria to grab a cup of coffee. My mom and I were alone in her room. I had taken her hairbrush out of the bedside table and was gently running the brush through her tangled hair, which besides a few gray strands matched the color of my own. She stopped me and pulled my head down to her chest. Petting the back of my head like she had done countless times before when I needed some comforting, she whispered softly in my ear so only I would hear.

"I'm so glad the three people that I love the most are here with me today. But, just remember, it's you that I love the most. I'll always be with you, baby girl."

I thought she was just scared that day in the hospital, but now I know that she knew she was sicker than what she was letting on. She was telling me goodbye. I'll never forget that moment, or her words. She will always be with me. No matter if I stay here in Michigan, or move to Washington D.C., her memories will always live within me, not in a particular city, or building.

It felt good to reminisce without feeling sad. Sure, I missed my mom tremendously, but it was time to move on. She would want me to be happy and to pursue the dreams that I had always envisioned for myself. If I couldn't be happy in love, at least, I could be happy in my work.

On Sunday morning, I dragged myself out of bed, popped my French vanilla flavored K-Cup in my new Keurig coffee maker, and sat down at my laptop to update my resume. After I had completed the resume, I wrote the sauciest cover letter and addressed the envelope c/o *The Washington Post.*

I had researched job openings the night before and saw they had a position open for a rookie reporter. Sure, I wasn't exactly a rookie anymore, but maybe they would decide they wanted someone with a little more experience. I had been doing the reporting thing for the last five years and covered every aspect from feature writing, local government and schools to reviews and opinion pieces. *Yes, they would want me – a seasoned reporter.*

The next three weeks went by and I had pretty much forgotten about my mailed application. They had probably decided to go with the rookie reporter to save on costs. I mean practically every business in corporate America is cutting costs these days.

It was a little after one o'clock when I heard my phone vibrate. I didn't recognize the out-of-area number that appeared on the screen and I almost sent it to voicemail assuming it was just another telemarketer wanting me to consolidate my debt. *Right, like they could handle my debt.* The call was on its last ring when I remembered the resume I had sent weeks ago, so I quietly picked up the call so as to not disturb my co-workers.

"Hello," I answered.

"Hello, Ms. Anderson?"

"Yes, this is she."

"Hi, my name is Caroline Murphy. I'm Mr. Davis's secretary with the *Washington Post*. He recently received your resume and is interested in scheduling an interview."

I couldn't believe what I was hearing, the *Washington Post* was calling. *Holy Fuck, the Washington Post was calling! Breathe and respond to the woman, Brooke.*

"Yes, that would be great. I would appreciate that opportunity very much."

"OK, great, how about next week? Would Tuesday work for you? Let's say eleven a.m."

"Yes, I do believe that would work just fine."

"Great, I will e-mail you with flight and hotel arrangements. If you have any further questions, please don't hesitate to call, or e-mail. Have a nice day, Ms. Anderson."

"Thank you," I said before ending the call.

Oh My God! Oh My God! Oh My God! This wasn't really happening. I couldn't contain my excitement as I exited my cubicle and ran through the office. I probably received a few blank stares, but I just couldn't help myself as I jumped up and down, even in my heels. I had to call Cassidy and tell her the incredible news!

Cass was as giddy with excitement about this interview as I was. She insisted on meeting me for dinner at our favorite bar sans Kaitlyn for the evening. It was like old times; I was so excited to spend some girl-time with my best friend. Kaity-bug was just as excited to spend the night with her grandma, so that helped ease my guilt for not including her, just a bit.

I arrived at Bubba's shortly before eight, and was surprised to see Cass already waiting for me in our old corner booth.

"You're early, lady!" I yelled from across the bar.

"Mom took Kaitlyn early, so I thought I would get a head start. I don't get many nights to myself so I wanted to take advantage."

Just as I was slipping into the somewhat tattered booth, our favorite bartender, Scott, walked over to take my order.

"Hey, beautiful ladies, long time, no see. What are you having tonight, Brooke?"

"Hey Scott, I'll have what she's having as I pointed toward Cass' nearly empty glass."

"One Long Island coming right up."

"A Long Island? Holy shit, Cass, you really did want to take advantage! I can only have one of those. You do realize it's a Wednesday and normal people still have to work tomorrow."

"Eh, that's the beauty of running your own business. My boss doesn't crawl up my ass if I'm late, or take a mental health day."

Cass had combined her knack for fashion and design with her business degree, and with a little monetary assistance from her parents, she was able to open her own wedding planning business. She was so wonderful at it, too. She had all the area's brides eating out of the palm of her hand. It really was shocking that she hadn't been able to plan her own wedding, yet.

Scott just stood there and watched our back-and-forth banter as if he was fully enjoying the show.

"Hey Scottie with the body, fill 'er up again, will ya?"

"Sure thing, ladies, two Long Islands coming right up. Oh, and Cassidy, might I add you are looking damn fine tonight." With that declaration, he walked away, leaving us both completely speechless.

After watching Scott and Cass flirt outrageously throughout the evening, I decided it was time to call it a night. Cass told me she was OK and that I could go on ahead without her. I made her promise to call me, if she couldn't catch a cab to get home.

She insisted on meeting me on Saturday to find the perfect outfit for my interview the following week. I couldn't very well tell her no once she gave me that puppy dog, pouty face. Unfortunately for me, she shared that identical expression with her daughter and they both knew that I always fell for it hook, line and sinker.

Chapter Six

There was a limousine waiting for me when I exited the terminal at Dulles International Airport, just a little after daybreak. I'd only ridden in a limo once before and it had been with *him*. I never imagined a potential employer going to such extremes for an interviewee. First, I received first-class boarding passes and now a stretch Hummer with my very own driver. This was certainly a few hundred steps above my current, small-town, reporting gig.

Even while riding in the lap of luxury, I couldn't shake the butterflies fighting in my stomach, or the incredibly sweaty palms that I kept wiping on my navy, pinstriped, pencil skirt. Thankfully, I decided to forgo breakfast before catching my red-eye out of Detroit. That would've made the butterfly situation a whole lot worse.

I could do this. I should have researched the editor, Davis, a bit more. Why didn't I think of doing it two days earlier? Where was the brown paper bag when you needed it? They were always so readily available to the broken heroines in the kinky romance novels that I enjoyed reading.

After what seemed to be a short drive, the limo began to slow down in front of a large building with oversized, tinted glass windows. Both an American flag and the flag of Washington D.C. flanked the entrance of my destination, the home of the *Washington Post*. Before the car came to a stop, I wiped my sweaty palms one final time, pulled my compact from my purse, applied a light pink lip gloss and took a deep breath. *Showtime!*

My driver came around and escorted me from the car. For that I was thankful, as I'm not sure my nervous, wobbly legs could have survived my new ankle-strap, cream leather Louboutins that I had purchased just for this interview. Sure, they may have cost me half an entire paycheck, but I wanted to look the part of an up-and-coming Washington reporter. My new shoes paired nicely with the vintage Valentino suit jacket that I found on clearance at my favorite consignment store and with my favorite go-to, pencil skirt.

I made my way up the front stairs, opened the heavy doors and headed toward the receptionist's desk. There sat a young blonde with what appeared to be a fake rack and an even faker tan.

"Hi, I'm Brooke … Brooke Anderson. I'm here for an interview with Mr. Davis."

The much-too-perky female handed me a visitor's badge and directed me to the twelfth floor where I was to ask for Mr. Davis's secretary, Caroline. I waited at the elevators for what seemed like an eternity before the doors opened and a group of people pressed forward.

A few suits exited the elevator on the sixth floor before the doors, pinging open on the twelfth floor, snapped me out of my nervous trance. I straightened my skirt and began to exit the elevator when I collided with all solid muscle and six feet three inches of him. And, that smell – why did this man smell so familiar? ... I hadn't smelled that perfect scent since ... it's then that I looked up and was greeted by those teal eyes. I'd never forget those eyes - those eyes that I never believed I would gaze into again. It was immediate déjà vu. I'd met him like this once before, only eleven years earlier. I had been a young and naïve student with so much to learn about life, love and heartache. I felt my heart begin to race and I feared that it might actually leap from my chest.

"Ms. Anderson. We need to stop bumping into each other this way."

Oh. My. God. Mr. Davis is Rich effin' Davis? How didn't I put two and two together?

"Brooke ... Are you all right?" he spoke again, stopping yet another potential panic attack from rising in my chest and throat.

"Yes. Fine. Thank You. ... Hello ... Ri—Um, Mr. Davis."

"Really, Brooke? Mr. Davis was my father. It's just me ... Rich ... Your Rich," he said, as his lips turned upward into what could only be described as a smirk. Rich knew he was getting to me and he was enjoying every minute of it. "Come ... with me."

Oh, the sexual innuendos came thick and fast and we'd only been together for thirty seconds. This was going to be a long and uncomfortable interview.

Rich reached out to grab my hand before walking toward what, I assumed, was the newsroom. He let go of my recently manicured fingers and ushered me through the area stuffed with tiny cubicles. His hand never left the small of my back as he introduced me to several reporters who were frantically typing away, trying to meet what I believed to be their early morning deadline. None of them seemed to be paying enough attention to notice Rich's hand on my back while we walked by, only muttering simple pleasantries.

We finally made it into a large office which overlooked the east side of the city. It wasn't the typical editor's cubicle that I had become accustomed to at my current job, this being far more than a cubicle. It was an expansive, corner office with a wall of windows looking out into the newsroom on one side and the city on the other. A chocolate suede couch with matching throw pillows sat against the wainscoting on one of the olive-colored walls, while a plush, cream chair sat in the opposite corner.

Near the outward-facing, floor-to-ceiling windows sat Rich's impressive, cherry wood desk. After seeing that desk, I may have entertained a few improper thoughts. A large, matching, coffee table sat in the middle of the room. The walls were adorned with framed newspapers, several Associated Press awards and Rich's diplomas. Rich was understandedly proud of his successful career without seeming overly conceited. Of course, I couldn't prevent the smirk crossing my face, knowing the real truth.

His office was fairly tidy, much more so than anything I'd ever seen in a newsroom. The only things that sat on his desktop were his all-in-one computer, a picture of a much younger-looking Rich sitting on his father's lap, and a digital voice recorder.

I was quite impressed because my own desk was cluttered with pens, notes and flyers from every event in town. The stacks of paper practically towered over the framed pictures I kept of my mom and dad on their wedding day and one of Cassidy, Kaitlyn and me taken on the day of Kaitlyn's baptism.

I momentarily wondered if I should tell him about my hatred for voice recorders. I had to explain myself to practically every one of my peers that I had ever encountered in the field. "I had a bad experience once and lost my entire recording," I always explained. "I was so embarrassed that instead of asking for a second interview, I simply stepped down from my internship position for a semester." Luckily, in the end, it still worked out for me, but to this day I would not rely on a voice recorder during my interviews.

I would go into all of my interviews with an old-fashioned reporter's notebook and pen. I may get strange looks, seeing as though it was now the twenty-first century, but it was what I felt comfortable with and most people understood. I was always accurate in my reporting and I think it actually made me listen and truly understand what my sources were saying. In spite of my messy desk and slightly dated reliance on pen and paper, I hoped that Rich would not question my competence. Of course, Rich would only know I was unorganized if he asked, and I would certainly not let that little detail slip.

"Your view … your entire office … it's exquisite," I said after soaking it all in.

"We haven't spoken in over nine years, and you want to talk about my view? But now that you mention it … my view is quite exquisite and I'm not referring to the skyline, or this office" he said, while licking his bottom lip. "You're just as beautiful as ever, Brooke."

"… … … Rich, why am I here?"

Rich walked over to his side of the desk and placed his palms flat on its surface as if bracing himself before speaking, his intense, teal-blue eyes looking directly into my soul. "You're here because when your application came across my desk, I knew it was a sign that I had to see you again … had to hear you laugh again … had to smell that sweet scent again. I've missed you, Brooke."

He took a deep breath before continuing, "Every time an application came across my desk I hoped that one day it would be yours. You always said this was it for you – your end game and your dream job. I'd be lying to myself and to you, if I didn't tell you that I came here and accepted this position, hoping that one day we'd find each other again."

"So, you only scheduled an interview because you wanted to finish what we never started ten years ago?" I asked in my most accusatory tone.

"Pshh, you would get that from what I just said, wouldn't you? No, of course not, Brooke. I wanted you to come for an interview, because I was impressed by what I read on your resume. You've had an impressive career and I think you would make an excellent addition to my editorial staff. Trust me, I'm not the only one who thinks that. Your resume made it through three layers of a selection process before it ended up on my desk."

"Oh ... OK. Well, thanks."

He looked at me with the most devilish grin before adding ... "It just doesn't hurt that I want to get to know you again."

I could feel the heat rising in my cheeks and expected that they had turned a bright shade of pink.

"Rich, I can't do this. I really do want this job, but if I accept the position, assuming that you are offering me one, I ... we can't do this. You'd be my boss. I can't and I won't be my boss's pet. No one would ever take me seriously. I wouldn't take me seriously. I've worked too hard for my career."

"I'm sorry, Brooke, I should have kept that to myself. I don't want to scare you away. How about this ... I don't offer you the position – today? We talk – you know, catch up – conduct a real interview. Then I'll send you on your way to your hotel. You will then eat at the restaurant where my secretary has already made dinner reservations for you. I'll just happen to show up and we'll meet once again. I'll just be Rich and you'll just be Brooke. We won't be interviewer and interviewee. What do you say, Miss Anderson? Sound like a plan?"

I had to give him credit; he sure did make it sound so easy.

"Sounds more like a date than a plan, Mr. Davis. You've really given this some thought. That truly is some proposition," I responded with a wink.

"I'll take your feisty response as a yes then. And, yes, I've been thinking about this since I left you on your doorstep, wearing that ravishing, purple gown over nine years ago. Now, the quicker we begin your interview, the faster we can get to dinner, the earlier I can get you to my place so we can make up for lost time. What do you say, let's begin your interview, shall we?"

"Ye-, Ye-s, sure … fire away."

I looked down at my watch and realized that two hours had elapsed as Rich asked dozens of questions about what I'd been doing after graduating from Western. He seemed impressed that I had earned a master's degree in journalism and had worked my way up to editor at my local newspaper. I was equally impressed to learn he had also earned a master's in journalism from a very well-respected university on the East Coast.

It was depressing to think that we had such similar backgrounds, yet he had made it so much farther than me. *You're here now, Brooke. That's all that matters. Forget the past … look toward the future.*

We talked a little bit about my family. Of course, he was devastated to learn about the passing of my mom. They had only met briefly once at a family picnic outing that the college had planned my junior year. He told me then that he had lost his dad about a year earlier.

So, he understood the pain that I still knew every day. It was in that moment when I think I felt a little closer to Rich. Sure, we had thick, sexual chemistry, but I was starting to notice an emotional attachment that I may have been missing when I first stepped into his office. It was then that I had to remind myself that this would never work, if I actually wanted to work at the *Washington Post*, my dream job. Of course, I wanted to work at the *Post*, but somewhere in the back of my mind, I wondered if I wanted Rich more. Was it possible to have both?

"Well, Brooke, I suppose I've taken up enough of your time for the day. Do you have any questions for me, or about the position?"

"No, I think we covered just about everything. Thank you for your time and thank you for considering me for the position. I'll see myself out, if that's everything."

"Brooke, don't forget about checking in with Ms. Murphy about your dinner reservations."

"Yes, sir," I said in my most seductive tone.

"Don't tease me, sweetheart. It's taking all my willpower not to rip that skirt off you and bend you over my desk right now."

And with that statement, I felt my lady parts quiver in anticipation for what I'd been dreaming about for the better part of a decade. *Was this really going to happen – tonight?*

Chapter Seven

I made it to my hotel suite shortly before two in the afternoon. Caroline gave me my dinner reservations and also provided a few options as far as the best boutiques in the area.

I had just a few hours to find the perfect cocktail dress that would wow Rich's socks off – or rather his entire suit and everything underneath. *What the hell am I thinking ... I can NOT have sex with Rich Davis. I want to work in his editorial department. This has always been my dream job and I can't mess that up now for just one incredible night under the sheets with him. Or, could I? Maybe we could just pretend to be strangers tonight ... as Rich had suggested. And, tomorrow would be a new day.*

I found the perfect dress in a small boutique in the most upscale area of D.C. Even though it was a bit out of my price range, I pulled out my credit card to pay for the purchase. Hopefully, I would soon have a better paying job and could afford to pay down the large amount of debt I had incurred over the years with my frivolous spending habits.

Arriving back at my hotel room at around four in the afternoon, I had just enough time to hop in the shower before getting ready for my dinner date with Rich. I still hadn't had time to call Cassidy to tell her about my interview, or my potential new boss, so I decided to shoot her a quick text telling her I would call her later with the details.

> *You'll never guess who I ran into today. I'm heading out to dinner in the city. I will call you when I get back. Love ya, girlie!*
>
> *Cass: What the fuck. You're going to dinner ... alone? You can't possibly have a date you've only been there what like six hours? You little slut! Who the hell did you meet in the city!?! You better call me TONIGHT, missy! Unless you're getting frisky! Make sure you stuff a condom into your purse. The last thing you want is a fun-sized Brookie showing up in nine months! ;) Xxoo*

Oh, Cass, always the drama queen. I tossed my phone onto the bed and padded into the bathroom to hop in the shower. After emerging, I applied some light makeup, slightly dried my hair before scrunching it up, so it would fall into loose waves over my shoulders. I opened my suitcase and was pleased that Cass had talked me into packing a sexy, black lace thong and matching bra.

I could hear her now, "You never know when you might need some sexy lingerie, Brookie. What if you meet the man of your dreams and instantly have to fuck him? Would you want him to see you in some granny panties? Or, heaven forbid, you get into a horrific, yet non-life-threatening, car accident and Doctor Hotstuff has to rip your clothes off in the ER?"

I chuckled at her infinite wisdom as I shimmied into my lingerie and then into the short, long-sleeved, sequined, purple cocktail dress that I had purchased earlier. I knew Rich had a thing for me in purple, after all, he did share that little fact earlier during the interview. I also added the silver, glittery, peep-toe, Jimmy Choo pumps that I included with my purchase and a pair of silver, dangly earrings that I brought along from home. *Who would have thought, I, Brooke Anderson, would buy a pair of Louboutins and Jimmy Choos in the same week?*

After checking myself once more in the mirror, I was pleased with the reflection staring back at me. It was approaching five o'clock and I needed to head out to make it to the restaurant on time. If I remembered correctly, Rich Davis was never late for anything.

As the taxicab pulled up to the Oceanaire Seafood Room, where Ms. Murphy had made reservations, I felt the same jitters that overcame me earlier that morning. I knew this was a premier restaurant in the city and briefly wondered how Rich could afford such an extravagant lifestyle. I'm sure he made a very nice living as editor of one of the world's largest newspapers, but I still knew how much journalists usually made and it wouldn't be enough for this type of restaurant, or the three-piece

Armani suit he was wearing earlier in the day. I made a mental note to ask him about that later.

I wiped my palms as best I could on my legs and took a deep breath before paying the driver and exiting the car. As I approached the building, I once again bumped into the hard chest of the one and only Rich Davis.

"You really do need to watch where you're going, Brooke. One of these days, I won't be around to keep you on your feet. Might I add, sweetheart, that you look ravishing. Simply a sight for sore eyes ... Mmmm ... edible, really. What I wouldn't do to skip dinner and just skip straight to what would probably be the sweetest dessert ever. I really do love you in purple – magnificent. You're just as stunning in purple as that day all those years ago."

I smiled as I mentally congratulated myself for listening so well earlier, despite the gorgeous man in front of me who had been doing most of the talking.

"Well, hello, to you, too, Rich. And, thank you. Might I add that you clean up pretty well, too." That was an understatement on my part. He looked so sexy in his black suit that he'd been wearing earlier in the day, paired with a shirt that matched the exact color of his eyes.

He had removed his tie and left the top button open which revealed just a small outline of sinfully sexy chest. His hair was a bit shorter than I remembered from college, but it was slicked back and so hot. I think that I, too, wanted to skip straight to dessert.

We enjoyed a pleasant dinner of the best sautéed scallops and shrimp and a few glasses of the house-specialty Chardonnay, as we exchanged much more personal information than we had earlier that day in his office. We also had a great time going back down memory lane. I reminded Rich of the time we worked together on our first writing assignment. He chuckled when I told him what a complete douche bag I thought he was at the time.

"I bet you still show up to everything twenty minutes early, don't you?"

"Punctuality is of utmost importance, Brooke – in life and in business. And, I bet you still sleep with that teddy bear that always sat on the end of your bed, don't you?

I glanced at him quizzically and with a raised brow before answering, "Uh, yeah. But, I don't ever remember you coming into my room. You always just stopped at my door and never made a move to come inside. How did you know I had a teddy bear on the end of my bed?"

"Oh, I have my sources," he replied with a devilish grin. "But, I was in your room briefly the afternoon of your sorority formal."

"Oh my god, I'm going to kill her. I can't believe Cassidy told you my deepest secret," I responded in a fit of laughter. "When did she tell you this?"

"Sure did. I believe it was the night of the sorority formal. You were still standing through the moon roof when she came down to get more champagne. I even understand his name is Reggie?"

"How ... how, after all of these years, do you remember my teddy bear's name? Even I can hardly remember his name!"

"I remember everything about you, Brooke Anderson – everything."

His words sent chills up my arms, but I decided it was time to broach a more serious subject while the waiter cleared the table as we waited for our desserts.

"Why did you break your promise, Rich?"

He looked directly into my eyes before answering, "I don't know what you're talking about, Brooke."

"You told me you'd keep in touch. It's been nine years, Rich. I haven't spoken to you since that day in the quad over nine years ago," I responded.

"That wasn't my promise, Brooke. What I promised you was that it wasn't goodbye for us that day. As you can see, I've kept my promise just like I intend to keep every promise I ever make to you. And, I can promise you this ... I plan on making several, sweetheart."

His words caught me off guard and I stared at him with my mouth agape for several seconds before I spit out the first question that came to mind.

"How did you get your position at the *Post*?" I'd been wondering this ever since I ran into him at the elevator that morning.

"Well, I started as a lowly intern during my last semester at Columbia," he said with a shrug. "I decided to come down here instead of working at the *Times* like most of my peers. I guess they just loved me so much that they gave me a job when the semester ended. I went back to New York to collect my degree and moved to D.C. the following week. I worked as a reporter for about a year before being moved into the editorial department. Eventually, our editor left and the rest, as they say, is history."

"That really is quite impressive, Rich, but how did you end up doing so well for yourself? I know journalists don't have the kind of money that you appear to be throwing around." *Shit, the words were off my tongue before I even thought about what I was asking ... and of my potential boss, no less. Real smooth, Brooke. Real smooth.*

A chuckle escaped Rich before he continued ... "Cut right to the chase, don't you." He took a deep breath before continuing, "My dad ... as I told you earlier, passed one year ago. We were always very wealthy growing up because he'd been very successful in his business dealings. He really knew how to invest his money. Due to his diligence, my mom, sister and I will never have to worry about money. It was still important for me to work. I worked very hard in school to have a successful career in journalism, but, as you just pointed out, the profession doesn't pay that well even in my position. But, thanks to my dad, I'm able to do what I love and still have the means to live a very comfortable lifestyle."

"That's nice that he was able to do that for you. He would be very proud of you, Rich."

"Thanks, I hope so. I know your mom would be proud of her baby girl, too."

"Thanks, but I'm not so sure. I really gave up on my dreams when she died. I think I was scared that I would fail and I used her death as an excuse. I'm tired of running scared from things anymore. I need to do this for me ... for her. It's what she would want me to do."

"Trust me, sweetheart. She would be very proud of the intelligent and beautiful woman that is sitting before me. It may have taken you awhile to follow your dreams, but you're here now. I hope I'm able to make each and every one of your dreams come true," Rich said reassuringly.

"Rich, you sound like a commercial for Disney World." I said, so matter-of-factly.

Now I had him in a fit of laughter as our waiter brought us two plates of tiramisu and two vanilla lattes with a hint of Bailey's Irish Cream.

"I've missed you, Brooke. Your wit. Your smile. Your laughter. Your beauty – Every. last. bit. of. you." Each word spoken between chuckles set off by my previous Disney World comment.

"I don't know if I can take a laughing man seriously, Rich."

He suddenly became very earnest as he spoke, "I'm serious, Brooke, very serious. Don't mistake my laughter as my not taking you seriously. It feels so good to be free and laugh around you. I love yo … your ability to make me laugh."

My mind was swirling a mile a minute after Rich's confession. *Was he just about to tell me that he loved me? How could he possibly know such a thing? We hadn't seen each other in nine years and we were never actually together then. I've never even had his lips on mine. Why, even with all of the rational thoughts, am I thinking that I could love him, too? Holy shit.*

An "OK" was all I was able to squeak out before I turned my attention to the tiramisu in front of me.

"Now that you've already asked me the tough questions, what do you say to a quick game of Truth or Dare. You know for old time's sake?" Rich inquired.

"I can't argue with a man who wants to play Truth or Dare," I replied, shaking my head.

"OK, I'll start. Hit me with a truth," he said.

"What's your biggest regret in life?"

"That's easy," he instantly answered. "Letting you walk out of my life all those years ago. I have thought about you every day for the past nine years, Brooke. That's the honest-to-god, truth."

His words were so raw, and so filled with emotion. I had to blink back the tears that had formed in my eyes.

"Wow, I wasn't expecting that, Rich. Maybe we shouldn't be playing this. I remember your questions and tasks were of a higher caliber in college, I can only imagine what they are like now," I said, with a chuckle.

"Just pick one, already. I promise to go easy on you."

"OK, truth for me, too," I said.

"Do you regret not kissing me – really kissing me when I dared you all those years ago?"

I took a deep breath before answering, after all, he did ask for the truth. "Yes."

"Interesting, very interesting – let's go with another truth."

"If you could have anything in the world, what would it be?"

"You," he said so matter-of-factly.

"I'm sensing a pattern here, Rich. Now I'll shake it up a bit and go with a dare," I said, flirtatiously.

"Strip," he said, without hesitation.

"Excuse me? You've got to be kidding, right? We're in a very public restaurant."

He said through his laughter, "I bet you thought I was going to ask for a redo on that kiss, didn't you?"

"Well I certainly didn't think you'd want me to get naked in public," I responded.

"Does that mean you forfeit ... again?"

"I – I didn't say that," as I bent down in my chair to remove my heel. *Two can play at this game.*

"Whoa, you can stop right there. Would you like to join me for a nightcap at my home? We can finish this little game there."

"I don't think that's a good idea, Rich. Given our current circumstances ... I mean, unless, you don't intend on offering me a position tomorrow?

"What did I tell you earlier, Brooke? Tonight we are old friends – reconnecting. We'll worry about tomorrow, tomorrow. Tonight I want you tangled in my sheets. I've dreamt about you in my bed for the last ten years, and I'm not about to let you board that plane tomorrow without hearing you scream out my name tonight. Now, what do you say about that nightcap?" He spoke all of that without any uncertainty in his voice. Rich was telling me how tonight was going to play out with no ifs, no ands, or buts. I was not about to argue; this was exactly what I wanted, too.

Rich settled the bill and escorted me out of the restaurant before his hand came to a rest on the small of my back.

"You know, sweetheart, I'm glad I didn't notice how short this dress of yours was before now. I'd have taken a swing at any guy, I thought was ogling that mighty fine ass of yours."

Suddenly, I felt his hand move away before I felt it slide under my dress and squeeze the globe of my rear end. He led me to his car with his hand once again resting on my back, but just a pinch lower this time ... When we made it to the car, I gasped at what I saw in front of me. I'm pretty sure it was the most spectacular car I had ever seen, let alone had the privilege to ride in.

"Holy shit you have a Maserati Granturismo? And, it's red ... and a convertible? Your car is fuckin' hot with a capital H, Rich," I exclaimed, as I stared in awe at the car.

"Yes, and we can even ride with the top down. One day we'll have to ride with more than one top down. But, not tonight ... too many people around here and I'm not sharing that view with anyone," he laughed, as I rolled my eyes at his suggestion.

Rich opened the door for me and I slid into the most gorgeous car on the planet. Oh, and that fresh leather smell. Seriously, Rich didn't even have my clothes off and I thought I could come from sitting in this car alone. Rich walked around the car, tossed his sport coat into the back seat and scooted into the driver's seat before turning the key and revving the engine a few times.

"Show off," I remarked.

"I can tell it's turning you on, sweetheart. If I knew my car would get you so excited we could've skipped the fancy restaurant altogether and got fast food to eat in the Maserati. Maybe we could've made use of my backseat, too."

With that suggestion, he lowered the roof and pulled out into traffic. He turned on the car's sound system and it immediately began playing "Too Close" by Next. Suddenly, I broke into loud, hysterical laughter.

"You actually remember this?" I asked him.

"I told you earlier, I remember every moment that I ever spent with you, Brooke. They were all special to me. I always wished that things could have been different between us. It just wasn't the right time for us, I suppose."

I really didn't know how to respond to him at that moment, so I just laid my head back to enjoy the starry night and the warm wind caressing my face.

"Oh, and baby ... you are making it hard for me."

I chuckled and rocked my head back and forth against the headrest.

The car slowed as Rich parked in front of, what I assumed to be, his apartment building. He let himself out of the car before coming around to open my door. He offered me his hand and I accepted it, as he helped me from the car.

The next thing I knew, my back was against the car and his lips were smashing into mine. I had dreamt of those soft lips and that cinnamon taste for what seemed like an eternity. He sucked on my bottom lip before parting my edges with a flick of his tongue. Rich moved closer into my front and I could tell that I really was making it "hard for him" as he had expressed with the song in the car. Our tongues danced together for several minutes, before I found myself panting for more.

"Not here, not yet, my little exhibitionist," Rich protested. "I just couldn't wait another second to feel your lips on mine. A decade was too damn long. And, sweetheart, it was everything I ever imagined it would be. Now let's get you upstairs and out of that dress, shall we?"

With that I grabbed for Rich's hand and he had me nearly sprinting to his apartment.

"Sweetheart, no offense, but those shoes are slowing you down," he said with a smirk.

Before he was done talking, he placed his hands on my back and under my knees and scooped me into his arms. He, too, began sprinting toward his apartment building and through the wide, double-glass doors. I tried to take in as much of the luxurious lobby as my eyes would allow. It was magnificent, from the high, vaulted ceilings and executive leather furniture to an elegant, Swarovski crystal chandelier hanging from the highest peak.

"You ... live ... here?" I managed to choke out in absolute awe.

"Yep, this is home," Rich said nonchalantly, as he continued to cradle me close to his solid chest.

"It's magnificent, Rich. Really ... amazing."

"Thank you, Brooke, but not nearly as magnificent as you. Now let's get us upstairs, shall we?"

I just nodded my head in agreement as he rushed us toward the elevator.

Once the elevator closed, he took advantage of our seclusion and parted my lips with his tongue once again. I could definitely get used to that taste ... *Stop, Brooke, you cannot, repeat cannot, get used to that taste. This is for one night. Tomorrow, Rich will be your boss and only your boss.*

Rich must have sensed my hesitation because he pulled away slowly and asked, "Are you all right, sweetheart. You just tensed up on me."

"Yes, Rich, everything is more than fine. Perfect really, just perfect."

He must have liked my answer because that Hollywood smile that I always adored, returned as his succulent lips engaged with mine once again. The elevator stopped on the top floor and Rich slid me down the length of his rigid body and led me out, firmly gripping my hand. He fumbled in his pocket with his free hand and removed his key to unlock the door to his penthouse. We made our way inside and Rich slammed the door, before we began making out against it, like horny teenagers. I suppose we were making up for over ten years worth of missed kisses.

"Unbelievable, Brooke. You taste so incredible. I can't believe this is happening right now. I'm so glad you've walked back into my life, sweetheart – so fucking glad."

"I know we were going to finish our game back here and I was going to let you do a little strip tease for me, but I can't wait to get you naked," he added, with his breath against my ear.

Rich wrapped his arms behind me and I felt him slowly unzip the back of my dress. He placed his hands on my shoulders and lowered the scoop neck of my dress, before extending both of my arms out to remove them from the sleeves. He slowly lowered the top half of my dress and when my bra came into view, I swear I heard a growl escape from his mouth.

"Absolute perfection," he mumbled again.

Once Rich had lowered the dress to my waist, he let go and it fell to the floor and bunched at my ankles. He stepped back and I watched his blue eyes take me in completely. Watching him watch me might have been the sexiest sight I had ever witnessed.

Rich took my hand in his once again and pulled it up to his lips for a gentle kiss, before leading me forward. I stepped out of my dress and followed him in the direction of what, I presumed to be, his bedroom. A surge of excitement ran through my body. This was it ... after all this time, this was finally happening.

I tried to hold back my nervous anticipation, but Rich was suddenly so close that my mind began to unravel. In this moment, I needed him and I needed him now. Rich pulled me into an embrace and walked me backwards until I felt the back of my knees touch his mattress. Before he had the chance to tip me backwards, I grabbed his broad shoulders, still covered in his crisp, white dress shirt, and pulled him into my body for another kiss. This time I took control and passionately parted his lips. As our mouths intertwined, I tore open his shirt and heard buttons clank as they hit the floor one by one. He pulled away and his shirt fell to the ground.

It was now my turn to take in the man that stood before me. His chiseled abdomen was everything I imagined it to be. His perfectly sculpted six pack led right down to that mouth-watering V on his hips. I wanted to use my tongue to trace the light line of hair near the bottom of his stomach that led to just below his belt. I caught myself whimpering as Rich came back forward. This time I didn't have his shirt to grab onto, as he lightly pushed me backwards onto the bed.

"Although these are lovely, sweetheart, they both need to go now," Rich said as he removed my bra with one hand and the other hand moved south to begin sliding my panties down my legs. "Oh, but those shoes ... those shoes can stay. Fuck ... you are the most beautiful woman I have ever laid my eyes on."

His words made me purr. I actually purred. The sounds coming from my throat told Rich to take me. Never hesitating, his mouth drifted south to my breasts. He took one in his mouth and slowly sucked before lightly biting down on my nipple. His other hand palmed the other and squeezed my sensitive bud between his fingers. He switched back and forth between both breasts for several minutes.

"We've waited for this for so long, Brooke. I want to make sure I pleasure you properly. I want to take all night pleasuring this beautiful body of yours. I want this image of you unraveling in my bed, ingrained in my mind for the rest of my life."

Rich's hands and mouth hadn't moved south of my breasts, but I was convinced at that moment I could come with that pleasure and his seductive words alone. Rich could tell I was about to fall over the cliff, as my body squirmed beneath him.

"You are so hot, sweetheart. I'm going to make you come. Concentrate for me, Brooke. Let yourself go."

I did as I was told and I put every thought into Rich and how his hands and mouth were pleasuring my sensitive and fully erect nipples. I wasn't sure if it was humanly possible to achieve orgasm through breast stimulation alone. Before I could think too much more about it, I felt my body quiver and my pussy spasm. I called out Rich's name in pure, ecstatic pleasure as my body jerked from the bed. I felt Rich's slacks rub against my legs, as my body lunged up in his direction.

"Rich ... Rich, you need to drop your damn pants and fuck me now."

"You're a demanding little minx, aren't you?"

I sat up in the bed and rested my weight on my elbows and watched Rich as he unbuckled his belt and slid down his dress pants. I licked my lips before whispering in my most seductive voice, "Let me do the rest ... please."

Rich got on his knees and crawled toward me. I sat up completely and reached out to touch his rock-hard abs. He looked at me with hooded eyes, before pulling me in closer for another kiss.

I moved my hands all the way down his body until I reached the waist of his boxer briefs. I lowered the elastic band just enough for his hard cock to spring free. My hands could feel his wide girth and I could see his that tip was already slick. Scooting forward and wrapping my legs around his kneeling body, I could feel the heat of his cock near my entrance.

"Tell me, sweetheart. Tell me what you want."

I just stared at him, unable to find my words.

"Playing coy now are you? Come closer. Whisper it in my ear."

I moved closer to Rich and blew lightly in his ear before whispering, "Please Rich, I'm so ready for you."

That was all Rich needed to hear before he straightened himself and removed his boxer briefs. Reaching over to his nightstand and pulling a foil-wrapped condom from the drawer, he unwrapped it and carefully slid it onto himself. He then gently pushed me back on the bed and lowered himself on top of me, resting his weight on his forearms. He suddenly plunged into me and I yelped out at his sudden entrance. I wiggled slightly beneath him in order to fully open myself to his size.

"Are you all right, sweetheart?"

"I'm great, Rich. In fact, I've never felt better," I moaned.

Rich began to pick up speed, jerking himself in and out of me. I could tell by his breathing that he was getting close to his own release.

"Touch yourself for me, Brooke. Take your finger and rub your clit for me."

I did as Rich asked, bringing two fingers to my clit and rubbing the sensitive nub in a circular motion, as he continued to slam his hard cock into my wet, slippery pussy.

"You are so amazing. So fuckin' amazing. I don't know how I could've waited for this for ten years. I know I'm never going to wait again," Rich gasped.

I could tell by the look in his eyes that he meant every word of it. Rich wasn't going to wait for me again. I couldn't think about any of that right now … Right now I just wanted to find another release with this man. I wanted to come together with him.

I continued to rub my clit, and Rich angled his body so he was able to bring his mouth to my tits once again. The simultaneous pleasure sent me over the edge, and I began to writhe beneath him. My walls began to tighten and spasm around his girth and I felt him pump into me twice more, before he groaned and let go of his own release.

We breathed heavily together for several minutes before Rich finally pulled himself out of my body and rolled over onto his side, before removing his condom and tossing it on the floor. Then resting my head between the pillow and his arm, I felt him stroke my hair with his other hand. I heard him lightly chuckle as he continued to pet my head.

"Something funny?" I asked.

"I was just thinking how I forgot to offer you that nightcap. Sorry, sweetheart, that wasn't very gentlemanlike of me."

I couldn't help but laugh at Rich's sudden concern.

"It's quite all right, Rich. We both know I didn't agree to come here for the booze."

"Well then, I hope you did get what you came for."

"Hmph, you know I did, stud. In fact, you were so amazing that you were able to allow me to achieve my first ever boobgasm. I had only read about them and didn't actually believe they were real. But, you taught me tonight that they are very much indeed the real deal."

"Wow, just wow. That was so incredible to watch, Brooke. You are also the first woman I have had the opportunity of pleasuring in such a way. I guess you could say we popped each other's boobgasm cherries."

We laughed and talked a bit longer before my earlier drowsiness returned in full force.

Almost drifting off, I felt the bed move next to me as Rich got up and walked to the bathroom. I heard the water running and just a few minutes later,

Rich came back to bed with a warm, soapy washcloth.

"I thought you might want to clean up before you fell asleep. Do you want me to do it for you?"

"Mmmhmm," was all I was able to mumble, before I felt Rich softly wiping my body clean of our sex.

I fell asleep shortly after I felt Rich sink into bed and put his arm around me. I could really get used to falling asleep like this, in this man's arms every night.

Chapter Eight

I woke up in Rich's bed just as the sun was beginning to rise above the horizon. Hearing my phone vibrate in my purse, I tried to get up in time to grab it, but felt the weight of his arm across my bare chest.

"You trying to sneak off already, sweetheart?" he murmured.

"No, I need to grab my phone, but I probably should get going, Rich. I have a flight to catch tonight and wanted to look around the city for a bit before heading back to the airport."

"What time does your flight leave?"

"I'm taking the last one out tonight at nine. I wanted to do some sightseeing this afternoon, so I scheduled it as late as I could."

"I'll take the day off and we'll spend it together then."

"Rich, we only agreed to last night. Today is another day and we can't continue to do this."

As I was trying to convince him that this was a bad idea, I could feel his hard length growing at my side.

"Oh, Brooke, after last night I'm not sure I can, or will, ever let you go. Just say you will spend the rest of the day with me and we can discuss what comes next when you are back home tomorrow."

Before he even let me speak, I felt his hands begin to slowly rub circles around my nipples. I felt my body begin to defy me as I started to lift myself up, making it easier for him to access my taut peaks. He took this as his victory and slammed his mouth against mine once again. He began teasing my tongue with his own as he continued to pinch and flick my nipples.

I felt myself already dripping with desire as he moved his mouth away from mine and latched onto my breasts, using the same pinching and flicking technique with his mouth. His hands began making their way down my abdomen to my slick folds, softly rubbing my clit with the same circular pattern, he had used before on my breasts.

"I don't know how you can say you want to deny me, Brooke. It's clearly obvious that your body desires me so much. You are so wet for me. So. Wet."

With that he plunged two fingers into my slit and quickly pumped them in and out while his thumb kept circling my clit, working me into a heated frenzy. I knew it was only a matter of minutes before I would explode.

"Rich, I need you."

"You have me, sweetheart."

"No. I.need.you.in.me.now."

"Just come for me, Brooke. I want to watch as you erupt on my hand. You are so fucking sexy right now. So fucking sexy. I didn't get to take my time with you last night. I didn't get to watch you fall apart."

With that, my walls tightened around his fingers as I felt the most amazing orgasm ripple through my body. With no time to catch my breath, I heard Rich tear open the foil wrapper.

"Rich, don't. I want to feel all of you this time." I heard his breath hitch at my request." I'm on the pill," I told him just to reassure him that I was safe that this was safe. "I trust you."

He looked at me with wide eyes as if he were registering what I had asked of him. Before I could get another word in, he rammed his bulging cock inside my already pulsating pussy. I had to reposition my body underneath him to allow him to fill me completely. Rich must have felt me move beneath him because, before I knew it, he had me flipped over and on top of him.

"Ride me like a carnival pony, baby."

I couldn't help but giggle before I realized he was being completely serious. I did as instructed and began bobbing up and down as he filled me with each thrust. He grabbed my neck and pulled me down, my tits rubbing against the perfectly sculpted surface of his chest, for the most passionate, yet aggressive, kiss of my life. As our tongues were teasing, I took the opportunity to run my hands through his shaggy hair. I was just about to come unglued when I heard Rich groaning.

"Harder, Rich. Don't stop … please," I begged.

With that Rich flipped us over again in one quick motion and began thrusting into me. He pumped even more deeply into me several times, before I screamed out his name one final time, as I came undone around him. My screams must have put him over the edge because, before coming down from my high, he grabbed my ass to pull me in closer, his liquid warmth filling me completely. He found his release and collapsed, breathless against my tender breasts.

Rich held me, my head on his chest for several minutes as our breathing evened out. I felt his fingers stroke my hair, just as he had done on the night that Jay and I had broken up, making me feel like a college kid again. I was young and carefree in Rich's strong embrace, as though the last ten years of my life hadn't happened.

As I ran my fingers up and down Rich's sculpted chest, I noticed a large, Celtic knot tattoo with a set of dates over his left pec muscle. Tracing the outline with my finger, I felt his breath hitch at my touch.

"What does it mean," I asked.

"The Celtic knot represents my father's Welsh ancestry. I added the dates – his birth date and death date – just recently," he answered with reflection in his voice.

I wanted to ask him about his father, but I knew he would talk about it, if he wanted to. I knew better than to push it. I couldn't stand it when people urged me to talk shortly after my mom died. I talked to a few select people and I wanted everyone else to leave me alone.

Just as I was starting to drift off again, I heard him ask …

"Does it ever get easier?"

"Does what get easier?" I asked, only half-awake.

"Your mom … I mean does the pain ever go away? Do you ever stop missing her?"

I had to take a minute to process what he was really asking me. Rich was taking our conversation to a much more intimate level. This was far past standard, pillow talk and I wasn't sure if I was ready for this. I had just thought about asking him about his father, and I guess he did want to talk after all.

"Rich," I said, blinking back the tears that were welling in my eyes, "I don't think we should discuss this right now."

"Come on, Brooke. I … I need to know if it gets easier. I don't have anyone else to talk to. No one else gets it. All of my friends," he went on, pausing for a moment to collect his thoughts. "All my friends, they still have their parents. Most of them still have their grandparents even. I don't know anyone else like … like us. And, I need to know if it gets easier. Please, just tell me … that it gets easier."

He was pained and he was pleading with me to take away the hurt of losing his father. He wanted me to promise something that I could not promise him. Sure, my pain had dulled from what it was six years ago, but it hadn't gone away and I was starting to believe it never would. I didn't think I ever wanted it to fade away. Once it was gone, would I forget my mom completely? Would I forget the sound of her voice, her smell, the look on her face when I brought home my report card chockfull of straight A's in the fourth grade? No, I didn't want the hurt to completely fade because then, too, would the memories.

I realized I had let some time pass, when I heard Rich ask me again, "please, Brooke."

"It's only been a year, Rich. The first year was the most difficult for me, too. I walked around in a daze for most of it. Honestly, I have no idea how I even finished graduate school. I don't even remember getting out of bed most mornings. I guess I was just surviving, doing my day-to-day tasks, and honestly, I wonder how well I did those things, looking back on it. Does it ever get easier? Yes, I'd say it does get easier; the hurt doesn't go away, though. At least for me it hasn't, but I don't think I really want it to go away – not entirely. If it does go away then it might mean I have forgotten her and there is nothing about my mother that I want to forget."

We were both quiet for several minutes before Rich tucked me closer against his chest and planted the most gentle, softest kiss behind my ear. The intimacy of the moment sent a chill up my spine.

"Thank you, Brooke," Rich said, tenderly.

"Maybe sometime you could tell me about him. It helps me to tell stories about my mom," I said the words before I even knew what I was saying.

"I'd like that, but right now we need to get showered so we can tackle this sightseeing list of yours."

I was a little disappointed and almost suggested we skip the sightseeing altogether and spend the day in bed, wrapped in each other's arms, until Rich moved away from me and peeled himself out of bed. In that moment, I felt empty without him.

As much as I didn't want it to, something had happened between us in that short span of time. I just knew that I had to get a handle on the situation while it was still possible. After thinking for a minute about what this would mean for my future, I looked up to see Rich standing next to the bed... completely naked.

All my previous thoughts vanished, as my bulging eyes attempted to take in a nude Rich, standing before me with a shit-eating grin on his face.

I hadn't seen all of Rich the night before in his darkened bedroom, and we were in such a heated frenzy, but the man was seriously a sight for sore eyes – all one-hundred-percent pure, male deliciousness. I could tell he spent much of his downtime at the gym. By daylight, I was convinced I had counted eight chiseled muscles on his sculpted abs that still led down to that delectable V – and below his waist ... *Sweet Jesus.*

"Enjoying the show, Brooke?"

" ... ... I ... wow ... I mean."

"I never thought I would see the day when I left Babbling Brooke speechless," he chuckled.

"Shut up. I am not a Babbling Brooke. I used to hate it when you called me that in college."

"I know," he added with a grin.

I grabbed the pillow from behind me and chucked it in his direction. He blocked my feeble attempt at bodily injury and laughed as he pulled me from the bed and into his embrace.

"I could hold onto you forever, Brooke Anderson. I know you have your reservations, but just know that I am not willing to let you slip away from me again. I don't care what I have to do to prove to you that this is where you belong."

Without saying another word, he grasped my hand and led me into his bathroom.

"I doubt we'll get out of here very fast, showering together, Rich."

"I don't care if we're here all day, Brooke. I'll be the one to wash every inch of your body this morning."

We stepped into Rich's spacious shower; seriously, it was easily big enough for six people. There were two large, shower heads attached to the modern, tiled wall. Rich turned on the faucet and a steady, warm stream of water began to trickle down his perfectly chiseled body. Feeling a shiver run down my spine, I wasn't quite sure if it was from the sight of him, or the cold air hitting my naked skin. Rich noticed my body quiver and he pulled me into a tight embrace.

"Step under the water with me. It's a lot warmer over here, sweetheart."

The hot water beating on my head, while wrapped in Rich's tight arms, was just what I needed to feel immediate satisfaction.

"Mmmmm. Perfect."

Rich's hands were instantly all over me. He pushed me up against the wall and nuzzled into my neck, while kissing me gently. I reached out and grabbed the bottle of conditioner that was sitting on a corner shelf of the shower. Squirting a dollop into my palm, I reached down to cup Rich's balls and gently stroked up toward his growing length.

Suddenly, Rich turned me around and pushed lightly on my back, so that I would bend toward the floor. As I rested my hands on the wet, acrylic floor, Rich guided my hips to meet his now fully erect length. Before I had time to register this steamy scene, unfolding before me, Rich entered me from behind in one, fluid motion. I gasped at his sudden entrance.

"Are you OK, Brooke?" Rich asked, as he began teasing my nipples with his fingers.

"Oh yes, please. don't. stop."

"Your wish is my command."

I loved how Rich had me bent over before him. This position allowed for the deepest penetration. I assumed that in this pose, he would be in complete control of my body, but I quickly realized that the farther I leaned over, the deeper he could go in. In order to slow Rich's movement within me, I adjusted my stance so that I wasn't bent over as far, and his thrusting became shallower. Within seconds of my orgasm, I folded my body over completely, as Rich thrust deeply within me a few more times. I felt Rich's orgasm ripple through him almost immediately.

"Wow," was all I heard escape his lips as I slowly stepped away from him and returned to an upright position.

"Whoever said the G-spot doesn't exist has never done that before."

Rich erupted in laughter as he pulled me into him once more.

"Oops, I can't believe I actually said that out loud," I said, feigning innocence.

After nearly forty-five minutes in the shower, exploring each other's bodies, we decided it was time to get out and get ready for our day. After all, I really did want to see at least some of the city. I was sitting on the edge of Rich's bed watching him prepare for our day in the city, when I heard my phone chirp once again with an incoming text message. I quickly got up and grabbed my purse, remembering that I was supposed to call Cassidy the night before.

Cass: You better be dead on a sidewalk somewhere because I am worried sick, Brookie. Seriously, text me back, or I will hunt you down and kill you myself!

Ack! Sorry, Cass, I'm a terrible friend. I'm fine. Just about to head into the city to do a little sight-seeing before I catch my flight back to Detroit. I'll call you when I land.

Cass: Thank God, you're OK! I thought I was going to have to come fight a bear for you. I'd fight a bear for you, you know? Not a grizzly, or brown bear ... or a koala ... But like a Care Bear? I'd fight one of those sonsabitches for you. ;)

OMG! I don't even know how to respond to that ... Are you drunk? At 10 a.m. in the morning?

Cass: Nope, I found that on that Pinterest site that I was telling you about. Isn't it hilarious? I just wanted to make my girl smile. Although, something tells me someone else has already taken care of that for me. Call me the second your flight lands! I need deets!

I will. Love you!

Cass: Love you, too! Safe travels, bbopof! Xxoo

I shook my head and smiled at my best friend's use of our nickname. We joked that we actually created texting terms years before cell phones were even on the market. We were probably still using crayons when we decided we'd be "Best Buddy O' Pal O' Friends" forever. It's always stuck and it's always been just for us. Just as I was about to turn my phone off and go back to concentrating on Rich, I heard my phone chime in once more.

> *Cass: P.S. If you find any other hot guys please pack them in your suitcase for your girl! ;)*
>
> *You really are a handful, Cass. Love you, bbopof! Xxoo*

I tossed my phone back in my purse and looked up to see Rich staring at me with a quirky grin, plastered on his face. Walking toward me, wearing only his jeans which hung low on his waist, he stopped just inches away from where I was sitting on the edge of the bed.

"What's got your face twisted all up, Davis?" I asked.

"I'm smiling at the most bewitching girl I've ever had the pleasure of seeing in my bed. Do you have a problem with that, Anderson?"

I felt immediate warmth on my cheeks and I was almost certain I was blushing at Rich's sudden declaration.

"Bewitching? That's a pretty fancy word, Rich," I replied.

"I am the editor of one of the world's most influential newspapers, sweetheart. My vocabulary is rather extensive. Just wait till I break out some of my words on you in bed."

"You've had me in bed. Not once, but … twice," I said as I held up two fingers. I let my fingernails trace down his rock-hard abdomen, taking extra time to admire that perfect V. "And, I don't remember you doing a lot of talking, really, just a lot of … groaning."

"Actually, Brooke, I've had you three times, if you count the shower sexcapade," he quipped, placing extra emphasis on the word "had."

"See, my math skills are pretty good, too. And, let's not forget my mad bedroom skills. I'm just a talented man, I guess. Oh, and I'll groan for you any time, any place."

"As much as I would love for you to have me again, Mr. Davis, we need to get out of here if I'm ever going to make a dent in my sightseeing list."

"Seriously, Brooke? I really don't know why you care about seeing the Washington Monument so badly. It's just a prime example of phallic architecture. I bet you're more impressed with the 'Washington Monument' in my pants, anyways."

"Oh my god … you are too much, Rich," I said, as I lightly smacked him across his chest. "Now put a shirt on and let's get moving."

Chapter Nine

The sun was beginning to fade in the distance and I knew my time in our nation's capital was quickly ending. Rich and I had covered a lot of ground during the afternoon, once I got him out of his penthouse, at any rate. We may have been distracted by his bed once more, before he finally put his shirt on and agreed to come on my little sightseeing excursion.

Along with taking me to see the Washington Monument, the White House and Lincoln Memorial, Rich insisted on taking me to his favorite deli for a late lunch where I indulged on the thickest sourdough bread and fresh tomato bisque.

After lunch, Rich argued with me for several minutes about my list, insisting that he knew of some much better areas of the city that weren't included on my list from *Frommer's* travel guide. I finally gave in to his pouty nature, pointing it out to him, and decided to give up my trip to the Smithsonian's National Zoo, in favor of his walk through historic Georgetown.

I would never admit this to him, but I knew he was right the minute we stepped off our DC Circulator Bus; the view of the stately homes, Potomac and Francis Scott Key Bridge were magnificent. I really had no words as we walked through the neighborhood. A small flea market and vendor area had been set up in the neighborhood as it was "Fall Harvest Days," as advertised on a banner hanging above the lampposts.

Rich grabbed my hand and pulled me toward the vendors. He bought us two caramel apples and a large, frozen, apple-cider slushie to share. Trying to avoid "brain freeze" from a large gulp of the sticky, sweet, frozen concoction, I glanced in Rich's direction to see him purchase a beautiful, handmade, beaded necklace. Returning to me, he soon wrapped the gorgeous purchase around my neck which had green beads of the most beautiful hues.

"I thought it matched the color of your eyes, at least today anyways, since you're wearing that emerald sweater. Your eyes have always intrigued me, Brooke. They're like the most exotic chameleon, always changing colors."

"You shouldn't have, Rich, but thank you. It's beautiful."

"You're beautiful," he added.

Before I got too distracted by Rich's charming words, I walked over to the next vendor booth. It was filled with all sorts of cheap baubles from toy race cars to fashion dolls with creepy, googly eyes. In one of the farthest bins, I noticed a toy that I hadn't seen in years. I reached over to grab the pink-foam top of the Ice Cream Punch Cone. I clicked on its release button just as Rich was walking toward me. I couldn't stifle the laugh as the foam top bopped him square in the face.

"Ouch. What was that for, Anderson?"

"Sorry, Davis. You walked into that one, literally. Wrong place, wrong time, I suppose," I giggled while giving him an apologetic shrug.

"Well, Brooke, I did walk right into that one, but whenever you are involved, it will never be the wrong place, or the wrong time.

"If I'm being honest though, that ice cream would be better if it was the real deal and I was licking it off your gorgeous body."

Rich had this ability of turning even the most innocent thing into my wildest, sexual fantasy.

"You and your lines, Davis," I said, as I swatted my palm against his chest. Damn the cool weather and the jacket that was covering Rich's hard abs and solid arms. I tried to act annoyed by Rich's flirtations, but I was trying my hardest not to soak through my panties. I had to get my mind off of Rich and what he could do, or rather did to me in bed. *Ice Cream Punch Cone, Ice Cream Punch Cone, Ice Cream Punch Cum ...* It became a chant in my head – anything to forget my desires.

"I'm sorry, but did you just say ice cream punch cum?"

Shit, I didn't even realize I'd said anything out loud. And," cum?" Crap I said, "cum?"

"No, I said ice cream punch CONE." I made sure to enunciate "cone." I continued to recall the memory in hopes of distracting Rich, or maybe myself.

"I haven't seen one of these in decades. I remember I begged my mom to buy me one at a storytelling festival we attended one summer. I took it home and bopped our cat in the face, repeatedly. As I recall, he growled, hissed and ran in the opposite direction." I couldn't help but laugh at the memory.

"Lucky for you, sweetheart, I won't hiss and run away, but I can't promise that I won't growl."

I had no words, but just rolled my eyes in Rich's direction.

I bought the pink punch cone for Kaitlyn and we headed back into the open neighborhood, losing track of time as we strolled hand-in-hand through the community.

"Is this up to your standards, Brooke?" Rich said as he caught me gazing up at the sky.

"What?"

"Do you like this area?"

"Oh, yes. Yes, it's beautiful here. I was just wishing that I didn't have to go back home tonight. It's been such a whirlwind these last two days. I almost feel like I'm dreaming."

"You aren't dreaming, Brooke. Everything you've experienced is real. Every place you have visited is real. I am real. And, most importantly, sweetheart, we are very real."

I swear this man knew exactly what to say that would take my breath away at that exact moment.

"We can't be too real, Rich, not if I intend to fly home tonight, pack my bags and move here to accept this job, this job that you are supposedly offering me in the morning … this job where you'll be my boss.

This job has been my dream longer than I can remember."

"We can make this work, Brooke." His eyes and his voice were almost pleading with me to consider what he was offering.

My dream job and my dream man ... all wrapped up in one pretty package. *Who am I kidding? ... One fucking gorgeous package. All I needed was the goddamn red bow.*

As much as it pained me to say it, I knew it could never work between Rich and me and I couldn't lead him on any more than I already had.

"It can't work for us, Rich – not for you and me. If we were going to make it work, it would've happened years ago. We'll be colleagues and nothing more. It's all that I want." I had to lie to him and hold back my tears all at the same time. I could see his chiseled jaw drop at my confession. He looked utterly crushed and that was all my doing.

"You know you don't really mean that, Brooke."

"I ... I should get back to my hotel to grab my bag. I'll understand if you'd like to say our goodbyes here."

"Don't be ridiculous, Babbling Brooke. You may have just gutted me, but my mother still taught me to be a gentleman," he said, with both sarcasm and dejection in his voice.

Chapter Ten

The muffled roar of the engine on my right was doing little to ease my nerves, as I sat aboard the plane, waiting to take me away from Rich and back to my tiny apartment in Michigan. I had never been much of a fan of flying and my nerves had already been through the wringer.

After our talk in Georgetown, Rich took me back to my hotel and waited in the lobby while I packed my suitcase. He insisted on driving me to the airport and luckily agreed to drop me off at the door. He gave me an awkward hug and a chaste kiss on the cheek before telling me I would hear from him in the morning about the position. I couldn't erase the pained look on his face from my memory as he drove away from the entrance. The cocky, conceited, and arrogant Rich Davis had never looked so defeated … at least not until that evening.

My mind was swirling faster than the engines … *"What if he changes his mind about offering me the position?"* Then my stomach sank upon realizing I might be more disappointed at not seeing him every day than at the thought of not getting the job for professional reasons. "*Can we make this work? Can I have both my dream job and Rich? What if we try and break up? Could I handle working with him after losing him? Is it going to be weird working for him after I just slept with him? Oh, crap, crap, crap … What have I done?*" I said, out loud to no one in particular.

Suddenly, a woman sitting next to me, and looking like she stepped off the set of *The Golden Girls*, spoke to me as if she were answering my questions. "Sounds like you've gotten yourself into quite a predicament, young lady," she said.

"Um, yes, I suppose I have. I'm sorry for bothering you. I hadn't realized I was talking out loud."

"Not to worry, darling. May I offer you a piece of advice? I never had a daughter. God blessed me with three sons. I always wanted a daughter, though. I mean I love my boys, but a girl would have been fun, I think. Someone I could shop with and gossip about boys."

"Sure, that would actually be nice. My mom was my best friend and I lost her several years ago. I miss gossiping about boys with her. She always knew exactly how to solve my problems. I feel a bit lost without her."

"Well from what I heard a few minutes ago, you need to follow your heart on this one, Dear," she continued. "Don't walk away from love. Love is more important than work. Jobs come and go, but true love may only happen once in a lifetime."

She smiled and the twinkle in her eye gave me goose bumps. It was like my mom had sent this stranger to tell me exactly what I needed to hear, at that moment, but I still wasn't sure if I should listen. My heart and my mind were definitely fighting World War III over this one.

The plane had already leveled off to its cruising altitude and the captain had turned off the seatbelt light, before I even realized it had taken off. At least my thoughts of Rich Davis and my subsequent conversation with the lady next to me had occupied my mind long enough to forget the typical "taking-off jitters" that I often experienced.

Flying was not my favorite mode of transportation. Cassidy often reminded me of the statistics about dying in a car accident versus dying in a plane crash. "Blah, blah, blah," I would always sputter back at her.

She was so mad at me when I made her make the twelve-hundred-mile road trip to Tampa for spring break our senior year at Western. "We are losing out on at least two good beach days," I remembered her whining, as we were packing up the back of my parents' Chevy Blazer. She still liked to remind me of the flat tire we encountered somewhere between BFE and Tennessee.

"Excuse me, Miss? May I offer you a beverage?" I snapped out of my deep thoughts and looked up to see the flight attendant hovering above me, holding a tray of tiny cups filled with various sodas. Wow, I thought, they really had downgraded these days. What happened to the cans of pop and bags of peanuts?

"Um, no thanks. I'm OK for now," I told her, before she walked toward the next row of seats.

The rest of the flight was uneventful and, before I knew it, the pilot was coming over the speaker to tell us to prepare for landing. I buckled my seatbelt, let out a deep breath and closed my eyes until I felt the landing gear connect with the tarmac. As soon as we got the all-clear from the captain, I turned on my phone and shot Cassidy a text.

I just landed. I need to see you right now. Please tell me you're still up.

Cass: Yep, just put Kaity-bug to bed. I'm just sitting here in my sweats with my two main men, Ben and Jerry. Be safe and I'll see you in a few. Love you, girlie.

Oh, ice cream and my best friend were just what the doctor ordered right now. I grabbed my car from the long-term parking area and headed straight for Cassidy's apartment. It was a little after eleven by the time I made it through traffic and to her tiny two-bedroom apartment. I didn't even bother knocking as I barged through the front door.

"You really should keep that locked, you know? I could be a deranged serial killer."

"Relax, I just unlocked it. Besides you couldn't care less about my cereal, you are just a deranged ice cream killer. Now get over here and spill it. This must be big if you are here and not in your own bed after what, I assume, was an exhausting interview process."

I couldn't stifle the laugh that escaped my throat. "Exhausting ... you don't know the half of it."

Cassidy just stared back at me with a confused look on her face. "What the hell are you talking about? You know how I hate all your cryptic stories. Talk!"

"OK, here goes nothing. The editor of the *Washington Post* is Rich Davis."

Her eyes got as big as saucers ... "Like, THE Rich Davis? Douche Monkey Davis? Hotty McAsshole?"

"The one and only. I ran into him, ironically enough, while I was getting off the elevator. He was the one interviewing me."

"Shut the front door! Holy shit, Brookie. Is he still hot? Please tell me he's still hot. Oh, and single? Please tell me he's single, too," she spit out without taking a single breath.

"Relax over there little bird, will ya? But, yes – he's single and gawd yes is he ever hot. I thought he was hot ten years ago, but he's so damn sexy now. He's just manly perfection at its finest."

"So did you fuck him on his desk then?"

"Jesus, Cassidy. No. I went there for an interview. I want this job."

She looked at me skeptically. "OK, fine. But, please tell me you had hot, passionate sex after the interview. Oh em gee! You did, didn't you? That's why you didn't answer your phone last night. You were getting busy with Hotty McAsshole!"

I didn't need to answer her. The minute she guessed, my face turned the brightest shade of crimson red.

"You little devil, you. So, are you two like together now?"

"No, I told him today that if I accept this job that we can't be together. This was a one-time deal. OK, maybe a four-time deal ... But, regardless, when I accept this job in the morning, he will be my boss and only my boss. I'm not in the business of being that girl who fucks her boss. I just can't. I can't, right?"

"You little slut! Four times?!?!!?!."

"THAT would be the part of what I just said, for you to focus on, wouldn't it?"

"I know what you think is best, Brooke, but do you like him? I mean aside from what, I assume, was mind-blowing sex."

"Yes," I replied without even needing to think about how I felt about Rich. "Of course, I like him; I've always liked him. I think even when I hated him, I liked him. I just can't. We can't. … Now hand me the damn ice cream."

Cassidy and I popped in *Can't Buy Me Love*, our favorite '80s movie, and downed two entire tubs of ice cream. We alternated between our two favorites, *Chunky Monkey* and *Karamel Sutra. The irony of the name was not lost on me that night.*

We laughed until our insides ached at the nerdy Patrick Dempsey all through the film. You would think we'd never seen it before, rather than quoting nearly the entire movie line by line. Oh, I remember the days when we both wanted to be the iconic Cindy Mancini.

"Who would've guessed Ronald Miller would become the one and only Doctor McDreamy," Cassidy swooned, as she hit eject on the DVD player.

"I know, right? Crap, it's after two, Cass. I need to get going. I'm exhausted. I can't wait to crash in my own bed."

"Of course, you're exhausted. You were too busy 'getting busy' last night to sleep."

I rolled my eyes at her use of air quotes.

"Whatever," was all I rebutted before getting up, grabbing my purse and making my way to the door.

"Give that little goddaughter of mine a kiss for me, won't you. Thanks for the talk, Cass. I'll sure miss you when I take this job. Love you," and with those words I left.

Chapter Eleven

I woke up to the sound of my phone ringing, shortly before eight the next morning. My head was pounding after my late night, spent with my best friend. I almost let it go to voicemail before I snapped to it and realized it was probably Rich calling to offer me the position he had nearly promised me the day before. I quickly coughed, hoping to rid myself of the morning frog that always took up residence deep in my throat.

"Hello, this is Brooke," I managed to get out, hoping I didn't sound as if I'd just been in the deepest of sleep.

"Hi, Miss Anderson, this is Mr. Davis' secretary, Caroline, calling."

I don't know why, but I was immediately saddened that it wasn't Rich on the other end. I missed the sound of his voice, already. I missed him.

Rich's secretary offered me my dream job on the phone that morning and I immediately accepted the offer. The salary was more than double what I was making at my current position and the benefit package was more than I could have ever imagined.

I knew the salary wouldn't be quite as impressive as it seemed at first. The cost of living would be much higher in D.C., than it was in Michigan, but my bank account would be padded with more money than ever before. Maybe I would finally be able to pay down the large student loans I had acquired while earning my master's.

Caroline told me on the phone that morning that Mr. Davis expected me to begin my employment in thirty days. That would allow me to give my proper two weeks' notice and also allow for an additional two weeks to find a rental in the city. I would also have to start packing my belongings and hire a company to move me hundreds of miles.

During Caroline's phone call, she also informed me that Rich wanted to personally cover all of my moving expenses as well as the security deposit and first month's rent at my new apartment. I almost declined his offer until I realized that I probably didn't have enough money in my savings account to cover it myself. I could always ask my dad for a loan, but that might wipe out his savings for awhile and I didn't want to put him in that position.

So, after briefly hesitating, I told her that I would accept his very generous offer, but on one condition: that it was only a loan and I had every intention of paying him back. I just hoped he wasn't using that as a way of getting closer to me.

I was excited by the new adventure, but scared at the same time. Not only was I apprehensive about leaving my comfortable job, the only home I ever knew, my dad and my best girls, but I was terrified at the thought of working in such close proximity to Rich. Would he pretend to not even know me around the other employees? Would he act like nothing happened between the two of us? Would he flirt with me incessantly? As much as I hoped he wouldn't, I knew I would be devastated if he acted as if nothing had happened during my night, or following afternoon, spent in D.C.

Fortunately, this fear was laid to rest later that night when my cell phone rang, just as I was leaving the office. My stomach began twisting in knots, the minute I saw Rich's number appear on the caller ID.

"Hi Rich." There was so much more I wanted to say, but the truth was that I didn't know how to say any of it.

"Hi Brooke." After a long pause, Rich continued, "Caroline told me that you accepted the position, as well as my offer to help you get settled into your new place. Just so you know though, sweetheart, I have no intention of accepting your condition, so you might as well drop that idea right now.

"But, Rich …" I managed to get out, before his deep voice stopped me once again.

"Please, Brooke, not another word on that issue. Aside from that, I am very pleased that we will be working together and I just don't want anything to be awkward for you. I meant every word that I said last night. I want us to be together, Brooke, but I understand if it's not the right time for you … for now, anyways. I just want it to be made clear, though, I don't believe for a second that we wouldn't work, or that you don't have any interest in me. Our time together wouldn't have been so easy, or so perfect, if that were truly the case."

He paused before continuing, "I will give you your time, but just know that one day … you will be mine."

My panties were dripping wet, maybe even literally dripping, and his words turned my brain to mush. "Rich …"

"Shh, you don't have to say anything. I just wanted you to know. I hope you have a wonderful evening, Brooke, and if you need anything, anything at all, don't hesitate to give me a call, sweetheart."

Before I even had time to say goodbye, he'd disconnected the call. For the rest of the night, I just kept replaying Rich's deep voice in my head … *You will be mine.* It was the memory of his words that lulled me to sleep that night.

The last two weeks at work flew by, and thankfully, my editor didn't really give me any large assignments, once I gave my two weeks' notice. He knew my mind was on bigger and better endeavors.

I'd decided to leave my car with my dad until I was sure I wanted to make D.C. my permanent residence, at which time, I would probably just sell my car for the extra cash. With good public transportation, someone could easily maneuver around without a car in D.C. So, without the additional cost of gas, insurance and parking, I could easily afford a nicer apartment.

Cassidy insisted on helping me pack my belongings and then drive me to my new home. She made arrangements to leave Kaitlyn with her mom and wouldn't accept no for an answer. Honestly, I was thankful for her assistance and company. I really don't think this was something I could have done on my own. I probably would make it as far as Ohio before turning my rental car around and begging for my old job back, the following Monday.

"Have you heard from Hotty McAsshole lately?" Brooke asked, as we were packing up the rest of my apartment. The movers had already hauled most of my furniture and larger items to a storage locker, thanks to Caroline's arrangements.

"No, not since the day I accepted the job. He said he would give me space, so I suppose that's what he's doing?"

Truth be told, I was thankful for the space, but I really did miss the sound of his voice ... his calming laughter. Even though I hadn't spoken to him in those two weeks, I heard him vividly each night in my dreams. Let's just say my B-O-B had gotten quite the workout recently.

"Why don't you call him?"

"I can't, Cass. You know I can't. This job is too important to me. You know this has been my dream for over a decade. I can't screw this up now – not for some fling with Rich."

"But, Brookie ... what if it's not just a fling? I mean, you know, I'm not the guy's biggest fan, but I remember the way he used to look at you and something tells me his feelings toward you have only intensified."

"I just can't, Cass. Just drop it, OK?"

"Sure, Brookie. I'll drop it ... for now."

Why does everyone keep saying "for now"? I thought to myself. Suddenly, I could hear Rich's words in my head once again. "I will give you your time, but just know that one day ... you will be mine."

The next morning we awoke bright and early to begin our road trip to the Mid-Atlantic. We had packed the car the night before, and I just needed to make one last stop before we were on our way. After showering and eating breakfast, we were in the car and headed to the place where saying goodbye would be most difficult.

As we turned the corner, the row of evergreen trees fencing in the backyard came into view, and I already felt the tears rolling down my cheeks. I envisioned Dad holding on to the banana seat of my purple Huffy bike, as I learned to ride without training wheels for the first time.

"Don't let go, Daddy. I'm scared," my five-year-old self pleaded.

"I won't let go, Princess," he promised.

My dad eventually let go, but not until I gave him the OK. I remember riding for a few seconds before losing my balance and toppling over, scraping both knees. I cried and told him that I was never going to ride again.

He taught me a valuable lesson that day, one that I have used several times since, including today. He taught me that it was OK to fall, but you had to pick yourself up and try again. Eventual success would make all the failures worthwhile.

Another vision flooded my memory. This time my mom was pushing me on the metal swing set in the backyard. As she pushed me higher, I leaned back and reached my toes toward the sky. My mother's infectious laughter resembled my own and our giggles (mine slightly higher-pitched) filled the sultry air of that long-ago, Michigan summer day. If I concentrated hard enough, I could still hear her giggles, mixing with my own. "I miss you, Mommy," I whispered, so only I could hear.

Cass parked in the driveway of the house I had called home for the first twenty-two years of my life. I hadn't even stepped out of the car and I was a blubbering mess.

"Hey, no tears. You know you will still talk to him every night and see him on long weekends and holidays. I'll take good care of him, I promise," Cass reassured me from the driver's side.

As I sat there, I was flooded with another memory. This time it wasn't from my childhood home, but from having to say goodbye. The scene of my parents saying goodbye on my orientation day as a freshman at Western played in my mind like a short feature film.

I lived on the third floor of my dorm and I remember stopping at every window on my way up the stairs just to watch their car drive off. It was hard for me to say goodbye then; it would be even harder to say goodbye now, more than a decade later.

I got out of the car and made my way to the front door, ringing the doorbell repeatedly and obnoxiously, as was my custom as a kid in pigtails. Dingdong, dingdong, dingdong, dingdong, dingdong, went the doorbell as I heard movement inside the house. I let out a small laugh as I pictured my dad's cat, pinning her ears back and bounding up the stairs at the chiming of the doorbell. "I'm coming, I'm coming," I heard my father shout.

He opened the door and immediately pulled me in for the tightest of hugs.

"Brooke, I'm gonna miss you."

"I'm gonna miss you, too, Dad," I said as my tears began to fall harder.

"No crying, baby girl. We will still talk every night and I will be out to visit before you know it. I'm so proud of you, kiddo. You've grown up to be such a beautiful and accomplished woman. Thank you for staying here with me for so long after we lost your mother, but it's time for you to go and follow your dreams now. I'll be fine here. I'm sure Cassidy will see that I eat right every day and fold my own laundry," he said, as he looked toward my best friend with a grin as wide as the Cheshire Cat's.

"Oh Daddy, I love you!" I cried out, with big tears rolling down my cheek.

"I love you, too, Brooke. Make sure you two travel safe and call me as soon as you get to your hotel. And, remember how proud I am of you. Your mother would also be so proud – so very proud, Brooke."

I didn't have any other words, I just fell into my dad's warm embrace. Cass had to nearly pry me away a few minutes later.

"Don't worry, Brookie. You know I'll take care of the old man here," said Cassidy reassuringly.

"Hey there, missy, who are you calling old?" My dad responded, with a wink to my best friend.

Those two had always liked to banter back and forth. Cassidy had always thought of my mom and dad as a second set of parents, and I felt the same way about her folks.

Chapter Twelve

November 2011

I didn't hear from Rich at all during the two weeks that I was in the city. I spent most of the first week apartment hunting. I was worried everything would be out of my price range, but decided I needed to splurge a little in order to meet my needs. I mean, in my world, it was a necessity to have a dishwasher and washing machine and dryer. I didn't live near my dad anymore and I couldn't stand the thought of lugging my dirty clothes to the Laundromat each week.

I also wanted something that I felt was safe and within walking distance of grocery stores, restaurants, theatres and museums. I could take a cab to work, but I didn't want the additional cost for simple things such as grabbing a gallon of milk, or taking in a movie.

I settled on a beautiful high-rise on the city's west side, if you could call it "settling" as the apartment building was fairly new with modern amenities such as a doorman, first-floor gym with an in-house tanning salon and a clubhouse area with an enormous, flat-screen television and billiard table.

It was a little out of my price range, but I was able to get a pretty good deal as the current tenants had to leave right away and were looking for an immediate subletter and would pick up a portion of the monthly rent for the next eight months.

I would have to decide at that point if it was something I could afford on my salary, or find something else a little more in my price range. I would have a better handle on the city by then, I thought, and this place was just too good to pass up right now.

Cass left me after the first week in D.C.; I spent the second week unpacking my boxes. I hired another set of movers once I signed my lease, in order to move my furniture out of storage.

It was Saturday evening; I was enjoying my last days of freedom before work would claim my life on Monday morning. I was just getting ready to pop a frozen pizza into the oven when my phone signaled with an incoming text message.

> *Rich: Hey Brooke, I know I said I would give you your space, but I just wanted to make sure you had found an apartment and were settling in all right. If you don't have any plans tonight, I'd like to take you to dinner, just as friends and soon-to-be co-workers, of course. I've asked a few other reporters to join us so you wouldn't think I had anything else in mind. I mean, I do, but space ... I promised you space. Anyways, I'm banking on the hopes that you have been*

surviving on frozen pizza this week and could use a night out on the town with good food, some drinks and a little human interaction. So, what do you say?

Frozen pizza? Does he have cameras in here? I chuckled before sending him a quick response.

Hey Rich, yes, I found a place on the west side and have settled in quite nicely. But, since Caroline already had the funds for the down payment and security deposit wired to my account, I assume you knew that I had already found something. Thanks for checking in, though. And, I would actually love to get out for a little bit before I have to start on Monday. How did you know I was about to eat a frozen pizza, anyways?

Rich: Ooops, caught red-handed. West side, huh? You're practically my next door neighbor then. Text me your address and I'll swing over and pick you up so you don't have to worry about a cab. Oh, and just a hunch on the frozen pizza, I remember you always eating that cardboard shit in college.

I sent Rich my address and quickly jumped in the shower. I hopped out with about 15 minutes to spare. I pulled on a pair of skinny jeans and paired them with a light, navy-and-white-striped sweater. The weather was starting to cool, especially at night, and I didn't want to freeze in case any portion of the evening would be spent outside on a bar porch.

Having little time to fully dry my hair, I decided to towel it dry and pull it up in a knot. I dusted on some powder, added some mascara and lined my lips with some gloss, before deeming myself presentable for my first night out on the town with some co-workers.

Just as I was about to head downstairs and wait for Rich in the lobby, my phone chirped with an incoming text. It was Rich telling me that is he was out front. I grabbed a light jacket, slipped on some nude, ballet flats and took the elevator down to the first floor.

As the doors opened to the lobby, I was surprised to see Rich standing inside the building waiting for me. I could have stared at him for hours. His jeans hung low on his hips and he was wearing a black T-shirt and black leather jacket. I hadn't seen this "bad boy" look on Rich before, but quite honestly, I liked it. I liked it – a lot.

As my eyes were surveying his body, I noticed his were doing the same. I felt exposed – he had seen every inch of me. There was no more hiding from Rich Davis. Looking at me with his smoldering eyes, burning with desire, he could see right through me.

Without even saying a word, I knew he was questioning what I had told him just a few weeks before. As I stared at him the words ran through my head, *"It can't work for us, Rich. Not for you and me. If we were going to make it work, it would've happened years ago. We'll be colleagues and nothing more. It's all that I want."*

"You can't hide from me, Brooke, not anymore. I know you're regretting what you told me earlier. I can tell your pretty little head is working in overdrive right now," Rich said, as he came closer to where I stood frozen by the elevator. "Don't worry about this … " he added, as he gestured to the heavy air between us. "We'll discuss 'this' later, but right now I just want to get you a drink and introduce you to some of your co-workers."

I couldn't find the right words to express what I was feeling, while at the same time, keeping it PG-rated, so I just nodded as Rich led me to his car parked at the front curb.

"What can I get you to drink, Brooke," Rich asked as we bellied up to the bar.

"I'll take my usual, please."

He chuckled before answering, "Babe, unfortunately, after all of these years apart, I'm not sure I know your 'usual.'" He replied, actually air-quoting me.

"My bad, I suppose you're right," I answered, blushing. "I'll have a mango margarita – my usual, you know for future reference." *Crap, did I just admit to Rich that I wanted to go out for drinks often with him?*

"Margarita, huh? Finally learned how to handle your tequila?"

"What can I say? I had a good teacher," I said with a shrug. "

"Yes, yes you did. I bet that instructor of yours could continue to teach you a thing or two," he added, with heated eyes before signaling for the bartender and ordering our drinks.

After our initial flirting at the bar, the evening seemed to be going quite well. Rich had kept his hands to himself as we shared an appetizer of loaded potato skins, deep-fried pickles and chili poppers. I let Rich eat all of the deep-fried pickles and he agreed to hand over all of the chili poppers. We really did work well together as a couple. I don't like pickles and he doesn't like chili poppers. It would always make ordering an appetizer easy. We'd never fight over who gets the last one. *Stop, Brooke. I reminded myself, before I let my imagination run wild about our couple-dom because of some fried foods.*

I threw back a few margaritas while Rich drank a few house draft specials. I laughed, chatted and enjoyed getting to know some of my fellow co-workers, too. Rich seemed to get along very well with most of them and it was great to see his jovial attitude around them. I must admit, after knowing what Rich was like when we first met at Western, I was a little worried that he might be a dick to work for, but his interaction with my fellow reporters put all of those worries to rest.

I was just about to tell Rich I was going to take a cab home, when an attractive man who I had noticed eyeing me from across the bar for most of the evening, approached our group. Rich was chatting with our co-worker, Brent, at least I think that was his name, when the stranger, dressed in tight jeans, a white T-shirt and cowboy hat, came up behind me, putting his hand on the small of my back. I'll admit, I found him attractive and a little intriguing. I didn't expect to see Mr. Tall-and-I-Look-Good-in-Wranglers at a city bar. *I giggled at my nickname for my mysterious stranger ... Maybe I'd had one-to-many margaritas.* In a way, he reminded me of my favorite country bar back home.

"Excuse me, but are you new around here?" he inquired, flirtatiously.

"Uhh, yes I am, but how did you know that, Cowboy?" I answered with a wink.

"This is a fairly small place and I've seen this group in here before, but you weren't a part of it. And, trust me, I would remember a beautiful woman like yourself," he said, as his hand drew circle patterns on my back. "May I buy you a drink, Gorgeous?"

I fidgeted on my bar stool at his touch and that's when Rich's attention turned back to me. I noticed his eyes widen and the veins in his neck throb when he looked over and saw the cowboy's hands on me.

Rich's mannerisms told me everything I needed to know. He was not happy that I was flirting with this stranger.

Already pretty tipsy, I figured one more drink probably wouldn't hurt anything. "Sure, that would be perfect. Another mango margarita, please," I responded.

"Are you sure that's a good idea, Brooke?" Rich hissed in my ear.

I turned to Rich and answered so only he would hear, "Thank you for your concern, Rich, but I'm a big girl and I know what I am doing. I'm not yours to worry about."

Rich winced as if my words had stung him. *I probably just bruised his big ego, I'm sure he'll get over it.*

The cowboy called the bartender over and ordered us another round, luckily not paying any attention to Rich. Before grabbing the stool next to me, he sauntered over to the jukebox and dropped in a few quarters. I wasn't surprised when I recognized a country song begin to play.

"Do you have a name, Cowboy?" I asked as he sat down next to me.

"Jared – and your name, Pretty Lady?"

"Brooke," I responded, noticing Rich's eyes turned in my direction.

"Nice to meet you, Brooke, care to dance while we wait for our drinks?" he asked, extending his hand, as I heard Luke Bryan's new single "Drunk On You" play through the speakers.

"Su--."

Rich interrupted before I was able to finish my thought.

"Get your hands off her," Rich hissed.

"And, what's it to you? The lady doesn't look like she needs a bodyguard, Pretty Boy."

"She's with me. That's what it's to me, Cowboy." Rich was practically growling; I could feel the anger radiating from his skin. I looked around hoping no one else was a witness to his sudden outburst. Thankfully, everyone was too caught up in their own conversation to notice Rich's sudden show of temper.

"Rich, stop it. Let's get out of here," I pleaded, in hopes of diffusing the situation before it fully erupted.

"Come on, Beautiful. You know you don't want to leave with him. He was paying you no attention, just five minutes ago. Suddenly, he wants to play Mr. Possessive. I don't see a ring on your finger, so as far as I'm concerned, you're fair game, babe."

"I'm sorry, Jared, but I think I should be going. I have an early day tomorrow and it's getting late. It was a pleasure meeting you."

I turned to Rich, adding, "Don't you dare follow me."

I didn't want Rich to give me a ride, I just wanted to walk the few blocks home and clear my head.

"Where are you going, Brooke?" I heard Rich growl, his breath heating the back of my neck, as I began walking away from the bar.

I turned and began walking backwards away from him, all while trying to blink back the tears that were pooling in my eyes. "I told you not to follow me," I yelled. "What the fuck did you just do in there, Rich?"

"He had his hands all over you. You're mine."

I must admit, if only to myself and certainly not to Rich, at that moment, as turned on as I was by his possessiveness and protectiveness, I was also seething; I wasn't his. I had explained that to him. He was my boss and he just embarrassed me. What if my co-workers – his employees – had heard any of what was said between us? How the fuck would I explain that one on Monday? I'd be the target of office gossip before I even stepped foot into the office. I would need to pack up my shit and crawl back home with my tail tucked between my legs.

"I'm. Not. Yours! How many times do I fucking have to tell you that, Rich? I can take care of my goddamn self. What if our co-workers had heard your little explosion? You just humiliated me. I can't even stand the sight of you right now."

"Fuck! ... I'm sorry, Brooke. I just ... I just couldn't stand that guy touching you ... I ... I just lost it. No one else heard anything, I promise. Let's just get into my car. Let me drive you back home. I can tell you're freezing out here."

"I'm not going anywhere with you, Rich. I'm perfectly capable of walking home. You're lucky I'm not resigning right now, too. I'll see you in the office on Monday ... Boss." I quickly turned in the other direction and began the descent toward my apartment. I could feel the heat from Rich's breath almost immediately.

"Brooke! Don't walk away! Let me, at least, get you a cab. It's not safe to walk alone at night. I would die if anything happened to you. ... I would die." He was pleading with me. I could hear the torment in his voice.

I was livid right now, but I didn't want to worry him, either. And, truth be told, he was right. It wasn't safe to walk by myself at this hour. I could hear my mother's voice in my head right now. ... "Always keep your wits about you," she would say.

"Fine, hail me a cab then," I snapped. "But, I don't want to hear another word from you until Monday and even then, it better be for professional reasons only."

I felt a twinge of sadness as I left Rich on the sidewalk in front of the bar. But, what he did was not appropriate; I was not his and he had to get that through his thick skull.

Minutes later, the cab dropped me off at the front of the building. Without greeting the night security guard, I ran through the lobby and up the stairs to my apartment. I quickly unlocked my door and ran straight to my bedroom where I crawled into bed and buried my sobs in the pillow. I felt so alone for the first time in my life. Usually, I would run to Cass and consume a big bowl of "Chunky Monkey" on her couch, but she was over five hundred miles away. The last thing I could remember was crying out loud to my mom before sleep consumed me.

I woke up the following morning, with raccoon eyes and tear stains smearing my cheeks. My hair was disheveled, never completely drying from the previous night, and I hadn't even bothered to change out of my clothes before going to bed. I was pretty certain my breath probably smelled like Pepé Le Pew on his death bed. Yep, I was the picture-perfect definition of a "hot mess." I'm pretty sure if Merriam-Webster added the phrase as one of its entries, my picture would be right next to it.

I took a quick shower and threw on some yoga pants and a sweatshirt before grabbing my cell to call Cassidy. I was in desperate need of best-friend therapy at that moment. I plopped down on my chocolate-colored, microsuede couch and entered my phone's security code. I noticed that I had four missed texts. I clicked on the message icon and saw Rich's name with the number four in the corner.

Two messages were from last night:

> *Rich: I hope you made it home OK. I really am sorry about what happened tonight, Brooke. I really did enjoy spending time with you like that, before things got out of hand. I really hope you can forgive me and we can go back to being just friends. I promise I will try harder and not overstep my boundaries next time. Please text*

me to at least let me know that you arrived home safely.

Rich: Brooke, it's getting late and I'm starting to worry. Please text me.

Before I had a chance to read the other messages from earlier in the morning, I heard a loud knock at my front door. I got up from the couch to see who it was. Thinking it was the doorman with a package or something, I opened it without even looking through the peephole.

"Brooke, thank God. I didn't hear from you last night and then not at all this morning. I was really worried."

"Rich, what the hell? I'm fine! I got home and went right to sleep. I woke up not that long ago and took a shower. I was just about to make a phone call and then take a walk to the farmers' market downtown to pick up some fresh produce before I'm stuck eating frozen pizza for the rest of my life – not that it's any of your business anyways," I fumed. "And, most importantly, how did you get past the doorman downstairs? I thought this place was supposed to be secure from UNWANTED guests!"

I was being overdramatic, but Rich was really getting on my nerves. I was not his to worry about, or his to protect; I moved to Washington D.C. to become an independent woman, not to get rescued by my knight in shining armor.

"Besides, I told you that I would see you tomorrow at work and I meant it. I don't think we should spend time together outside of work, for awhile anyways."

"I'm sorry, Brooke. Your doorman let me in because he and I know each other," he shrugged apologetically. "We ran a story about the contractor and owner of this complex, his boss, before it was built. I guess you could say he was doing me a favor. I can behave, though, I promise. Let me walk you to the market and then maybe we can stop for a quick bite to eat. Too bad I learned last night that you don't like pickles, because I'd offer you mine – again. What are your feelings toward sausage?" he said with a wide grin.

I couldn't help but blush at his suggestive nature.

"I don't want your pickle – or your sausage, Rich. And, remind me to have a chat with security about allowing guests access to my door without my prior consent," I huffed.

"Your rosy cheeks would suggest otherwise, Miss Anderson."

"See Rich, you're just proving my point that we can't do this. I don't even think that we can be friends, for now at least. I'll just see you at work tomorrow," I said, as I lightly closed the door in his face.

My heart broke for the second time in less than twenty-four hours. Stopping in the kitchen first to pour myself a glass of wine, I headed straight back to my couch and dialed Cass. She answered on the second ring to the sound of my heavy sobs.

Cassidy provided me with the best-friend therapy that I needed so desperately. We talked and laughed for the next two hours. I told her about the events of the previous night and she referred to Rich with her standard "Douche Monkey Davis" on more than one occasion.

She also told me about the latest "Kaitlynisms" before we ended our conversation. I swear she could write a book using just the lines that her kid came up with. Just last week, they were at the grocery store checkout when the clerk asked Kaitlyn what her mommy was going to make for dinner to which she replied "vagina" instead of lasagna.

I spit out the wine I'd been drinking when Cass threw that little gem into our conversation. Really, I must have laughed hysterically for, at least, five minutes. Kids really do say the darndest things.

I just had an hour to spare to make it to the farmers' market before it closed for the evening. Opening the door, I found a dozen red roses sitting at my doorstep. I picked them up, knowing exactly who they were from, but, nevertheless, opened the attached card which read:

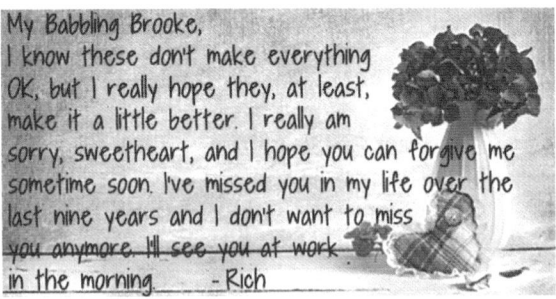

My Babbling Brooke,
I know these don't make everything OK, but I really hope they, at least, make it a little better. I really am sorry, sweetheart, and I hope you can forgive me sometime soon. I've missed you in my life over the last nine years and I don't want to miss you anymore. I'll see you at work in the morning.   - Rich

My alarm woke me up shortly before sunrise. I hadn't slept well the night before. It was one of those restless nights where I'm not really sure if I slept at all, but figured I must have dozed off at least for a few minutes at a time. I wasn't sure what I was most nervous about – starting my dream job, or working for the man of my dreams.

I crawled out of bed and walked to the kitchen to pop a K-Cup into my Keurig. While waiting for my coffee to brew, I quickly dialed the closest taxi company and requested a cab out front in about forty minutes. I drank my coffee then headed to the bathroom to start getting ready for the first day at my new job with my new boss.

I stepped into the scalding-hot shower in hopes of waking myself up after my fitful sleep. After about twenty minutes of letting the water run down my back, I figured it was about time to step out in order to avoid an obscene water bill.

I wrapped the towel around my body and began to blow dry and straighten my naturally wavy hair. I dusted on some light powder and neutral eye shadow before glossing my lips with a sheer glaze.

I slipped into my black lace bra and matching panty set before dressing myself in the pair of slightly flared-leg, charcoal pants and lightweight purple, fitted sweater that I had set out the night before. I decided to pair the casual look with a simple gold chain and small, diamond-studded earrings that my mom gave me for my high school graduation. It would be a simple reminder of her, being with me, if I needed her today. My phone rang just as I was slipping on a pair of black heels, which nicely completed my look.

"Hello, this is Brooke."

"Miss Anderson, the taxi you called for just arrived," said Roger, my doorman, through the line.

"Thank you, Roger. I'll be right down."

I grabbed my briefcase before heading out the door. It held my brand new tablet that my dad insisted on buying for me as a congratulatory gift. I was perfectly happy with taking my old laptop, but he insisted that it was the tablet that all the up-and-coming journalists on television were using. Who was I to argue with my father? After all, I was now the proud, new owner of a shiny, new Apple iPad.

I made my way downstairs and greeted Roger with a friendly hello before hopping into the cab that was waiting near the sidewalk. I rode in complete silence for the twenty-minute ride through town. I must have been in a complete daze as I hadn't even noticed we'd pulled up to the *Post*.

"Your destination, ma'am. That'll be eleven dollars and sixteen cents," the cab driver said.

I pulled my wallet out of my briefcase and grabbed my credit card to swipe through the driver's scanner. I exited the cab and stood at the bottom of the steps, looking up at my future.

"This is it, Brooke. You're finally here. It's not just a dream anymore," I whispered to myself.

Just as I was about to take the steps up to the front door, I felt a familiar, warm breath against my neck.

"Prompt – just how I like it, Miss Anderson. Did you receive the flowers I sent over yesterday?" Rich asked.

"Yes, I did." I wanted to be short with him. I didn't want him to feel what he was doing to me. Truth be told, my heart was racing and my palms were sweating. Just this man's breath was getting me all worked up. *What the fuck am I going to do?*

"May I carry your bag for you?" Rich offered.

"No, thank you, Mr. Davis. I think I can handle it."

"What did I tell you about that 'Mr. Davis' shit, Brooke?"

"Yes, Mr. … I mean, yes, Rich."

He put his hand on the small of my back and escorted me up the stairs, through the doors, and to the elevator.

"I figure if I accompany you on the elevator then you won't be able to crash into me once we exit, even though I like it when you crash into me. I do want you to know that I know your rules. I may not like them, but I will respect them … If I must."

"You must."

Rich walked me to my office which, coincidently, shared a wall with his. It was relatively small, but I was actually surprised I had an office at all. Most of the other reporters simply had a small cubicle set up in the large newsroom.

"This is nice. Thanks, Rich."

"I asked Caroline if she would move out into the lobby area. I thought it would be more beneficial if she could greet guests as they come up to the newsroom for interviews. You can have her office; it will give you a bit more privacy than one of the cubicles. I'll give you some time to get settled. Please meet me in my office in fifteen. I'd like to go over some story assignments with you before we have our daily staff meeting at ten."

"OK, I'll see you in fifteen, Boss."

"Don't toy with me, Brooke, or I'll be forced to break YOUR rules on the very first day."

I watched Rich leave my office as I pulled out the few picture frames that I had packed in my briefcase. The photos were of my parents and me at my college graduation and of Cass, Kaitlyn and me at Lake Michigan last summer. I added a framed, crayon drawing that Kaitlyn had given me before I left earlier in the month. She insisted it was a picture of her cat, Simon, but I wasn't so sure.

There was a light knock on my door, as I was unpacking the rest of my belongings: a few notebooks, pens, tape recorder and batteries.

"Come in," I said.

"Miss Anderson, I have a delivery for you."

I turned around to see Caroline holding the most beautiful bouquet of Gerbera daisies. I smiled immediately knowing who sent them.

"Thank you, Caroline. Please set them on my desk."

I was opening the card as Caroline turned to leave.

"Oh, and Miss Anderson, welcome. If you need anything at all, please don't hesitate to ask," Caroline added with a warm smile.

"Thank you. That's very kind of you."

I glanced quickly at my phone, to check the time, realizing I had just enough time to take a peek at the card before I needed to be in Rich's office.

Brookie,
We hope you have a fantabulous first day. You are going to knock 'em dead, girl. Cut Rich some slack and follow your dreams. Both of them!!! Love you lots, bbopof!
Your two best girls,
Cass and Kaity-bug

I shot Cass a quick text.

Thanks for the flowers. They are beautiful! And, I'm not cutting Rich any slack. He's my boss and that's that. Now please drop it! I will call you tonight and let you know how it goes, bbopof! Love you both! Xxoo

Cass: Glad you got them! And, STOP being so damn stubborn, will ya? Talk to you later. I'd hate you to get caught texting on your first day of school, errr work! Xxoo

I had just a minute to spare as I lightly knocked on Rich's office door. I heard him on the phone, so I quietly let myself in and took a seat on his couch. He was standing with his back to me, looking out toward his view of the D.C. skyline. He was always sexy as sin, but watching him in his element – our element – was spectacular. His suit coat was unbuttoned and hiked up around his waist. I could see the definition of his ass through his loose, black slacks which hung low on his hips. *Pure, unadulterated sex on a stick.* Just as I was coming back to reality, I heard Rich end his call.

"Sorry about that, Brooke. It was a call from the advisor of the Department of Homeland Security and it couldn't wait. I'm working on a series of enterprise pieces and when one of my sources returns a call, I have to make myself available right at that moment," he said, as he turned to face me.

"Trust me, Rich. I understand. I've been in this business awhile myself, you know."

"Right, of course, I didn't mean to offend you, Brooke," Rich said, as he took a seat next to me on the couch. He wasn't touching me, but I could feel the heat radiating from him, almost as if we would fuse together at any given moment.

Rich spoke first, breaking the tension that was growing between us. "Brooke, I have your first assignment. As I'm sure you know, Thanksgiving is next week and I was hoping you could write up something about Black Friday and all the hoopla that surrounds it. You're a girl; I'm sure you've stood outside in line for some crazy deal, right?"

I couldn't believe that Rich was talking about Black Friday. Had I entered into some sort of parallel universe? I quit my job covering real, albeit small issues, to come to the *Washington Post* to cover shopping? I had avoided covering fashion bullshit my entire career and now, I'm here at my dream job covering exactly what I'd spent the last five-plus years of my career avoiding.

"I'm sorry, Rich. I must be misunderstanding you. You want me to write an article about Black Friday deals? What's next, the fucking White House Christmas tree?"

"What? It's a legitimate story, sweetheart. Call a few senators, or their wives. Better yet, give the first lady a shout. Maybe she's taking her daughters to Target at four in the morning," he responded, rather flippantly.

"First of all, DO NOT call me 'sweetheart' at work. When we are in this building I am Brooke, or Miss Anderson, unless, of course, you want me to file a sexual harassment suit against you. Actually, on second thought, just drop the sweetheart altogether. OK, pookie?" I responded snidely. "Secondly, you are punishing me, aren't you? Because I won't fuck you anymore, you are going to give me the worst possible assignments? I am better than this, Rich, and you damn well know it. You wouldn't have hired me, if you didn't know it."

"I'm not punishing you, Miss Anderson, and I don't appreciate your accusations. This story needs to be covered and right now you are my most available reporter. And, actually, if you'd like, you can also take a crack at that White House Christmas tree story you suggested," he said with a sly smirk on his lips. "Oh, and, Miss Anderson, one more thing … you will fuck me again. Whether you want to admit it or not, you can't deny this chemistry that's floating in the air between us right now."

I just stared at him with my mouth agape.

"I have no words, Rich. … No words," I mumbled. "But," I said with a bit more voice, "I will take your Black Friday story and I will make the most of it. It will be the best damn Black Friday story this newspaper has ever seen. I might just use your idea and give the first lady a call. If that's all, I'll be leaving. I have an assignment to cover."

Without giving him an opportunity to respond, I got up and stormed out of his office. Rich had crossed the line, we both knew it. What we also knew is that I would never do anything about it. Even if I did file a sexual harassment complaint against him, which I wouldn't do, I would just end up losing my job. I was the new kid and he was the seasoned editor whom everyone loved. Rich Davis had me where he wanted me, and he knew it.

Chapter Thirteen

Over the next two weeks, I begrudgingly covered the stories that Rich assigned to me on my first day and on the mornings that followed. I didn't have the opportunity to interview the first lady, or any senators' wives for the Black Friday story. Turns out, they aren't the easiest contacts to make. Secret Service makes that a little difficult and the White House press secretary was less than forthcoming when it came to the shopping strategies of the first lady and her daughters.

So, I stuck to the basics and contacted some of the local retailers and took the "shop local" approach to the article. It might not have been my finest work, but I was satisfied with the completed story. It had a little more "meat" to it than just a shopping column and for that, I was pleased. Rich had to leave town to work on his enterprise piece on the Department of Homeland Security, but the news editor, Kyle, who was a step below Rich in the editorial department's pecking order, seemed pleased as well.

It was Thanksgiving morning, and I was fortunate to have the day off. Only a few reporters covered the shift on holidays and many chose to work in order to get the additional holiday pay. I only had the one day off, though, so I wasn't able to go home for Thanksgiving, my favorite holiday, and I was really missing my dad and the girls.

I woke up around nine, sleeping in a few extra hours, and made my way to the kitchen where I turned on the small TV I had placed on the counter. I flipped the station to the Macy's Thanksgiving Day Parade just as Snoopy was making his way through the crowd.

Feeling a silent tear rolling down my cheek, I thought about watching the several televised parades with my mom and dad every Thanksgiving morning. It would be different this year. It was just me.

I decided a few days before that I was still going to make the most of it. I had bought myself a small turkey and planned to prepare the traditional fixings. I even bought the ingredients needed to bake a pumpkin spice pie for dessert.

I had just removed the slimy, nasty innards of my bird when I heard a knock on my door. I quickly rinsed my hands in some hot water and wiped them on the back of my jeans before seeing who was there. My mind drifted momentarily, as I wondered who would be at my door at this hour of the morning on Thanksgiving.

My thoughts immediately centered on Rich. After all, he had managed to get by Roger, my doorman, on other occasions. *Ugh, why do I keep going there?* Truth be told, I hadn't heard from Rich in over a week, and I missed him. He hadn't called, texted or even e-mailed an intra-office memo. My head returned to the here and now, when I heard another knock, although a bit louder this time.

"Coming," I hollered, while scurrying to the door.

Before opening the door, I looked through the peephole, but was surprised when I didn't see Rich on the other side. Actually, I wasn't sure who stood there because all I could see was my Black Friday article cut out of the paper in the shape of a turkey. Perplexed for a minute, I heard two, girly giggles coming from the hallway. I swung the door open and before I could utter a word, Kaitlyn was jumping in my arms, with her mom not far behind.

"Surprise," they both shouted in unison.

"Ahhhhhhhhhhhhhh, I can't believe you two are here!" I gushed.

"We wanted to surprise you!" My best friend exclaimed.

"I missed you, Aunt Brookie!"

"Aw, I missed you too, Princess. I'm so glad you and your mommy are here. ... But, how?" I said, directing my question to Cassidy.

"Well, your old man helped a little. He wanted to come too, but I kind of sprung this on him at the last minute and he'd already made plans with his lady friend."

"I'm sorry; did you just say that my father has a lady friend?" I replied.

"Ummmm, maybe? But that story is for another time. Right now, you're going to tell me where the effin' toilet is because this momma has got to pee."

Cassidy helped me prepare the rest of our Thanksgiving dinner, and the three of us enjoyed our meal along with stories from the last few weeks. I hadn't realized how much I had missed these two until they were right there with me.

Kaitlyn fell asleep on her mom's lap while we were watching the annual showing of *The Wizard of Oz*. After the movie, I offered to put Kaitlyn to bed in the guest bedroom while Cass finished up the rest of the dishes. I read a groggy Kaitlyn a bedtime story and tucked her in, snug-as-a-bug-in-a-rug, before heading back into the living room, ready for an inquisition.

"OK, I can tell you've had something on your mind all day," I said, as I entered the room. "Let me have it."

"OK, I'll cut right to the chase," agreed Cass, "but only after I devour another piece of that scrumptious pumpkin pie."

"Seriously, how do you stay so damn skinny? You've even had a baby! It's so not fair." I complained – only half-jokingly.

"Whatever, are you having another piece with me, or what?" She asked casually.

"Well, that's just a silly question. Cut the damn pie!"

We plopped down on the couch ready to gobble down the pie with heaps of whipped cream, when Cass began to grill me.

"How are things going with Rich?" she asked.

"Honestly, not well. He's been gone the last few days and when he left we weren't even really on speaking terms. He punished me with that stupid Black Friday assignment because I won't be with him and I let him have it. Then he left to work on one of his own assignments."

"Brookie, you know I love you, but why are you fighting this with him? I think you're making a huge mistake. I was never really Rich's number one fan, but I know you cared for him and it's obvious that he did and still does care for you, too."

"I'm not … I mean … I can't be … interested. I love my job. I've followed my dreams and I'm so proud of myself for that. Rich wasn't part of my dreams, Cass – not my current dreams, anyways. He was nothing, but a distant memory. I can't jeopardize my career for a relationship with Rich. It would more than likely fail, and then I would have to quit in order to avoid the drama. It's simply not worth it."

"If you say so, Brooke, but it sounds to me like you're trying to convince yourself. Just remember, he's not going to wait around forever. Don't let him slip away from you, again. I think you'll regret it someday," my best friend warned.

"I'll think about it, Cass. But, I really think I just need to concentrate on my work right now," I said. "Now on to other topics … tell me about this lady friend of my father's?"

"Um, you should ask him about that, Brooke. It's not my story to tell."

The White House staff was much more helpful when it came to arranging the appropriate contacts for my story on the White House Christmas tree. They really made a big deal about this "Blue Room Christmas Tree." I was ecstatic to finally be doing a story with White House personnel, maybe even with the first lady, even though it was just about a decorated tree. It was the freakin' first lady. Isn't that every journalist's dream? *I finally made it!*

I mean, sure, I'd love to interview the president about his upcoming healthcare bill, but I need to take baby steps. I just set foot in Washington D.C. and I had already made it onto the White House's list of media contacts. I'd say I'd done quite nicely. Cass wasn't around to give me my standard pep talk and "Way to go, Brooke," so I was left with giving myself a pat on the back.

After all, Rich wasn't about to do it. He'd been a little cold toward me since he returned from his business trip after Thanksgiving. Sure, we talked every morning, but it was all business. He would meet with the staff to go over our weekly assignments and dismiss me with the rest of them without even making any friendly small talk.

Rich was giving me exactly what I wanted, but it still hurt. I thought a lot about what Cass said when she visited over Thanksgiving, but I just couldn't go through with it. Rich and I couldn't be anything more than just colleagues. Besides, I even had my suspicions that he was dating Janine – you know the much-too-perky, big-breasted bimbo from reception. I didn't really have proof of that, yet, though. I was just relying on my womanly intuition.

After scheduling my interview with White House personnel and giving myself that proverbial pat on the back, I hung up the phone and decided I would go share my good news with Rich. I was hoping he would at least be pleased, if not for me, for the *Post*. It would be a good feature story, anyways. Besides, I had to get the green light for a photographer to accompany me on the assignment.

I ran straight from my office right into Rich's, without stopping to knock. I realized as I barged into his office unannounced that he wasn't alone. Sure as shit, there sat Janine rather cozily, on the edge of Rich's desk, as he stood over her reading a memo that she had brought up from downstairs. *Score one for womanly intuition.*

I took a few steps back and knocked on the door to announce my presence.

"Uh, Rich, I don't mean to interrupt, but I'd like to talk with you about this assignment."

"Sure, we're done here, come take a seat, Brooke," he said, as he pointed to one of his office chairs.

"Janine, thanks for your help with … that matter. I look forward to your further assistance," he said as she sashayed out of his office. His eyes stayed locked on her ass until she giggled and closed the door behind her.

I took my seat and cleared my throat, hoping to ease the tension that I felt building in the air.

"What can I help you with, Miss Anderson?"

"Are you two dating, or just fucking?" I couldn't stop the question, slipping from my lips. I lowered my head and covered it with my hand just as I realized what I'd asked Rich – my boss.

I heard Rich chuckle before answering, "What I do in my personal life really isn't any of your concern, now is it, Brooke? If I didn't know any better, I would think you are a little jealous. You, however, have made it perfectly clear, on more than one occasion, that you aren't interested. So, if you don't mind, I'd rather just discuss this article of yours. I mean, correct me if I'm wrong, but isn't that the reason you just barged into my office unannounced?"

I stood there with my mouth agape, yet again, not prepared for Rich's response to my sudden verbal diarrhea.

"Cat got your tongue, Miss Anderson? I don't think I've ever left the infamous Babbling Brooke speechless. This is one for the record books."

Yep, there he was – the Rich I first met all those years ago. Call him what you want, Hotty McAsshole, or Douche Monkey Davis. He was back and in full force. There was no denying the tears that I was trying to hold back. *I missed Rich – my Rich.* The intense, yet caring man, I had come to know.

I quickly blotted my eyes, hoping Rich wouldn't notice the lone tear escaping down my cheek. I didn't want him to know that he was affecting me this way – again.

"You're right, Rich, I apologize. Who you see in your personal life is none of my business. I just came in here to tell you, I will be meeting with White House staff tomorrow to discuss the infamous Christmas tree. I may even have the opportunity to interview the first lady. I was told I could bring a photographer along and I was wondering if you knew who might be available around one o'clock to accompany me, that's all."

"That's fantastic, Brooke – nice job. I never doubted you, though. And, of course, I will be sure that one of our best photographers will attend the interview with you. Now, if that's all, I have some pressing business I must attend to."

"Yes, that's all, but …"

"But, what, Brooke?"

"Nevermind, thanks again, Rich." I wanted to tell him in that moment that I was having a change of heart; I didn't want him seeing Janine, or whatever he was doing with her, but I just couldn't. It wasn't the right time, and it probably wouldn't ever be. I just had to focus my energy on my job.

Forget about Rich, you're interviewing the friggin' first lady tomorrow! Easier said than done, brain, easier said than done.

Chapter Fourteen

My first month at the *Post* had come and gone. I was happy with my job performance, and Rich seemed to be as well. He even had assigned me a fair number of more serious articles to cover. Ever since I made my way into the White House, even though he was trying to sabotage me with fluff, he knew I was an asset to his editorial team. After all, he was a talented journalist and an even more talented editor, and he wanted his best reporters working on the hardest news.

So, since that day before Thanksgiving when I threw a temper tantrum in his office, he was only assigning me hard news assignments. The most recent one I covered was regarding the billions of dollars that the Internal Revenue Service had lost in fraudulent tax refunds to identity thieves.

Chills ran up and down my spine when I saw my article in print that day. I ran my finger across the inky paper, just like I told Cass I would do all those years ago. The byline read: *Brooke Anderson; Washington Post staff writer* and the article appeared on the front page above the fold. I was the star of that day's paper and I couldn't have felt more gratified.

As I perused that day's paper, I heard knocking on my office door.

Looking up, I saw Rich standing in the doorway, "Penny for your thoughts, Miss Anderson?"

"Oh, hey, Rich. I didn't even see you walk up. Sorry, I just can't believe that I finally have the main story on the cover of the *Post*. Do you know how many people are going to read my work?"

He chuckled before answering, "Yes, Brooke. Actually, if you're looking for a number, it's probably near a half million. That's not why I came to see you, though. I would like you to accompany me on a business trip to New York City. I'm working on a story out there and I think you would be the perfect addition to my byline. We always worked so well together in college that I thought the dynamic duo could give it another go. What do you say?"

"Are you asking me, Rich, or are you telling me that I'm going?" I asked.

"Well, you're right. I am your boss and I am requesting your presence. I would rather you go willingly, not that I am opposed to handcuffing you and dragging you screaming onto that plane," he said with that all-too-familiar, sly smirk of his.

"You won't need the handcuffs, Rich. I will go on the trip with you, but it's ALL business," I reminded him.

"Yes, Brooke. Sadly, I know all your rules. Now go home and pack your bags. We leave later this evening," he said in his most authoritative voice.

"SERIOUSLY?" I asked him wide-eyed. He simply nodded a yes in response. "Crap, OK, I have so much to do!"

I caught a cab home and immediately began throwing some of my clothes in a suitcase. I didn't even know what I'd need to wear, or how long we were going to be gone. I probably should have asked Rich for those details before I hurried out of the office.

Oh well, I guess I would just have to wing it this time. I threw in some business-casual items, a pair of skinny jeans, a few sweaters, sweatshirts and my favorite little, black dress. I could also hear Cassidy's nagging voice in my head as I threw in a few lacy panties and bra sets. *Definitely not for Rich ... what if I ran into George Clooney while I was in the city? After all, didn't I just read in my trashy magazine (don't judge, old habits are hard to break) that he was single again?*

Just as I was drooling over Clooney, I heard a knock on my front door. I looked out my peephole to see Roger standing on the other side.

"Hello, Roger," I greeted, as I opened the door.

"Hello, Miss Anderson. There is an airport limousine waiting for you outside. Would you like assistance with your bags?"

"Oh yes, thank you, Roger," I responded.

Roger rolled my suitcase out the door as I pulled on my puffy, pink coat and grabbed my carry-on bag. I was just slipping on my gloves when I saw Rich exit the back of the limo to assist Roger with my bag.

"Brooke, you look gorgeous tonight, as always."

"Thanks, but I'm wearing my comfy, flying clothes, Rich. I'd hardly call yoga pants and a sweatshirt - gorgeous."

"In my eyes, Brooke, you are ALWAYS gorgeous," he said with emphasis.

"And, you, BOSS - are ALWAYS a flirt. Now, don't we have a plane to catch?" I asked with a quick, and somewhat, flirty wink.

We boarded the first class section of the plane and were waiting for the captain to signal for takeoff, when Rich noticed my jittering knees and legs beside his.

"Are you OK?" he asked.

"Yes, I'll be fine. I just hate flying. I do this every time. I'll be OK once we're in the air. Sorry if I'm making you uncomfortable. Cass hates flying with me because of it," I replied.

"Don't be silly. I love having you by my side. So, any place you want to see while we're in the city? We have some downtime while we're waiting for our interviews that I've already scheduled."

"Oh, I haven't really thought much about it. Someone decided to spring this on me pretty last minute. I'm a bit embarrassed to admit this, but I've actually never been to New York City," I replied sheepishly.

"What?!?!" Rich exclaimed, with a dumbfounded look on his face.

"Really, NYC virgin right here," I confessed.

"First I got to pop your tequila cherry all of those years ago, then your boobgasm cherry and now you're NYC cherry, huh? I'm such a lucky guy." *And, there was that damn wink again.*

I ignored his previous comment and continued, "I would like to see all of the 'must sees' I suppose. Although, I didn't have time to buy a *Frommer's* guide before I left, I'd imagine it would tell me to visit Central Park, Times Square, the Empire State Building ... Oh – and the Christmas tree at Rockefeller Center!"

"You and that stupid *Frommer's* guide! Don't worry; with me as your guide, you won't need that damn book. Did I steer you wrong in D.C.? Those are some great places that you've mentioned. I have a few others in mind as well," Rich said.

Before I knew it, the plane had already leveled out and I had missed takeoff all together, once again.

"You were distracting me, weren't you?" I asked.

"Maybe, did it work?"

"Yes, thanks, Rich," I managed to get out, through the yawn that escaped me.

"You tired? Why don't you take a nap? I'll wake you when it's time to land," he promised.

After what was probably just a few minutes, sleep overtook me. I dreamt of Rich and the amazing sex we shared all those months ago. I woke up awhile later with Rich stroking the top of my head. Crap, I fell asleep with my head on his shoulder. *Oh my god! What if I drooled on him!*

Rich must have noticed the sudden terrified expression on my face.

"What is it, Brooke? Something wrong? You looked so happy and content while you were sleeping – and now you just look petrified."

"I didn't drool on you, did I?" I asked worriedly.

Rich broke into a full-out, belly laugh. "That's what's got you so scared? No, of course not, Brooke – just relax. We'll be landing in just a few minutes."

We had a driver waiting for us outside of JFK. Rich wouldn't tell me where we were staying. The only hint he shared was that it was someplace in Manhattan. Never having been to the city before, this little piece of information didn't mean much to me.

"The Plaza?!?! We have rooms at the freaking Plaza Hotel?" I couldn't contain my excitement as our limo pulled up to the grandest hotel in New York City. I felt like Kevin McCallister in *Home Alone 2* when he got lost in New York. "Let me guess, next you're going to take me to Duncan's Toy Chest?"

"I have no idea what you're talking about, but yes we have a suite at The Plaza. I only stay at the best, and this hotel is the best around."

"Back up – Duncan's Toy Chest is from the *Home Alone* movie series. You have seen *Home Alone* right?"

He chuckled again before answering, "I swear, Brooke, sometimes I think you're a nine-year-old girl trapped in a grown woman's body – albeit a hot, sexy, gorgeous, grown woman's body."

I felt my cheeks flush as he held his hand out to help me out of the town car. Rich explained to me as we were checking in that he had booked us to stay in the hotel's Royal Terrace Suite. Although we would be sharing the same space, we would each have our own bedroom.

The concierge helped us with our bags up to the hotel's twentieth floor where he showed us to our suite. I resisted my urge to tip him with my chewed gum, as in the movie. I'd probably be the only one to find that funny; besides Rich was already taking money out of his wallet before I had time to reach into my purse for some cash.

"I know it's getting late, but I'm pretty hungry and was thinking about ordering something from room service, if you'd like to come relax in the living room and have a bite with me? I promise, no funny business – Boy Scout's honor," he said, trying to assure me.

As if right on cue, my stomach grumbled. "Well, OK. I guess I am pretty hungry."

While Rich was placing our order with room service, I took the opportunity to really look around. The lower level featured an elegant, spacious living room that overlooked Central Park, a dining area and a large powder room. There was already a roaring fire blazing in the living room's restored, marble fireplace.

Rich walked up behind me, put his hand on the small of my back, and led me to the couch that faced the fireplace. We sat with my body nestled into his and made small talk while he waited for our food to arrive. It reminded me so much of that day spent in the *Eagle's* office all those years ago. I had so many déjà vu moments with this man. It was becoming more and more difficult for my head to tell my heart "no." I was getting comfortable – almost too comfortable with Rich.

As I was relaxing in his arms after a long day, I began thinking about what Cass had said at Thanksgiving. *"Don't let him slip away from you, again. I think you'll regret it, someday."*

But was he already slipping away? He'd looked rather cozy with Janine recently. Maybe he's just trying to get lucky this weekend when he already has a girlfriend back at home, or maybe he is just trying to be my friend. Maybe he was trying to give me what I wanted. Now, if only I could figure that out for myself.

A knock on the door, followed by the pleasant aroma of food, woke me from my thoughts.

"That smells divine," I told Rich, as he walked over with a tray of food.

I dug right into the Portobello flatbread pizza while Rich started in on the Red Wine Short Rib Tacos. We also opened the house-specialty Cabernet that the waiter had brought up with our meal.

"This is simply delicious, Rich. Thanks for suggesting dinner. I was even hungrier than I thought."

"I hope you saved room for dessert. I asked the dining room to prepare chocolate-covered strawberries just for us," said Rich temptingly.

I smiled at the memory of a much younger Rich serving Cass and me gooey pizza and chocolate-covered strawberries in the limo on the way to our sorority formal. So much had happened since then, yet here we were – together again.

"You know I can't turn down a chocolate-covered strawberry."

I was stuffed to the brim after eating nearly the entire flatbread pizza on my own as well as a half dozen strawberries – at least. My insomnia along with my food-induced coma was putting me on the brink of unconsciousness.

"I think I'm going to go find my bedroom. Thanks again for dinner."

"Please take the master bedroom upstairs, Brooke. You'll love the view. It overlooks Central Park."

"OK, thanks. What time do we need to begin working in the morning?" I asked Rich.

"Our first appointment is scheduled at nine o'clock, and with the heavy traffic, it will probably take about thirty minutes to get there. Would you like to meet downstairs at The Palm Court around eight? They serve fabulous omelets," he informed me.

"Yes, that sounds perfect. Thanks, again, Rich – for everything," I said warmly.

"No problem, Brooke. Goodnight, sweetheart."

I was so exhausted when I finally made it upstairs that I hardly had enough energy to wash my face and pull my hair into a high ponytail. I was already dressed in my comfy clothes from the flight so I just decided to jump into bed without changing. As I began to drift off, part of me wished that Rich would come knocking on my door, but when I awoke to the sound of my alarm that next morning, those wishes had not been realized.

Chapter Fifteen

Rich and I spent several hours the next day working on our assignment. We'd traveled to New York City to do research on an article concerning the inner workings of the stock market. Rich had set up several interviews with Wall Street bigwigs before we arrived in the city.

His goal for us was to write a series of articles beginning with Wall Street's history to the recent crash of '08 to its current rebuilding. We had met with several sources throughout the day when Rich suggested we take a break for the rest of the evening.

Rich made dinner reservations at Eleven Madison Park. After waiting a few minutes in the lobby, the hostess took us to a table near the back of the restaurant. I looked at Rich quizzically when I noticed four place settings.

"I hope you don't mind, but I invited my friend Blake and his wife, Alyssa, to join us. Blake and I went to Columbia together for its journalism master's program and he stayed here in the city after graduation. He has an editorial position with the *Times*."

"Really? I don't mind at all. I can't wait to meet a friend of Rich Davis. I was convinced, after all these years, that you were incapable of a male friendship. After all, I've only seen you in the company of co-workers, or ladies."

Just as I was heckling Rich about his bromance, I heard someone whooping and hollering as a loud, booming, male voice got closer.

"What's up, Hot?" said the man who, I presumed, was Blake.

I looked at Rich and mouthed, "Did he just call you, Hot?"

Rich just started laughing and whispered in my ear that he would explain later as he fist-bumped his friend.

I could tell that Blake commanded a room. He was huge; I mean maybe, even literally, a giant. I thought Rich was tall, but Blake had at least five inches on Rich's six-feet-three-inch frame. His arms were probably the size of an average man's thighs. To put it simply, he was a tree, and not just any tree – a very mature oak tree. Although his size alone might terrify most, I could tell by his bright, green eyes and deep dimples that he was nothing but a big teddy bear.

The woman standing at his side, who I assumed was Alyssa, was the complete opposite in stature of her wall of a husband. Even with her black pumps, she didn't reach my height. I smiled when I realized that her usually tiny frame was carrying a very large, protruding baby bump. She looked like she was about to fall over. *How in the heck was she still wearing heels? It was a mystery that I would never understand.* She was beautiful though as she looked up at her husband with nothing but pride gleaming in her eyes.

"Early!" Rich exclaimed. "It was always like you to show up at least fifteen minutes late to everything. It's a wonder you didn't get kicked out of grad school."

What the hell, did Rich call the guy "Early," yet he was late, and evidently is always late? I really need to get more information on these nicknames.

"Whatever, Hot. I have to make my appearance known whenever I enter a room. You know I can't just blend in with the losers who always show up on time. Now, who is this stunning lady at your side?"

"Blake, this is my colleague Brooke Anderson. Brooke, this is my good friend Blake Mitchell and his beautiful wife, Alyssa."

I shook both their hands while noticing that Rich only introduced me as his colleague and not even as his friend. That's what I wanted though, right? Even if it's what I asked of Rich, I still felt some disappointment at his introduction.

While waiting for our food to arrive, Rich caught up with Blake as I talked about babies with Alyssa. The two of them were going to welcome their first child, a daughter, in about three weeks. I gushed about my precious goddaughter and told Alyssa stories about Cassidy's pregnancy and labor. After all, I was like the surrogate daddy in the delivery room.

"So, what brought you to D.C., Brooke?" Blake asked, as the waitress was bringing our calamari appetizer. "Hot mentioned that you two knew each other during his undergrad days in Michigan? I assume that's where you're from?"

"Yes, but before we talk about me, can we back up a bit? Would you two please explain these nicknames of yours … I mean 'Hot' and 'Early?' I think I'm missing something here."

Alyssa couldn't resist laughing and chimed in, "Oh, honey, these two have their own language. When Blake and I first met, I didn't know what they were talking about half the time. I've slowly figured it out and now even catch myself using it."

"Whatever, Lys. It's simple, Brooke. Everything is pretty much opposite of what we're actually saying," Rich explained.

"Exactly, so I call this guy 'Hot' because he's so damn ugly," Blake said, as he elbowed Rich in the rib.

"Yep, you're just jealous that I always got all the hot chicks at Columbia," Rich shot back. "Blake earned the name 'Early' because he's always at least fifteen minutes late for EVERYTHING, as I pointed out before."

"Come to think of it, though, I should've just called him 'Hotter.' You better pray your kid takes after your wife in the looks department," Rich chaffed.

"You two are both crazy," I said, as Alyssa nodded her head in agreement. "But, to go back and answer your question – yes, I'm from Michigan. Rich and I met as undergrads at Western. I always wanted to work for the *Post*, and thanks in part to Rich, I finally have that opportunity."

We continued our conversation throughout dinner. I learned that Blake met Alyssa while he was studying at Columbia. She was actually in the law program and they met during a media law course that Blake was taking as part of the journalism program. They were both originally from Upstate New York, but decided to stay in the city where Blake now worked for the *Times* and Alyssa was a partner in a prestigious law firm in Manhattan.

Blake and Rich continued to razz each other about anything and everything. It only became slightly uncomfortable when Blake asked Rich about his social calendar.

"So, Hot, seeing any pretty ladies these days? Since Brooke is only your 'colleague'; I assume it isn't for your lack of trying."

Rich cleared his throat before answering his friend's very direct question. "Actually, I do hope there is one special lady in my life. But, we're still working out the terms of our relationship."

Is he talking about me? Suddenly, I became nauseated at the thought that Rich wasn't talking about me, but, most likely, Janine.

"If you'll all excuse me, I need to head to the ladies' room." I had to regain my composure. I couldn't let Rich know that he was getting to me this way.

I made my way back from the restroom just as Blake and Alyssa were standing up to leave.

"Sorry to leave you alone with this punk, Brooke, but Alyssa's pretty tired. It was a pleasure meeting you and please let us know the next time you visit the city."

Rich and Blake gave each other a one-armed, man hug.

"Hey, keep your hands where I can see them, man," Blake joked to Rich, when he gave Alyssa a warm, friendly embrace.

Ignoring his friend, Rich said to Alyssa, "Take care of yourself, Lys. Don't let this asshole make you go into early labor. And, make sure he lets me know when my niece enters into this world."

Rich and I had been in New York City for two entire days, and he hadn't tried anything more than snuggling with me on the couch. This could only mean one thing – he was, in fact, dating Janine. I didn't want to come right out and ask Rich because the last time I did that, he practically scolded me in his office. We were having a great time and working well together and I didn't want to make the rest of our trip uncomfortable for either of us.

We spent the morning, once again, interviewing some of Rich's contacts at the Exchange. It started snowing just as we were exiting the building for lunch. I pulled my red, wool peacoat tighter to my chest and wrapped my knitted, white, infinity scarf closer to my neck. I was glad that I chose my knee-high boots rather than the black pumps I had originally unpacked this morning.

"Why don't we skip our afternoon appointments and play hooky this afternoon," Rich said. "I have the perfect idea."

"Did Rich Davis just suggest playing hooky?" I questioned in disbelief.

"Shockingly, I did," he answered amusingly.

"You've come a long way since you referred to me as the 'slacker-type.'"

"You never let me forget my arrogant ways, do you Miss Anderson? Now, let's go have some fun, shall we?"

How could I argue with this playful side of Rich?

"Lead the way, Mr. Davis," I said with the widest possible smile on my face.

We took a cab back to The Plaza where Rich insisted I change into something warm and comfy. I went into my bedroom and changed into a pair of skinny jeans and my favorite white, cashmere sweater. I pulled on my pink Ugg boots and completed my ultimate snow-bunny look with my matching pink, puffy jacket. After wrapping a scarf around my neck, I added a knit headband to cover my ears. I figured I would be prepared in case Rich was planning an outdoor activity.

I headed downstairs to the living room and noticed that Rich was already waiting for me, dressed in his winter gear. I tried my best to hide my disappointment after seeing his ski jacket covering so much of his sexy body.

"Where are we headed, Rich?"

"That's my surprise, Brooke. You said you'd never been to the city before and I thought we could have some fun and maybe tackle a couple of those locations that are probably in your precious *Frommer's*."

I soon realized, when Rich didn't immediately hail a cab, that we were walking across the street to

Central Park. Rich's hand clung to mine as we made our way through the gates and headed toward the signs that pointed toward the Wollman Rink.

"Oh my god, are we going ice skating?" I questioned, as I began jumping up and down on the sidewalk.

"Somehow, I knew you would love this. Is this part of your Home Again movie, too?" he asked.

I couldn't help but laugh at Rich's error. "First, it's *Home Alone* and no, no ice skating. I've just always dreamt of skating in Central Park. And, we're also so close to the zoo."

"Well, I'm not sure if we'll have time to make it to the zoo. If memory serves, it closes fairly early in the winter. But, I do have another surprise planned for this evening."

Rich and I rented skates and glided over the ice for several hours. The snow started coming down more heavily as the afternoon flew by. After I was certain that my nose was going to fall off, Rich pulled me into a warm embrace. I gazed into his eyes and knew he was going to come in for a kiss. In that moment, I desired his kiss more than my next breath, but instead of letting my heart win, my head pulled away from Rich's arms. "*Just colleagues,*" my inner voice whispered.

Although no words were spoken between us, the carefree atmosphere that had lingered between us all day began to fade away. I had ruined what would have been the most beautiful and romantic kiss in the middle of the Wollman Rink in Central Park.

If our lips had met, the falling snow would have coated us both in a light dusting. My already rosy cheeks would have further flushed as a result of his tongue dancing with mine. But, I had ruined that picture-perfect moment. Instead, I just wanted to go back to my room and sulk. *Why do I have to be so damn stubborn?*

Even though I wanted to head back to the suite, Rich wouldn't hear of it. He may have lost some of his earlier, carefree spunk, but he was still determined to show me the "right way to play hooky."

"If you're gonna be a slacker and play hooky, you might as well do it up right," he kept saying.

"Go big, or go home," I added.

We grabbed hot cocoas and hot dogs, minus the pickles for me, from a street vendor, before Rich waved down a cab to take us the few blocks to his surprise destination.

I laughed to myself when I realized we were stopping at Rockefeller Center. "Hey, this one is in the movie," I said, as I lightly nudged him in the side.

"I figured. Any Christmas movie set in NYC has to include the tree here."

It really was beautiful. As I stood there in Rockefeller Plaza looking up into the tree, illuminated by thousands of tiny white lights, I began thinking about how perfect this day had been. I didn't want to leave because I was afraid of what tomorrow might bring. I didn't want to think about Rich's possible relationship with Janine, my career, or my reservations about us. I just wanted to stay here with Rich – forever.

Chapter Sixteen

I was lucky that as a new reporter I was able to get the holiday off, but I think I was getting a little special treatment from Rich. Under normal circumstances, I wouldn't appreciate his giving me this special treatment, but I was so thankful to be going home that I was willing to let it slide just this once.

I was so excited to be going home for a few days to celebrate Christmas with my dad, Cass and Kaitlyn. Although I had just spent time with the girls, I hadn't seen my dad in almost two months; although we talked almost every day, I still missed him like crazy. I also couldn't wait to give Kaitlyn the teddy bear I bought her while in New York.

I chuckled at the memory of Rich taking me to the final destination on our trip before we headed back to the airport on our last day in New York City. When I walked into FAO Schwarz, I felt like a kid in a candy store.

"I googled that Duncan's place you mentioned, but I didn't come up with anything. I figured this was the next best option," Rich said, as I stared in amazement.

We walked around for at least an hour looking at the aisles upon aisles of dolls, puzzles, games, remote-controlled cars, stuffed animals and action figures. I finally settled on the famous store's signature teddy. I knew Kaitlyn would be beyond thrilled with her gift.

After sliding the last of my gingerbread men into the oven and with my dad stringing lights on the tree, I began to fantasize about what I'd be doing now if Rich were here with me. We'd probably spend most of the day at the mall Christmas shopping for our families. He'd make me sit on Santa's lap; then we'd stop at the Christmas tree farm to chop down the perfect Fraser fir just like the Griswold family. (*I can't help it; I'm a sucker for classic holiday flicks*). Granted, it would look nothing like the tree we saw at Rockefeller Center, but it would be our tree.

We'd come home and sit in front of the glistening evergreen, while sipping on my dad's specialty hot chocolate. I was always so disappointed as a kid when I had to drink the powdered stuff while all of the adults got to drink his "special" recipe. Little did I know, until many years later, that he always added a dash (more if we were on Santa's Nice List) of peppermint schnapps to the adult version.

We'd end the night, cuddling on the couch munching on popcorn balls and homemade sugar cookies, while we watched my all-time favorite holiday film, *Holiday Inn*— not the colorized version either, but the original black-and-white film starring Bing Crosby and Fred Astaire. It was one of my mom's favorites, and we watched it as a ritual every season while we decorated the tree, or wrapped gifts.

After the movie, Rich would take me upstairs where he would unwrap the gift that I would wear and had purchased especially for him – a black lace nightie with a red ribbon tied in a loose bow right under my breasts. ...

The oven's timer announced that the cookies were done and snapped me out of my Rich-induced reverie. Just as I was slipping on my oven glove, my dad sauntered into the kitchen. I saw his hand grab one of the cookies that were already cooling on the counter.

"You know you have the same eyes as your mother? I could always tell when something was bothering her – just like I can tell that something is bothering you right now. What's going on in that pretty, little head of yours, Brooke?" he asked.

"It's nothing, Daddy, really. Let's just eat the cookies I baked and watch a movie, or something. I bet if we surf through enough channels we will come across *Elf*. Oh ... or we can always watch that old VHS copy of *Christmas Eve on Sesame Street*."

No matter my age, I would never be too old to watch Big Bird trying to figure out how Santa Claus fits down that "skinny, little chimney." *Rich was right, I was a nine-year-old girl, trapped in a grown woman's body.*

"I do love Buddy the Elf, but right now I really think we should talk, baby girl. Is it that boy from college, that editor of yours?" Dad asked caringly.

"How – how do you know? Let me guess? Cassidy has been feeding you the gossip, eh? How much has she told you?" I questioned.

"Not too much, just that you are being stubborn as usual. You get that from your mother, too, you know?" Dad said.

"I just can't, Dad. You know how much this job means to me. I've finally made it. After all these years, I'm there. I'm at the *Washington Post.*"

"Yes, Brooke, and I'm so proud of you for that, but I can tell in your eyes that something is missing. Maybe you should give it a try. What's the worst that can happen?"

"I could lose it all. I could lose my job and I could lose Rich. At least this way, I get to keep my job." I answered dad's question as truthfully as I could.

"Or, you could keep your job and live happily ever after with the man of your dreams."

"Did you just watch *Beauty and the Beast* with Kaitlyn, Daddy? You sound like freakin' Walt Disney."

He laughed before adding, "No, Brooke, I'm being serious. It already sounds like you think that you and this Rich fellow would fail. Why do you think that?"

"I don't know, Dad. I guess I don't think that; I'm just afraid, that's all."

"Do you remember that saying that's framed in your old man's office?" he asked.

"Of course, I do. Mom and I had it framed for you as a Father's Day gift when I was just a kid. She said it was always one of your favorite quotes. I remember we even wrapped and hid it, but you still managed to open and rewrap it before I gave it to you. You never were one for surprises."

My dad laughed, before adding, "But, do you remember what it says, Brooke?"

"Yeah, if I remember right it was something Bobby Kennedy said, 'Only those who dare to fail greatly can ever achieve greatly.'"

"Yes, that's exactly it, Brooke. You need to dare, take a leap, do what's in your heart because it could be great. And, if it's not, then you have gained vast experience already in your short time with the *Post*. Other superb newspapers in the country would want you in a heartbeat."

I sat there for a minute in silence, really thinking about what my dad was saying. After what felt like several minutes, I finally nodded my head in agreement. "You're right, Daddy. I need to give this a chance. I need to give Rich a chance. Thank you." With that, I rose from the couch and walked over to my dad to give him the biggest hug. "Really, thank you, Daddy." I said lovingly.

"Anything for you, honey – anything for you."

"OK, enough of this gooey sh – show of emotion," I added with a giggle.

"So, I guess the movie of choice tonight is actually *Home Alone*, huh," questioned my dad, with some disappointment in his voice.

"Can you believe Rich has never watched *Home Alone*?"

"Well, we'll need to make sure he's here next year to watch it with us then, won't we?" My dad said, with some sarcasm in his voice.

"Whatever, Dad, you know you love it as much as I do," I chuckled back.

"If you say so, Brooke, if you say so," he said, shaking his head.

With that, my dad and I did settle on the Macaulay Culkin classic that I remembered watching for the first time at the theater with him when I was only about nine. So much had changed since then, but I was still thankful for the time we shared and the advice he was still able to give me these many years later.

Cass was delighted to hear that my dad had finally been able to talk some sense into me. She insisted on taking me to Victoria's Secret on the day after Christmas to shop for some sexy lingerie.

"He can't see the same old stuff, Brooke. Besides, their semi-annual sale starts today. You can't pass up BOGO panties."

"Did you really just say, BOGO? You really have been watching too many TV commercials. You know you can fast forward through that shit these days, right? Welcome to the twenty-first century, Cass." I said with a giggle.

"Whatever, don't change the subject, bi-atch," she exclaimed while giving me the finger. "Now, we are finding you the sexiest outfit, so you can bang, err ring, in the New Year in style." She got this wild look in her eyes before adding, "Oooooh, or we can skip the lingerie store all together and head straight for the adult store, maybe even pick you up a naughty nurse outfit, or a Playboy bunny … the possibilities are endless," Cass added.

"OK, OK. I'll agree to the new lingerie, but stay classy, Cass – Victoria's Secret ONLY." I made sure to emphasize the "only" so she wouldn't get any more over-the-top ideas.

The typical jitters that I usually experienced, boarding the airplane flying back to D.C., didn't occur this time. Maybe the green beads that hung around my neck were helping to ease my jitters. I wasn't nervous, only anxious to get back to Rich and tell him that I wanted to try and work something out.

In order to preserve the integrity of our professional relationship, I thought we should take things slowly at first, but I still wanted a relationship with him. I couldn't wait to see the look on his face when I told him the news. My flight was scheduled to arrive at around three in the afternoon and I knew he was scheduled to be at work.

As soon as my flight landed, I collected my baggage and hailed a cab to the office. After paying the fare, I made my way up to the twelfth floor. I opened Rich's office door, and there he stood, on the phone, gazing out his window. I probably should have announced my presence, but I just stood there in awe at the man before me.

He had removed his suit jacket and haphazardly thrown it across his chair. His broad shoulders filled out his light green, button-down shirt which was loosely tucked in at his well-defined waist. He had rolled up his sleeves to the elbows, showing off the definition in his tanned forearms. Oh ... and his perfectly tailored pants fit his fine, firm ass to perfection.

Rich's deep voice broke my trance as he spoke to the mystery caller. I decided to stand in the doorway so as not to disturb his conversation. I probably should have returned to my office and waited, but I just couldn't stop myself from eavesdropping on his conversation.

"No, I don't have plans for the weekend, yet. What did you have in mind," he asked, and then paused to let the caller continue. "Yeah, I think that sounds perfect, actually. I haven't gone skiing in awhile and I think it would be the perfect opportunity for us to get away from everything. I'll book a flight out to Vermont later tonight and meet you in the morning," he said before pausing to listen again.

I had never been skiing before. I usually avoided those types of activities since I wasn't even all that coordinated on flat surfaces, but I imagine I would give it a try for Rich. Besides, we could spend most of our time cuddled in front of the roaring fire at our cozy little inn. We would ring in the New Year with the finest champagne and a kiss at midnight; maybe even with that bang that Cass had not so subtly suggested.

I was deep in thought about playing the role of Rich's ski bunny when I heard him say those three little words to his mystery caller.

"I love you. I'll see you in the morning," Rich cooed.

I must have let out a louder-than-intended gasp because Rich turned around to see me standing in the doorway, just as he was ending his call.

"Brooke, I didn't realize you'd been standing there. How-how much did you hear?"

"Sorry, Rich. I didn't mean to eavesdrop. I just-I just came to tell you that I was back in town."

"It's good to see you made it back safely. I hope you had a nice Christmas with your dad and friends."

"I did, thank you. I couldn't help but hear you making plans for New Year's, I assume?" I asked distractedly.

"Yep, I'm going to head out later today for a ski trip. So, obviously, I will be out of the office for a few days. I sent you an e-mail earlier today with a few story assignments. You may report to Kyle with any questions, or concerns." Rich added.

"Oh, OK. Well, I guess happy New Year, Rich. I'll get started on these assignments and see you in a few days."

"Happy New Year's to you too, Brooke." Rich replied casually.

Before I headed back into my office, I couldn't help but take a quick peek at the vacation schedule which was posted in Caroline's cubicle. Sure enough, my suspicions were confirmed when I saw that Janine, too, had some scheduled vacation the exact same time as Rich. He was doing this to me again. The first time he said he would wait for me, but he ended up with Aubrey Sullivan; now he was with big-breasted Janine.

I wanted to run back into his office and yell at him – shake him, even. *How could he do this to me again? He promised me he would wait for me all those years ago and instead he shacked up with Aubrey. Now, he feeds me all that bullshit about me not dreaming – that we're real. Then just weeks later he's telling fuckin' Janine that he loves her? Right again, Rich – not only am I dreaming, but it's a fucking nightmare! Oh, and Happy New Year – my ass.*

Instead of waltzing back into Rich's office and letting him have it, I decided to take the higher ground and moped back into my office. I wouldn't let him see me like this. I couldn't control the tears that fell from my eyes and clouded my vision as I tried to access my e-mail.

Cass was right when she said he wouldn't wait for me forever. *Why did I always think I knew best? I had fallen in love with Rich, maybe even ten years ago, and there wasn't anything I could do about it.* With my right hand, I began rubbing the beaded necklace that I had tucked behind my sweater before I entered the office. Just thinking again about Rich's kind gesture that day only months ago, brought more tears to my eyes.

February 2012

Weeks had passed since I heard Rich professing his love for Janine over the phone. I gagged each time I was forced to watch those two flirt endlessly. I always knocked before entering Rich's office for fear of walking in on them getting busy on one of Rich's couches, or spread out naked across his expansive desk. The image conjured up in my mind was so depressing to me that I was convinced, if I actually saw it with my own two eyes, I would jump from the 11th Street Bridge, if given the opportunity. *OK, perhaps, I'm being overdramatic, but point is – it hurt like hell.*

I had decided in the weeks following New Year's Eve that maybe Washington D.C. wasn't the place for me after all. I missed my dad, Cass and Kaitlyn, like crazy, and I thought that I might be able to move closer to them while still staying at a newspaper in a larger market. Besides, seeing Rich and Janine together just made it that much harder for me; I just couldn't take the pain anymore.

The irony didn't escape me, either. I had avoided Rich in the beginning because I wanted my career at the *Post* more than I thought I wanted a relationship. Turns out, less than six months later, I wouldn't have Rich, or my job in D.C. and not because it didn't work out between us. Truth is – I did this. I never even gave us a chance. And, now he had moved on with someone else – again.

I had applied for a few reporting jobs throughout the Midwest – a couple in Detroit, one in Cleveland and another at the *Chicago Tribune*. It was just another ordinary Tuesday morning around the office. I had just gotten back to my desk, after covering a small-scale political rally just blocks from our building, when my phone rang. I didn't recognize the number that flashed on the caller ID.

"Hello this is Brooke," I answered.

"Hi, Brooke, this is Melissa with the *Chicago Tribune*. We have received your resume and would like to schedule an interview with you at your convenience. Would next week work with your schedule?" she asked.

"Oh, yes, thank you for the opportunity, Melissa. Next week would work with my schedule. If you could please just send an itinerary to my e-mail, I will be sure to make it work." I assured her.

"Thanks again, and I look forward to my interview in Chicago," I added, before completing the call.

Just as I was hitting end on my iPhone, I looked up to see Rich standing in my doorway. Before I could explain, I saw his face redden as he turned and abruptly exited my office. It wasn't my intention to hurt Rich, but I needed to escape. This was all too much for me. I never expected to meet him again after all these years and it was more than I could handle. I had been an emotional wreck since the holidays and I needed to find my place again. And, unfortunately that place was without Rich Davis and without the career and city that I had always hoped for. I allowed myself to giggle momentarily when I secretly wished my next editor would be a sixty-year-old man with a receding hairline and potbelly. *Please, I can NOT handle any more Nick Lachey look-a-likes!*

After taking a few minutes to compose myself, I walked the few feet to Rich's office and abandoned my new protocol of knocking first. Much to my surprise, I saw Janine sitting in one of Rich's office chairs with him sitting on the other side of the desk, looking visibly upset. Before I had time to take in anything else, I heard her utter the words I never expected to hear – "I'm pregnant."

I wanted to walk away, rather run away – take a cab to the airport and take the next flight out of this goddamn city. I don't care where it took me, I just needed to escape. Instead, my feet wouldn't move. They remained planted in Rich's doorway. *Why did I keep walking in on his private conversations? I wasn't trying to be a glutton for punishment.*

Rich looked up and saw me standing there, probably hearing the bated breath finally escaping from my lips. Walking to the other side of his desk, his knees rubbed up against *hers*. "Don't you worry about a thing, we'll work this out – together," he added as he looked at me.

I escaped his office just as abruptly as he had left mine just moments before – I had to leave. I couldn't stay here in the same building any longer. I would just go home and wait for my e-mail from the *Tribune*.

I went home that afternoon and called in sick the next two mornings. Honestly, I wasn't sure if I intended on ever stepping foot inside that building again. My interview with the *Tribune* was scheduled on Monday and if that didn't work out, I was considering just moving back in with my dad for awhile. Maybe I could crawl back and beg for my old job. Sure, it wasn't glamorous, but no one broke my heart in all the years spent there, either.

For the third consecutive morning, I called Caroline and told her I was still suffering from the flu. I think she suspected that it was just a lie, but she didn't push it – especially on today, of all days. Valentine's Day wasn't typically a favorite of mine anyways and the entire Rich situation just made it seem that much worse.

In the years since Mom died, whenever I became sad or depressed about anything, I always missed her even more than usual. It's probably because she was always my constant – my rock. As a little girl, whenever I had an earache, stomach ache, or skinned knee, she would always seem to make it better. If I woke up in the middle of the night with a bad dream she would chase the monsters away from underneath my bed. As I got older, when I got a bad grade on a test, or if my crush didn't invite me to a dance, she would always find a way to cheer me up.

I found myself sitting on my bed that Valentine's Day, missing my mom even more than losing Rich.

My mom's little presents that I used to look forward to on Valentine's Day after Jay and I had broken up hadn't been an option for a number of years. She would always send care packages when I was in college that were chockful of jelly hearts, conversation hearts, red and pink socks, glittery stickers and a little mom, love note. One year I even remember a heart-shaped necklace in the package.

The boys in my life never seemed to top my mom's gifts. Jay tried once. He ordered me flowers through some mail-order company when he should've just called a local florist directly. I remember how disappointed he was when I told him the flowers had arrived half-dead. I guess it was the thought that counted, but I still wasn't very impressed. I always envisioned him showing up at my doorstep with the flowers in hand, but it never worked out that way.

This year wouldn't be any different. It took all my effort to take a shower that morning, but since I hadn't showered for the last three days, I decided it was time to wipe away the sadness. I spent the rest of the afternoon cleaning up my apartment and packing for my trip to Chicago. As evening approached, I decided to watch sappy chic flicks, drink wine and eat chocolates until they made me sick. My only date consisted of some FaceTime with Cass and Kaitlyn.

After running out to complete a few errands before my trip, I came home and changed into an oversized, hooded sweatshirt and black yoga pants before popping *Hope Floats* into my DVD player. Harry Connick Jr. and his sexy southern swagger always made my heart flutter a bit. I had just sat down with a large glass of Moscato and a big bowl of popcorn when my phone buzzed next to me. I looked at the screen and saw my favorite little face looking back at me. I quickly connected the call so I could talk to my two favorite ladies.

"Hi Aunt Brookie. Happy Valentime's Day," Kaitlyn chirped through the line.

"Hi, Princess. Happy Valentine's Day to you, too. Did you get any flowers from your boyfriends?" I asked.

"Eew, boys have cooties, Aunt Brookie. Mommy told me so," Kaitlyn replied with disgust.

I chuckled at my goddaughter's innocent response. "Of course, she did, Princess. Speaking of your mommy, where is she?"

"I'm right here. So, tell me …" she said, as she lightly pushed Kaitlyn out of the view screen "did Mr. Boss-man try anything today? I figured if he was going to use any day to make a grand gesture to win your affection it would be today," Cass said.

I had avoided talking to Cass for the last few days because I just didn't feel like hearing her tell me, "I told you so." But, I guess there was no time like the present to get it all out there.

"No, Cass. He didn't try anything. Actually, I haven't been to the office in three days. I'm actually thinking about moving closer to home, too. I have an interview in Chicago on Monday," I informed her.

"You what? What the hell happened, Brooke? And, why am I just now hearing about this?" she shot back.

"He's still too busy with that blonde bimbo, Janine, from reception. I never told you, but I heard him tell her that he loved her when I came back after

Christmas. Well, it was over the phone, but I know now that it was certainly her. In fact, I overheard her tell him she was pregnant earlier this week."

"Shut up! That really sucks, Brookie, but you sound pretty bitter for the girl who told him on more than one occasion that she wasn't interested," she said with an arched brow. "I mean you know you could be getting laid right now, instead of talking to us about his pregnant girlfriend?"

"Mommy what does 'getting laid' mean?" I heard a little voice ask in the background.

"Oh, nothing honey ... why don't you go play in your room and let mommy talk to Aunt Brookie, OK?" Cass suggested to her daughter.

"Crap, I always forget she can understand me now. She's probably going to repeat that to her grandmother. I swear she's a little sponge," Cass said, after Kaitlyn had scurried to her bedroom.

I shook my head and tried to muster a laugh before answering her previous question about Rich ... "I knew the 'I told you so' was coming, I guess I just thought you'd be a little less harsh about it, Cass. You know that I tried to tell him I had changed my mind about us when I came back after Christmas. Remember, my grand idea for New Year's Eve that exploded in my face? I know it's my fault, but yeah, I guess I'm a little bitter. But, it's time to dust myself off and move on. He clearly has – again." I explained regretfully.

"Are you trying to convince me, or yourself?"

"Whatever, just let it go, will you? None of it matters anymore. I know I messed up, but there is no happily ever after for us. That shit just doesn't exist in my world. I couldn't let it."

"Whatever, it will happen, Brooke. I just want you to be happy. I saw that sparkle in your eye when you came home from your interview. I hadn't seen that same sparkle since Mom died maybe even be--." Cassidy was cut off by the sound of my doorbell.

"Let me call you back. Someone is at the door. Probably just a pizza delivery man at the wrong unit, or something," I said.

I quickly ended my call and sat my glass of wine on the coffee table before making my way to the front door. I checked the peephole to see what appeared to be a man holding at least two dozen, vibrant orange roses.

"What in the hell," I said, to no one in particular, as I opened the door.

"Not quite the greeting I was looking for," I heard the familiar husky voice answer behind the roses.

"Rich? Wh—What are you doing here?" I asked, perplexed.

"Don't act so excited to see me. I'm here to bring you these. A little birdie told me that it was Valentine's Day and that you were sick. I would've brought you some chicken noodle soup, too, but I had a feeling that you weren't really all that sick," he answered.

"Why aren't you spending Valentine's Day with your Valentine then, Rich. And, actually, I haven't felt well the last few days, but you're right - a broken heart can't be cured with chicken noodle soup."

"That's what I'm trying to do here, sweetheart. I want to spend this day with my Valentine, that is, if you'll finally let me in." I sensed he meant much more than into just my apartment. "I have a feeling I can help mend that broken heart, too, but, once again, only if you'll let me in," he said with emphasis.

"But, what about Janine? How can you come here with roses for me when your girlfriend, who you love, is pregnant, Rich?" He was just making me mad now. I was mad for her and I was even more pissed for myself.

"What about Janine? We were never together, Brooke," he insisted.

"What do you mean 'What about Janine?' I heard her Rich. She's pregnant with your baby for fucks sake and you told HER that you loved her? I shouldn't even be talking to you about this right now. You're a bigger asshole than I thought you were even all those years ago." I said, with more than a hint of bitterness in my voice.

 "I never told her that I loved her. I may have flirted around her in your presence, but this is all a big misunderstanding. If you'll let me, I'd like to explain."

"Fine – I can't wait to hear how you are going to try and weasel your way out of this one. I know what I've heard," I shot back.

"Listen to me, Brooke. I don't want Janine from reception. I don't want Lyndsay from accounting. I don't want Deb from production and I don't want Allison from advertising. The only woman I want in my life is Brooke Christine Anderson from my past, present and future."

I wanted this, just six weeks ago. I wanted to hear those words and he unknowingly broke my heart. But, now he's going to be a father.

"But, Janine – she's pregnant, Rich," I yelled, as I pushed against his chest.

"Pregnant, yes, but her baby is not mine. We were never even together, Brooke. I sound like an asshole saying this, but I just used her and acted cozy at the office to make you jealous. Little did I know, she's in a pretty serious relationship. When you overheard her telling me that she was pregnant, you just misunderstood. She was telling me because I'm her supervisor. I need to make arrangements for her maternity leave. She certainly wasn't telling me because I'm the baby's father."

"But, when I came to your office before New Year's, you were making plans for your ski trip together and you told her – you told her that you loved her." I said, swallowing back the lump that had formed in my throat.

"Brooke, I went on that ski trip with my sister and her family. I was talking to my sister, Jennifer, that afternoon. I told my sister that I loved her. Don't you see, Brooke, this is all just a big misunderstanding. When I overheard you the other day, scheduling an interview for another job – I just can't take this anymore, Brooke. I can't lose you – either as my employee, or my girl. I knew I had to come to you, I just needed to figure out the best way so that I wouldn't scare you off even more than I already have – please understand," Rich begged.

With that statement, Rich pushed twenty-four long-stemmed, orange roses into my chest.

"Why orange? Were they out of red, Rich?" I asked teasingly.

"Don't get sassy, Brooke. Will you invite me inside? I have something else here for you with a letter inside that will explain it all." Rich said with relief sounding in his voice.

With Rich standing in my doorway asking for my permission to let him enter my apartment, my life and my heart – I took him all in.

It looked like he hadn't shaved in a few days and the sexiest stubble outlined his chiseled jaw line. I don't ever remember seeing Rich with facial hair before, but goddamn was it ever sexy. He was still wearing his charcoal dress slacks and white, buttoned-down, dress shirt that I assumed he had worn to work that day. He had already unbuttoned the top two buttons. Holy Hell, what I wouldn't do to see his rock-hard chest again. *Get a grip, Brooke. The last thing you need is to let Rich catch you drooling over him again. That will certainly send him the wrong idea. It is the wrong idea, right? FUCK, why do I keep questioning this? I thought I had lost him, not only once, but twice. And, now this confession – what does it all mean? Don't overanalyze this. Just jump …* *I heard my dad's advice resonate in my head.*

I motioned for Rich to come in as I made my way to the kitchen to fill a vase with water for the roses.

"They are beautiful. Thank you, Rich," I told him, as I breathed in the fresh, floral scent.

He slid a brown-colored box across the counter. It strangely resembled the care packages that I used to receive from my mom while in college.

The box was taped shut and had my address written with black Sharpie on the top. I grabbed a knife from the drawer and carefully cut through the tape. I gasped and put my hand over my mouth as I opened the lid. Inside were a bunch of jelly candy hearts, conversation hearts, playing cards, Valentine-themed socks, cherry flavored lip balm and a temporary tattoo that read "be mine."

UNWRITTEN

Also among the contents were three folded pieces of notebook paper.

> My Sweetest (but still Babbling) Brooke,
>
> Since the day you slammed into my life, nearly twelve years ago, I knew I needed you to be mine. I thought I lost you once, forever. Now that I have you in my life, I'm not letting you go, ever again. I don't care how much you resist. I am not giving up on you—on us. You are probably wondering why I picked orange roses to give you when red roses obviously symbolize love. For starters, I tried red once and it didn't really work out so well for me. Secondly, that seemed far too easy. Red roses are simple and don't take much thought. I want you to know that I do think about you … always in my heart and always on my mind. The florist told me that orange roses are the embodiment of desire. You are certainly what I desire, Brooke. I desire your mind, body and soul. The florist also told me that orange roses often symbolize passion and excitement and are an expression of fervent romance. Do you get what I'm trying to say here?

I am passionate and excited about a romance with you, sweetheart. We are hot together; there is no denying that, is there? But, I want so much more than a hot tryst with you.

Along with the roses to show you how passionate I am about us, I brought you a simple package to show you how much I care — how I know you better than you know yourself.

I remember just a few months after we met, you came up to the Eagle's office to work on an assignment. I happened to be up there working on an assignment of my own. It was Valentine's Day and you walked into the room carrying a small brown box. I remember assuming it was from your boyfriend, but instead you gave me a heart-shaped cookie from the box and said it was baked with love from your mom. You dumped out the rest of the box and showed me each item from the variety of baked goods and candy to a deck of playing cards and cherry lip balm. I tried to recreate that box as best as I could remember because I know how much those memories of your mom mean to you. I want to bring the spark into your eyes that existed when I saw you open that package ten years ago. Please say you'll give me a chance, Brooke. Please stop running from this ... Running from us.

Brooke, I love you. I think I loved you all of those years ago, I probably even loved you when you weren't even in my life. But, since you came back into my life, I have known that I am head over heels in love with you—always and forever.

Rich

Tears fell like raindrops from my eyes and down my cheeks, as I looked up into Rich's piercing blue eyes which were also brimming with his own tears.

"You - you mean - you really did - you waited for me?" I stammered.

"I'll always wait for you, Brooke." Rich promised.

Without saying another word, I walked back into the kitchen and grabbed one of the orange roses I had just placed in a vase. I pushed a single orange rose into his chest and whispered through my tears, "Yes, I'll give us a chance, Rich. I'll quit running. And, I'm just as excited and passionate as you are at this very moment – about us. And, just for the record, I was ready to jump in six weeks ago, but ... well, that's a story for another day. Just kiss me now, Rich. Please just kiss me." I begged, choking back the tears.

He just sighed and pulled me into his strong chest. I nuzzled into his neck as he breathed in the scent of my hair against his face.

"I love you, Brooke," he said, as he placed light kisses on the top of my head. "I want to make love to you. I want to worship your body ... every inch and every curve. I want us to be together body and soul."

I pulled back slightly and looked Rich straight into his icy, blue eyes, noticing the corners of his mouth turn upward into that Hollywood smile that I adored.

"What's that for?" I asked curiously.

"What?" Rich asked.

"That smile of yours."

"I just saw it," he said as he planted a butterfly kiss on the tip of my nose.

"Will you, please, tell me what you're talking about?" I begged, as I nudged him in the chest.

"That spark, sweetheart. It's back," he replied with a chuckle.

"It's because of you, Rich. You've reignited me. Now take me to bed and make love to me." I pleaded.

"You don't have to ask me twice."

Rich picked me up and began showering my face and neck with soft, simple kisses. I could tell he wanted to take his time with me tonight. Unlike the other times which were filled with heated passion and need, he wanted to prove to me that he truly loved me.

A chill ran up my spine with just that thought. Rich carried me toward the bedroom as I squealed in his arms. He stopped in the hallway and pulled my sweatshirt over my head and dropped it on the floor in a heap.

"Holy fuck, Brooke. I didn't know you were naked under that thing. You need to give a guy some warning. I might fuck you right here in this hallway." Suddenly, Rich's mouth came crushing down to suck on my already hardened nipple. I whimpered as Rich carried me the rest of the way into the bedroom where he sat me down on my silk sheets.

"Scoot your bottom back and lift your hips up. Those pants need to go. I need to see you Brooke. All. of. you."

I did as he asked, and he growled when he saw I was just as naked down below as I had been up top, after he removed my one and only layer of clothing.

"Were you expecting someone tonight? You seem to have been prepared by your lack of undergarments."

"Just hoping the most amazing, hottest, and sweetest man would show up at my doorstep with roses in tow. But, you'll do," I said, with a laugh, as I looked up into his eyes gazing down on me.

"So, naughty."

Before I could get another word in, Rich had knelt by the bed and placed his hands under my ass to drag me forward on the cool, silk sheets. I glided across the smooth fabric as my legs parted at Rich's face. I leaned up on my elbows and watched him as he started placing sweet kisses on the inside of my thighs. His newly grown stubble tickled my inner legs which caused me to squirm beneath him. Rich took that as his cue and moved up from my thighs and began gently sucking on my clit.

"So fuckin' delicious, Brooke," he said, as he continued to suck on my overly sensitive bud. So fuckin' sweet. ... My sweets," he moaned.

My, I thought ... I finally belonged to Rich Davis. My mind had finally given in to what my heart had desired for the last ten years. I suddenly felt the weight of the last ten years lift from my shoulders. I was just that twenty-one-year-old girl again who was in love with a boy.

With each nip, Rich brought me closer to ecstasy. I felt my muscles tighten and begin to constrict as my orgasm intensified, rippling through my body. Rich let me come down to Earth before placing sweet kisses all the way up my abdomen and breasts. He crawled up onto the bed and hovered over me.

I then brought my hands up and slowly began unbuttoning his shirt, after which I trailed my lengthy nails down the thin line of hair that adorned his chest. I stopped at his beltline, where I took both hands and unbuckled his belt, before unzipping his pants. I could see his hard cock begin to spring free from the opening of his red boxer briefs.

"Rich, get up and drop your fucking pants and stand by the edge of the bed," I hissed.

"I love it when you get bossy, sweets," he answered, between heavy breaths.

Rich didn't argue as I heard his pants and shirt fall to my bedroom floor. I got up and adjusted myself. My head was now at the foot of the bed looking up at Rich in all of his naked glory. Oh, how I would never get tired of looking at this man … MY man. A smile began to form on my lips.

I stretched my arms out over my head and cupped my hands around Rich's tight ass. I pulled him closer to me as I lifted my head up off the bed and opened my mouth to take in all of him. Rich reached out and began fondling my breasts, as I continued to work his cock with my mouth.

His groans only pushed me to take in even more of him as I began to work his crown with my tongue. I slowly licked circles around his tip as he continued to squirm.

"Ahhhhh-mazing, Brooke. So damn amazing."

Knowing Rich was on the brink of his own release, I took as much of his length in my mouth as I possibly could and worked his balls with my hands. He slowly rocked his hips back and forth before I noticed his rhythm picking up a much quicker pace.

"Brooke, I'm gonna come. You need to get out of the way."

When I didn't move, I heard Rich moan out … "oh, shit, I didn't think it was possible for you to be any more perfect. Always full of surprises, sweets."

He continued to groan as he pumped himself into my mouth a few more times before I tasted his warm, salty essence on my lips. I have to admit that I wasn't really much of a fan of blow jobs in my previous relationships, but with Rich it felt different. I wanted to taste him. I wanted to lick every last drop of his cum off him.

"Oh, baby, that was perfect, but I need more of you now. I need to feel you when I make love to you for the first time," Rich said, breathlessly.

I didn't move as I watched Rich walk around to the other side of the bed, his cock still fully erect. His eyes never left mine and he reminded me of a mountain lion stalking its prey. I was so turned on, knowing that I was his prey.

Suddenly, he was straddling my legs and using his knee to spread my legs apart before he positioned himself at my entrance.

"Meeting you that day by the elevator was fate. Becoming your friend was by choice which took a whole lot of work, might I add. But, falling in love with you was beyond my control, sweets," he whispered in my ear, as he hovered over my body with his hard length tormenting my swollen clit.

"Falling in love with me might have been beyond your control, but making love to me right now is certainly very much in your control," I growled back. "Make love to me, Rich. Please, baby, please make love to me now," I begged breathily.

"Brooke, I thought you'd never ask. Your wish is my command."

Rich entered me slowly, taking his time, filling me to the brim. I could tell that he wanted to savor this moment between us. We weren't fucking, like months before; now Rich was telling me with his body that he loved me.

After what felt like hours of Rich pleasuring every inch of my body, we were finally curled up in each other's arms. I felt the happiest I'd been in months, maybe even years. If someone had asked me all those years ago if I truly loved Jay, I would have told them yes. But knowing now how I felt about Rich, I knew, without a doubt, that he was meant for me. I knew in that moment that I loved this man, holding me in his arms. Some may say that it was too fast. We had only just solidified our relationship, but we were twelve years in the making.

"Something on your mind?" Rich asked, as he placed a gentle kiss on my temple, pulling me tighter to his chest.

"Just us – I can't believe we're finally here – together," I replied.

"Mmmm, I like the sound of that – together. Speaking of which – you are planning on canceling that interview of yours, right?"

That's when my mind began to race. *Crap, I forgot all about my interview in just a few short days. Maybe I should still move. Maybe it would be better for my relationship with Rich. If he wasn't my boss, I wouldn't feel uncomfortable around him at work. What if our colleagues found out? What would they say? I would be nothing but water cooler talk.*

As if Rich could sense my inner turmoil, he said, "Shhh, stop overthinking this, Brooke. We'll make it work. We can even keep it a secret for awhile if you'd like, but you are canceling that interview with the *Tribune*. That decision is final and closed for discussion. Understand?" he said with finality.

"Yes, boss."

"Now that, that's settled, let's get some rest. You haven't been at work in three days and your assignments are piling up on your desk."

I couldn't help but laugh as I playfully punched Rich's bicep. "Do you always have work on the brain, Mr. Davis."

"No, I usually have you on the brain, but now that you are MINE, I can start concentrating on my work again. Actually, I think tomorrow, I'll need to see you in my office. I've been fantasizing about bending you over my desk since the day of your interview with me – be sure to wear a skirt tomorrow."

I shook my head and kissed his chest, "I love you, Rich, even if you are a demanding boss."

Chapter Eighteen

March 2012

It was my thirty-first birthday, or the second anniversary of my twenty-ninth birthday as I liked to remind my friends; I couldn't help but remember celebrating my birthday a decade ago. It seemed only fitting that I had celebrated then with Rich, too.

This time, though, instead of downing tequila at a local hole-in-the-wall, we'd be drinking champagne, and rubbing elbows with the Who's Who of Washington society at the annual White House Correspondents Dinner. Rich had attended each year since starting at the *Post*, but this was obviously my first time.

Having searched for weeks for the perfect ensemble, I finished putting on my makeup, while sitting at my vanity, and looked in the mirror; I smiled at the reflection staring back at me.

Rich was right about the sparkle being back in my eyes, and it wasn't because of the shimmering eye shadow I was wearing, either. He had done that

… all by himself. We had come so far in our relationship since I'd allowed him back into my life and heart a month ago.

The awkwardness that I feared would exist at the office, never happened. We kept things low-key for about a week, before Rich decided we were being ridiculous and sent out an intra-office memo. I must admit, it was a little awkward seeing the subject line – **Brooke Anderson = MINE**, come through over e-mail. I nearly choked on the French vanilla latte I was drinking at the time.

For being such an articulate man, Rich really wasn't very eloquent when it came to addressing our relationship status with colleagues.

I marched right into his office with the intent of letting him have it, but when I opened the door and saw him leaning against his desk with his shirt unbuttoned, bearing his abs, I melted into a puddle of goo.

"Excuse me, Mr. Davis, but what if someone else had just walked into your office," I recalled asking him.

"I assume you didn't read the entire memo, Miss Anderson, because if you had, you would've seen the last sentence advising my staff that I would be unavailable for the next hour. You see, I knew your pretty little behind would come in here acting angry with me. I would need to calm you down for the first fifteen minutes before I used the next forty-five for some hot, make-up sex right here on my desk," he replied with a wink.

Rich really did love bending me over his desk. I blushed thinking of the number of times he'd worked me into a frenzy over that thing – including that day.

While fantasizing about bending over Rich's desk with my panties bunched at my ankles and skirt around my waist, my mind returned to the present when I heard the sound of a key unlocking my door.

Just a second later, I heard Rich yell toward the bedroom. "Just me, sweets!"

"I should hope it's just you, baby. I don't go around giving my apartment key to many strangers," I laughed.

"Oh, Miss Sassy Pants tonight, huh?"

"Whatever," I quipped. "I'm almost done. I'll be out in a sec. Make yourself at ho--."

Before I had time to complete the sentence, I heard the snap and fizz of Rich opening a can of Bud Light and plopping on my couch, followed by the jingle that I've come to know as SportsCenter play on TV.

"Don't get too comfortable, though." I said as I walked out of the bedroom.

Rich looked in my direction and a smile quickly formed on my lips after seeing the expression on his face and hearing him mouth, "Whoa."

He stood up from the couch and my mouth dropped in similar fashion as I took in his crisp, black suit, light pink, collared shirt and gray and pink, striped tie. It took some work, but I was finally able to convince Rich that "real men wore pink." I'm so glad he gave in because – *dayum he looked sexy.*

He walked over to me, grabbed my hands and pulled me close to where I could feel his breath on my lips. He looked deep into my eyes before pulling me in closer to his lips. His tongue licked my bottom lip as it seemed to be asking permission to enter. My lips parted and our tongues met together in a dance.

I loved the taste of this man, which was better than any flavor of Ben and Jerry's. He was my own perfect flavor. I giggled a little at that thought and Rich pulled back to gaze into my eyes once again.

"When I look into your eyes I know that it's true; God must have spent a little more time on you," he hummed, in his off-key Karaoke voice.

My giggle turned into hysterical laughter. "Busting out the Justin Timberlake lyrics, eh? You must think you're getting lucky tonight."

"One, I'm always lucky when I'm with you," he said as he held one finger in the air. "Two," he continued while adding a second finger, "it's not just J.T., it's 'N Sync. You know, Justin, Chris, JC, Lance and that fat-one guy." I swear I thought he was going to throw a 'duh' in there just to prove his point.

I spoke before giving him that opportunity. "Wow, I'm almost impressed, but it's Fa-tone. Joey Fatone."

"It's true though, Brooke; they broke the mold when you came in this world."

"Seriously? What's with the 'God Must Have Spent A Little More Time On You' serenade?" I asked with a raised brow.

"I heard it this afternoon on Throwback Lunch. It reminded me of you."

I just smiled and gave him a simple peck on the lips. We were already running late and didn't have time to get ready all over again. The last thing I wanted was to be late for the White House gathering. "*Sorry, we're late to your party, Mr. President.*" – Uh, I don't think so.

Rich grabbed my right hand and twirled me around like a ballerina. I was wearing a strapless, pink chiffon dress with a black sash tied in the back that hung just above my knees. I completed my look with a glittery, pink-and-silver pair of ballerina flats. Who said fancy couldn't be comfy? That was Cassidy's motto and I was starting to think that she was on to something.

"Did I tell you that you look simply elegant tonight, my love?"

"Thanks, baby. You look pretty handsome yourself," I said with a grin.

I had been looking forward to this event for months. I just never imagined that when I RSVP'd several months ago that my "plus one" would be Rich. As our limousine pulled up to the front of the Washington Hilton, I felt those familiar, pesky butterflies take up residence in my belly once again. This place was swarming with notable reporters – the same ones who I'd been idolizing for years. Aside from the journalists, many politicians were expected to be in attendance including the vice-president, first lady and president.

Following dinner, each year, the event included a comedy roast of the president. This year's Master of Ceremonies was Jimmy Kimmel. *I would actually be in a live audience of a Jimmy Kimmel comedy show – someone pinch me now!*

"Are you OK, Brooke?" You seem a little distant."

"Yeah, I'm great, actually – just a little nervous that we are going to be in the company of all these celebrities."

"You'll be great. You always know how to charm a crowd. Look how well you got along with the first lady during your White House Christmas tree debacle," Rich chuckled. "Here I was trying to set you up, and you sure proved me wrong. Just one of the many things I love about you," he added, as pulled me closer, placing a light kiss on the tip of my nose.

The chauffeur opened the door and Rich slid out of the car. He turned to me and we walked hand in hand into the building where we were directed into the extravagant dining room. Rich and I found our name cards at one of the main tables nearest to the stage. I suppose my name was bumped up on the guest list because I was being escorted by the editor of the capital's leading newspaper.

Just as I was reading the names of other guests seated at our table, my attention was drawn to a beautiful, leggy blonde who was making her way to our table. You've got to be kidding me. Aubrey effing Sullivan was walking toward our table with an equally attractive man at her side.

How was she so freaking skinny? I thought to myself. *Note to self: go to the gym in the morning, better yet, maybe I'll take up running. I hate running, even the idea of running makes me want to barf, but really maybe it's a necessary evil, and would do me some good.*

And, her boobs! How were those things not pointing at all to the south? If it's even possible, I think they point more to the north than a decade ago. If she hadn't had a boob job then, she most certainly has by now.

Just as I was thinking about implants and a running schedule, I heard her sickening sweet voice. "Oh my, Rich – Rich Davis is that really you? And, your friend – well if it isn't Brooke Anderson. This is just a great, big, college reunion, isn't it?" she giggled.

Friend, friend? Did she just refer to me as Rich's friend. Was he going to correct her? Should I correct her? Better yet, I should just punch her in the throat, I mused to myself.

"Hello, Aubrey. Long time, no see. And, yes, this is Brooke – my girl friend," he told her as he squeezed my hand, as if sensing my internal panic. "What are you doing here? I've been to several of these as a representative of the *Post*, but I haven't seen you here before."

Thank goodness, Rich was just as surprised as I was that she was here. I felt my heart rate begin to return to normal with that revelation.

"I took a job with the *Times-Picayune* about a year ago. I took some time away from the journalism field after college and got into public relations, but I'm back at it now," Aubrey answered. "And, I never thought I'd see you again, Rich," she added, in her most flirtatious voice.

I just wanted her to finish her pleasantries and vanish – vanish from the dinner and from our lives, but to make the situation so much worse, I realized the name card next to mine read "Aubrey Sullivan and guest." We learned after we all took our seats that Aubrey's guest was just a colleague of hers from the *Times-Picayune*. Much to my disappointment, he also paid more attention to my boyfriend than he did to the beautiful blonde at his side.

It appeared that Aubrey was single and had her sights set on MY MAN! I just wanted a perfect birthday with Rich and here I was again sharing my night and my man with Aubrey freaking Sullivan. *Relax, Brooke. The difference is that tonight Rich will leave with you. He's not interested in Aubrey; he's only interested in you – you're his Brooke Anderson of his past, present, and future. I just had to keep reminding myself of that fact each time I saw Blondie batting her eyelashes at Rich.*

The rest of the evening went by in a bit of a blur. I laughed when Kimmel made jokes about the president and I greeted all of the political bigwigs as they visited our table, mainly to talk to Rich, but I never got comfortable because all I could really see were the googly eyes Aubrey kept making at my boyfriend. I couldn't wait for her to get on a plane back to New Orleans! It was bad enough thinking that she might come into contact with Rich more often now; I needed her out of our damn city.

Finally the night came to an end and Rich and I said our goodbyes. Rich must have picked up on my unease as he helped me into the limo.

"You don't have anything to worry about, Brooke. I love you. My time with Aubrey is in the past," Rich said, trying to ease my fears.

"But, you chose her over me once before, Rich. How can I be sure you won't choose her again?" I questioned.

"First of all, I always wanted you. It's only been you that I've ever wanted. I just never wanted to be your rebound guy. I wanted to be it for you. You were still in love with Jay. As much as you said you weren't, I always knew that you were. He hurt you deeply. I only went out with Aubrey because I needed to get my mind off you. So many times I just wanted to kiss you, make love to you, but I knew it was too soon."

"If I thought that your heart had been ready for what I felt for you then, it would have been you. It was and will always be you," he declared with absolute certainty.

I put my hands in Rich's thick hair and pulled him in for an affectionate kiss. In that moment, I knew that I would never have to worry about Aubrey Sullivan, or any other woman for that matter. This man at my side loved me and only me. And, I loved him, more than I even believed was possible.

Just when I thought this night couldn't get any more perfect, Rich pulled out a small, black, jewelry box from his right pocket. My eyes became as wide as saucers with what I thought was going to happen. *Holy shit! Was I ready for this? Rich and I had only been together for a month. But, I did love him. Yes, I was ready for this!*

"Relax, sweets. I know you probably aren't ready for THAT, yet … But, you will be my wife one day – soon," Rich said as he opened the box.

Inside was a beautiful, sparkly pair of tear-drop, diamond earrings. "I know it's almost over, but Happy Birthday, Brooke," Rich said with his perfect Hollywood smile.

Even though they were absolutely stunning, I couldn't help but feel a wave of disappointment course through my body. *We'd only been together for a month and I already wanted to marry this man. The realization hit me harder than walking into a wall of bricks.*

"Thank you, Rich. They're gorgeous and I will treasure them forever. Now, please, take me home and make love to me. Make my birthday wish come true," I purred.

Chapter Nineteen

July 2012

It was the Fourth of July when Rich and I traveled back to Michigan to spend some time with our families. I hadn't seen his mother or sister since his graduation ten years ago, and it had been even longer since he'd seen my father. I was most nervous, though, about Rich seeing Cassidy again. She'd never been his biggest fan and although she'd been fairly supportive of our relationship, she didn't want to see me get hurt. She'd been especially worried since I told her about our run-in with Aubrey Sullivan on my birthday.

"Why does that skank always have to ruin my bbopof's birthday? I wish I'd been there – I would have cut a bitch," she said, the day after our little reunion.

I reassured her over and over again that day that I had, in fact, fallen head over heels in love with Rich. I even told her I thought he was going to propose and that I'd been disappointed when he hadn't.

I stayed in bed a little later that morning, but crawled out when I smelled my favorite coffee brewing and heard conversation and laughter coming from the kitchen. I threw on my purple, fluffy robe, pulled my disheveled hair into a knot, and took care of business in the bathroom, before making my way to the kitchen.

"Mr. Anderson," Rich said, clearing his throat before continuing. "I love your daughter and I want nothing more than to make her my wife. She loves you and respects your opinion more than you will ever know. I understand that we are really just meeting here for the first time, but I would appreciate your blessing in asking for Brooke's hand in marriage."

Holy shit! Rich just asked my dad for his blessing to marry me. I should go back to the bedroom. I shouldn't be listening to this private conversation. Ahhhh! I can't help it. I have to listen. It's like gawking after a car accident. I just can't stop!

"Rich, please, call me David," Dad said. "I had a long talk with my daughter over Christmas and I could tell then that she really cared for you. I'm glad that the two of you were able to work things out. I want nothing more than her happiness and if she agrees to be your wife then I will happily welcome you into my family as my son-in-law."

Daddy said yes! Is Rich going to propose today? He did say something about the beach and fireworks over the lake at sunset. How romantic! All of those places would be the perfect setting for a proposal. This kind of stuff only happens in romance novels! Oh my gosh, I need to call Cass ... What do I wear? I'd want pictures and I want everything to look perfect – including myself!

I rushed back to the bedroom, hoping that I hadn't been caught eavesdropping and went right into the bathroom and started to shower. I stayed in a little longer than normal, hoping that Rich would join me, but he never came. *He must still be talking with my dad; the thought of those two actually hitting it off sent tingles up my spine.*

Just as I was leaving the bathroom, Rich entered the bedroom.

"Mmmm, you're still wet ... just how I like you," Rich said, not taking his eyes off my towel-wrapped body. "Come closer so I can lick you dry," he added lasciviously.

I walked into Rich's warm embrace, and he started nipping at my earlobes before beginning to lick the droplets of water that had fallen on my neck and shoulders.

"I was waiting for you in the shower," I said seductively.

"Too bad I missed that, but I'm here now," he said, as he opened the towel and let it fall to the floor, exposing my nude body for his viewing pleasure.

He continued his assault on my body by licking my cleavage before lapping and nipping on my already alert nipples. I moaned in pleasure which just caused Rich to clamp down a little harder on my taut peeks.

"Why am I the only one naked here?" I said between moans.

"Mmmmm ... Probably because you're the only one who just got out of the shower," he quipped.

"Being difficult this morning, I see," I said, as I began unfastening Rich's belt which I continued to work on as he reached behind himself and pulled off his black, Polo shirt in one swift motion. *Seriously, I think that is the sexiest move any man can make ... especially, my man.* Watching me fumble a bit, Rich made quick work of stripping his belt, khaki shorts and boxer briefs.

"Now we're both naked. Whatever should we do?" he asked, faking cluelessness.

"Oh, I have plenty of ideas," I offered, as I began to drool over his perfect abs, sexy-V and growing length.

"We'll get to your ideas, but first I want to show you mine."

Rich picked me up, cradling me in his arms and carried me to the bed. Gently laying me down, he continued licking and lapping my breasts and moving down to my stomach, paying extra attention to my belly button. I began squirming underneath him as the warmth began radiating from my core.

"Rich, please," I begged.

He swirled his tongue around my navel a few more times before kneeling at the foot of the bed, parting my sensitive thighs with his roughened hands. Once settled, he began licking each thigh, one at a time. After teasing me a bit longer, he finally brought his mouth to my clit and began sucking the delicate bud. Just when I thought I couldn't endure any more pressure, Rich plunged two fingers into my pulsating center.

I uncoiled beneath him, screaming his name over and over again. I could even see stars as I began to come down from the intense high. Once I gained control of my senses, I looked up to see Rich about to pounce. I scooted back onto the bed, hoping my damp hair was spread out beneath me, as Rich crawled up to kiss my mouth, allowing me to taste my orgasm on his lips.

"Fuck, Brooke! I'll never tire of the sight of you coming undone. You. Are. So. Beautiful." He said, as he plunged his hard length into my already drenched pussy.

I let out a deep moan at his sudden entrance. He began rocking his hips, filling me deeply with each thrust. I moved with him in complete synchronization. We knew every intimate detail of each other's bodies. I swear, he could make me unravel by just looking at my vagina.

"Oh my god, yes, I'm going to come again, Rich. Please … touch me," I pleaded.

Rich knew exactly what he needed to do as he brought his fingers to my clit and began rubbing them in a circular motion, causing friction to build between our bodies.

"Ahhhhhhhhhhhhhh," I screamed as a second orgasm rippled through my body.

Rich pumped into me a few more times as my pussy clenched around his hardened length. He let out a deep moan as he let out his release. He held me tightly for a few minutes as we both came down from our high.

"Who needs fireworks on the beach when we just had our own show here in the bedroom," Rich joked.

"Whatever, smartass, I've told you over and over how much I love watching the Fourth of July fireworks show on the beach. Now let's get going, or we're going to get stuck with a crappy view, plus I need a little sun time."

I caught Rich ogling my curves as I walked down the stairs after changing into my pink and white polka dot bikini. He licked his lips as I tied the matching, pink sarong around my waist.

"See something you like, baby?" I said, using a line from his book.

"Do we have to go to the beach? I'd rather stay here and taste my sweets."

"Yes, we already promised your family we'd be there. Now put your tongue back in your mouth and let's go," I said, pushing him toward the door.

"Fine, but I hope you stretched this morning because I plan on working you out later," he said as he lightly spanked my backside.

This man always knew what to say to render me completely speechless. At that moment, I really wished we could skip the day at the beach altogether and just head back upstairs.

Rich and I made the two hour trip from Dad's house to Grand Haven. The beach was crowded with families, tourists and locals enjoying the Fourth of July holiday. Rich unloaded our beach bags, chairs, umbrella and picnic basket as we made our way from the parking lot to the sandy Lake Michigan shoreline.

I saw a young girl, with a smaller boy chasing her, running toward us at warp speed.

Rich dropped our belongings, as the two children tackled him to the sandy ground.

"Uncle Rich! We missed you!" They shouted in unison.

"I missed you rugrats, too. Help me up, I want to introduce you to someone."

Rich let the children pretend like they were lifting him off the ground when in fact his bulging calf muscles were doing all the work.

"Leila … Nate … This is Uncle Rich's girlfriend, Brooke."

"Hi Leila, I remember seeing you when you were just a baby. You've grown up to be such a pretty young lady! And, Nate, I've heard so much about you. You're such a handsome little guy, aren't you?"

The two just looked from me to Rich with adoring eyes.

Leila poked Rich's arm and pulled him down to her level so she could whisper in his ear, "Uncle Rich, I like her. She's pretty!"

"She is pretty, isn't she? Truth is, Uncle Rich likes Brooke a lot, too. Now, can you two kiddos show us where your mommy is sitting," Rich asked the children.

The two began running in the sand toward the water, Rich picked up our stuff and headed in that direction before stopping when we reached his family.

They were all as I remembered, sans the family patriarch.

Rich made the introductions, as we began unloading our beach necessities. The children ran off with their father toward the water, carrying a Frisbee.

I took a minute as Rich caught up with his mom and sister to take in the view. The Great Lakes, including Lake Michigan, had always amazed me – miles upon miles of endless, crystal blue water. Many of my friends who I'd met recently while living in D.C. didn't believe that you couldn't see to the other side of the lakes. I'd explain to them that it was like looking out at the Atlantic, but they just didn't grasp the vast beauty. The Great Lakes had so much history, so many stories and so much mystery. I felt a chill run down my arms just thinking about these lakes that were created nearly ten thousand years ago, at the close of the last Ice Age.

The beach here in Grand Haven was magical, all on its own. The waves made a hypnotic sound as they crashed along the beach's pier. The two lighthouses were picturesque, standing like sentinels now in the waters of Lake Michigan, and were connected by the pier's lighted catwalk. I made a note for Rich and I to take a walk over there after darkness fell. *It seemed like a prime spot for a proposal, I thought to myself.*

"Do you need help with your sunscreen?" Rich asked, presumably for his own benefit, breaking me out of my thoughts.

"Sure, baby, but before you get any wild ideas, don't forget that your mother and sister are sitting less than five feet from us."

"Unfortunately, I'm well aware. I'm just looking out for you, Brooke. I don't want you to be complaining of sunburn for the next week because you were trying to tan."

I situated my towel in the sand before lying on my stomach. Rich straddled my backside and began massaging my shoulders and sides with the oily lotion.

"Can I help with the front, too?" he asked as I felt his length harden against my backside.

"That's probably not a good idea, babe. I'm already turned on and I can tell you are right there with me. I have some 'special' lotion that I packed, maybe we can try that out later," I suggested.

I rolled over, with Rich now straddling my hips; His cock teasing my clit through the fabric of my bikini and the fabric of his board shorts. I groaned as he came down and parted my lips with his tongue. We became consumed with each other's lips for several seconds before the sound of his mother clearing her throat brought us both back to reality.

"Sorry, Mom," Rich said as my face reddened.

"I'm so embarrassed. Please forgive my behavior, Mrs. Davis. It certainly won't happen again."

"Don't be ridiculous, Brooke dear. When my Michael and I began dating we had our fair share of trysts right here on this very beach," she informed me with a wink. "And, please call me Brenda."

"Gross, Mom. We really didn't need to know that," Rich and Jennifer said in unison.

"Don't be ridiculous, kids. You are both grown adults. I figured you would both know about the birds and the bees and where babies come from by now. In fact, I'm pretty sure I was the one to have that talk with each of you," she said, rolling her eyes and pointing at her children.

"Maybe so, Mom, but we like to think that you and Dad were exempt from that little story. I like to think that we were both immaculately conceived, right little brother," Jennifer suggested.

"OK, I think I am done with this conversation," Rich gagged. "I think I'll go play Frisbee with Connor and the kids. You ladies can finish your dirty talk in private. Hey, Brooke, why don't you tell them about that fifty shades of whatever that dude's name is that you were reading the other night."

"It's *Fifty Shades of Grey*, baby, and I doubt your mom and sister want to hear about my 'smut addiction,' as you like to call it."

I was wrong, after Rich ran off in the direction of the shore in search of his brother-in-law and kids, his mom and sister were all over me wanting to learn more about the infamous "Christian Grey," they both had heard so much about from their girlfriends. After sharing some of the details of the book, I promised I would mail them my copy once I returned home from our vacation.

After about an hour of sunbathing, I heard the laughter of little ones and the husky voices of Rich and Connor returning from their game of Frisbee. I was beginning to feel hunger pangs and was relieved when I saw Brenda pull a package of hot dogs and hamburger patties from their cooler. Connor grabbed the dogs and burgers from his mother-in-law and walked to the grill that was located in the park just south of the sandy beach area.

Rich helped his mother unpack the buns, condiments and chips while Jennifer opened the plates, napkins and utensils. I unfolded a few blankets and placed the extra coolers on the corners to hold them in place. Several minutes later, Connor returned with the grilled meat and we all sat down to eat.

Brenda shared stories of her children and grandchildren and I laughed uncontrollably at her stories of Rich as a rambunctious toddler and troublesome teenager.

"Rich Davis caused trouble?" I asked. "You were such a perfect college student that I just assumed you were always a brownnoser."

"Ha! Yes, I was quite the handful for a few years, but Ma here put the fear of God in me after I came home one afternoon with my tattoo. She was so pissed. Dad couldn't care less, he had a few tattoos from his days in 'Nam, but Mom yelled and cried for hours. I guess that night I was scared straight, you could say."

"Always full of surprises, aren't you, babe. I didn't know that my boyfriend was such a hard ass."

He chuckled, "Yep, that's me. Rich Davis – hard ass extraordinaire."

"Honestly, I'm glad you were a bit of rebel. As you know, I happen to love that tattoo of yours," I whispered in Rich's ear.

"I may not have liked that atrocious thing at the time, but I think you've turned it into a beautiful tribute to your father," Brenda said as she blotted the few tears that had rolled down her cheeks. "He may not have said it a lot, but he was proud of you Rich – all of his children, Connor included, and grandchildren. He loved his family very much, and he would be so very happy that you're here with us now, too, Brooke. He was just smitten with you when we all met at Rich's graduation all those years ago. He talked about that 'beautiful, green-eyed brunette' for weeks," she added with a warm smile.

After we cleaned up our picnic area, we all headed to the shore for a game of Capture the Flag. We had an uneven number of people, but we all agreed that the children would probably only count as one adult, anyways. Jennifer, Connor and the kids played on one team while Rich and I played on the same team as his mother. I think I should've actually been considered the handicap, instead of the kids, as it was obvious Rich's family had a long-standing tradition of Capture the Flag.

After several failed attempts, Connor finally sneaked past Rich and was able to snatch the flag from our side of the court. Loud cheers erupted for the opposition, "Nah na nah, Uncle Rich, we beat you and Grandma, too!" the kids cheered.

"Yes, you did, rugrats," Rich exclaimed as he ran toward the kids – picking them up and swinging them each in the air. "You got lucky. You better believe I won't let it happen again!

"Why don't you two head up to the beach and start setting up for the fireworks," Brenda suggested to the children.

We positioned our blankets on a small, sandy hill toward the back of the beach, directly facing the pier. Rich grabbed our portable radio and synced the station to follow along with the colorful blossoms erupting in the clear, night sky. It was difficult at times to hear the patriotic favorites over the crowd, gasping in amazement with each explosion.

I chuckled to myself as I remembered always wanting to be one of the Bayside kids in one of my favorite episodes of *Saved By The Bell*. I always dreamt of being the one to kiss Zack Morris under the fireworks at the Malibu Sands beach resort. At this moment, I was just thankful to sneak several quick kisses from Rich, as his niece and nephew's eyes remained glued to the sky. *Who needed Zack Morris when you had Rich Davis, I thought to myself.*

After nearly twenty minutes, the sky lit up in a sea of color as the fireworks danced across the night sky as part of the grand finale. The children sat in their mother's lap in complete awe at the show. I snuggled closer into the crook of Rich's arm, not wanting the day to end, just as I saw the last rockets begin to smolder in the night air.

"We should get going, son," Brenda said to Rich as she began picking up the last of their beach gear. "The children are rubbing their eyes which means it's bedtime."

"No sleepy! We want to stay and play with Uncle Rich and Brooke," Nathan said, trying to suppress the yawn that escaped his mouth.

"I don't know, little buddy. I think maybe you should listen to your grandma and go get some sleep," Rich told his nephew. "I promise, we'll see you again real soon," he added, as he kissed the top of Nathan's blonde head.

We said our goodbyes to the rest of his family, before Rich suggested we stay and stargaze for a bit before making the drive back to Dad's house.

"I've dreamt of this day – this moment – for over ten years," Rich whispered in my ear.

I paused for a minute before the realization dawned on me. "You're unbelievable!" I exclaimed. "You just recreated my perfect date. The one I told you about during that silly game of Truth or Dare all those years ago! It's been amazing, Rich. Today really has been perfect – your family – the beach – picnic – the fireworks – stargazing – just perfect. Thank you!" I said, peppering his lips with kisses.

"I'm just glad that no one beat me to it. How many times do I have to remind you that I remember everything about you, Brooke Anderson? I knew one day, I would create this moment for you – for us. So, now that this perfect date is out of the way … what else do you have in mind?" he said with a wink.

"I just can't believe you are real sometimes. You are just amazing, Rich Davis. I love you."

"And, I love you, sweets – forever."

"Now can you take me home? I want to make love to you, but I don't want to be cleaning sand out of my whooha for weeks," I said with a giggle.

"Your whooha?" Rich said with a raised brow. "I think you've been talking to Cass too much."

As we walked back to the car, I was a little disappointed that Rich hadn't asked me to marry him on the pier that day, or even under the stars, but I knew that Rich only had even grander plans up his sleeve for his proposal.

Chapter Twenty

It was our last day in Michigan and I was starting to think that Rich wasn't going to propose until we got back to D.C. I was a little disappointed I wouldn't be able to show my bling off to my best friend, but I could also show her over FaceTime.

While making a pot of coffee in Dad's kitchen, Rich found me and told me he'd made us plans for the afternoon. I was a little miffed as I'd been home nearly a week and still hadn't seen my two best girls. Cass had been busy with clients all week; July was the busiest time of year when it came to wedding planning.

She had planned on coming to visit earlier in the week, but I'd been feeling a bit under the weather. I chalked it up to lack of sleep and constantly being on the go since our arrival. I missed my own bed and my own place - I needed sleep. I loved being back in Michigan and spending time with my dad, but truth be told, this didn't feel like home anymore. When I was with Rich in D.C., I was at home.

Of course, I video-chatted with my girls at least every other day, but I was sure I would be shocked to see how much my little princess had grown. Rich must have seen the disappointed look on my face because he quickly added, "Don't worry sweets, my plans involve Cassidy and Kaitlyn, too."

"Really?"

"Yes, really. I know how much you miss them so I asked them to join us for the afternoon. But, that's all you're getting out of me. Now go throw on a pair of jeans and a sweatshirt – it might get chilly."

Even though it was July, the Michigan weather had been a bit unpredictable.

"Have I mentioned that I love you, Mr. Davis?"

"Mmmm, not in the last twenty minutes, Miss Anderson," he growled in his husky voice.

"Well, I do, Rich. I love you – to the moon and back."

"What I wouldn't do to make sweet love to you to the moon and back, but, since your three-year-old goddaughter will probably be storming through that door any minute now, and we're in your father's kitchen, that's probably not a good idea. But, you better be ready for me to pleasure every inch of your body later in the privacy of our bedroom," he added, with his signature smirk that instantly soaked my panties.

"Thanks, baby. Now I need to change my panties, too."

"Well, go baby. I don't want us to be late," he said, as he spanked my ass and lightly pushed me toward the bedroom.

I quickly changed clothes and was making my way back to the kitchen when I heard squeals coming from the living room.

"Long time no see, Davis," Cassidy said as she entered from the hallway.

"Hmmph, nice to see you too, Cassidy," Rich said, exchanging pleasantries.

"And, this must be the lovely Kaitlyn," Rich said, as he kneeled to get closer to the pint-sized toddler who was hugging her mom's leg for dear life.

"Who are you?" Kaitlyn asked.

"I'm Rich. I'm your Aunt Brooke's boyfriend. You must be Princess Kaitlyn. I've heard so much about you. It's so nice to finally meet you, Beautiful."

"Eew, boys have cooties! That's what Mommy says."

A deep belly laugh escaped Rich as I approached the three of them.

"She's definitely your daughter, Carpenter," he managed to sputter out between laughs.

"Aunt Brookie!" Kaitlyn exclaimed, as she broke away from her mom and ran toward me, grabbing my leg this time.

"Hey, Princess. Look how big you've gotten. You're almost as big as I am."

"Am not, Aunt Brookie. You silly," Kaitlyn giggled.

"Are you ready for our afternoon out? Rich here has a surprise for us girls."

"We're going out with ... a boy?"

I chuckled to myself; this poor little girl had so much to learn about boys. Her mother's warped feelings toward the opposite sex would need to change drastically before Kaitlyn became an angry teenager.

"Yes, Princess. We're going with a boy. His name is Rich. Can you say 'hi' to Rich? I promise he doesn't bite."

I heard Rich let out another laugh behind me, but chose to ignore his obvious innuendo.

Kaitlyn looked toward Rich with questioning eyes. "O----K, I guess. As long as he doesn't have cooties. Promise he doesn't have cooties, Aunt Brookie?"

"I promise."

"Hiiiiiiiiii, Rith," she squeaked out in her shy little voice. I could tell when the look in her eyes turned to pure bravery as she let go of my leg and ran into Rich's now open arms. *I swear in that moment I felt my ovaries flop inside my belly.*

It took only a few more minutes before Kaitlyn had made Rich her new, best friend. I collected my purse which I'd forgotten in the bedroom and upon returning was delighted to see that Kaitlyn was already riding on Rich's shoulders, as they all headed out the door. I stepped up my pace and quickly met up with them in the parking lot.

Cassidy scooped Kaitlyn off of Rich's shoulders and placed her in the car seat that Rich had already so thoughtfully placed in the back of our rental car. He opened my door and I slid into the passenger seat, then he placed a soft kiss on the top of my head before shutting the door.

"Where are we going?" I asked Cassidy, before Rich had made his way around the car.

"Ha! That's not my secret to tell, Brookie."

"Ugh, since when are you on HIS side?' I sighed in frustration.

Just then Rich opened his door. "She's not on anyone's side. She just knows who's boss," he added with his sexy wink.

"You two are evil! Just evil. Can't I have a little hint?"

"You'll have fun … how about that?" he quipped back.

"You're incorrigible."

"You love me anyways," he added teasingly.

"Hmph, you got me there," I said, as I stuck my tongue out in his direction.

"Better be careful, or I might just bite that tongue of yours."

"You wouldn't dare. Besides, I already told Kaitlyn that you didn't bite."

We drove most of the way while playing car games with Kaitlyn. Rich immediately suggested Truth or Dare, but I was familiar with his version so I quickly suggested the License Plate Game. Thankfully, Kaitlyn went with "Aunt Brookie's" suggestion.

Her infectious laughter filled the car each time she spotted a license plate from a different state. She asked if "Uncle Rith," as she almost immediately dubbed him, could play on her team. He agreed to both the game and his new moniker.

After about an hour had passed, and the team of Kaitlyn and Uncle Rich were kicking our butts, we arrived at, what I believed was our destination. I'd been so distracted by the game that I wasn't entirely sure where we were. I thought it was somewhere near Detroit, but, I honestly didn't really know.

Rich pulled into a deserted parking lot and I looked at him with a questioning stare.

He chuckled at my confusion before pulling what appeared to be a blindfold, from his pocket.

"What the heck are you doing to me?" I asked, a bit irritated.

"Relax, sweets. I don't want you to know where we're going yet. Let me put this on you, please."

"Just let him do it so we can get this show on the road," I heard from the backseat. "Yeah, Aunt Brookie," Kaitlyn chimed in, joining her mother.

"Great, now you have the peanut gallery on your side … again!"

They all erupted in laughter before I finally agreed and bent in Rich's direction so he could tie the silk around my head and over my eyes.

"Is it comfortable, baby? Can you see?" Rich questioned.

"Yes and no. Now let's go!"

I heard the car start and we were once again en route to our destination as I hoped we were. I felt the car come to a stop after another twenty minutes, or so.

"Can I take this thing off yet?"

"Not yet. I'll come help you out of the car." Rich answered.

"You've got to be kidding me," I huffed.

"Is that a big Ferris wheel with baseballs?" I heard Kaitlyn ask from the back seat.

Suddenly, I registered our location with the assistance of my inquisitive goddaughter.

"The jig's up, Rich, and company. We're at Comerica Park. You can remove the blindfold now, baby." I sputtered, as I stuck out my tongue in what, I hoped, was his direction.

"Be careful, sweets. I warned you earlier, I might just nip on that delectable tongue of yours."

Rich agreed and untied the scarf. He threw it in the backseat before we all exited the car and made our way to the entrance. I still hadn't forgotten about Rich's "secret" conversation with my father, nearly a week earlier.

Every time he had taken me out this week, I'd prepared myself for his proposal. I was starting to think it wasn't actually going to happen, at least, not any time soon. In fact, I knew it wasn't going to happen here of all places. Rich knew about my baseball experience with Jay and I was a little confused as to why he would choose this as a date for the short time we were home.

He always tried to convince me to watch a Tigers game with him when they were on local TV playing the Nationals, but I didn't want him getting any wild, idiotic ideas so I always graciously declined. I didn't want Rich to sense my disappointment though, because it appeared as if he'd put a lot of thought into our little "family" outing.

Kaitlyn, however, was in love with the entire adventure. The only thing about this afternoon that was putting a smile on my face was Kaitlyn's expression when Rich stopped to buy her a foam finger, hot dog, a pop, nachos, popcorn and cotton candy.

"I really hope that isn't all for her," Cassidy asked Rich, hesitantly.

"Nope, the nachos and popcorn are for us to share … and, maybe the cotton candy, but something tells me she won't be so willing to share that one," he chuckled, as we all looked toward Kaitlyn who already had her tiny fist in the plastic bag.

Cassidy grabbed the tray of food as Rich once again hoisted Kaitlyn onto his shoulders. She actually did share a bit of her airy confection as her tiny fingers dipped down to Rich's mouth.

"He's really great with her. I'll admit, I didn't think Davis had that 'daddy factor,' but he does, and it's pretty damn sexy," Cassidy said, as she gently punched my side.

"Yes … he is definitely pretty damn sexy. I think my ovaries are about to explode just watching him interact with her. He was the same way with his niece and nephew earlier this week."

"You are such a dork. I can't believe you just said that … I mean, really, who says that?" Cassidy remarked, shaking her head in disbelief.

We made our way to our seats, which of course, were amazing – thanks to Rich.

I actually found myself having a good time when I heard cheers erupting from the audience. It was between innings so it wasn't until I looked over to the Jumbotron that I realized the applause was for the kissing cam. I watched as several couples locked lips when suddenly I saw Rich's deep blue eyes and Hollywood smile staring at me from the big screen.

The crowd erupted once again and I knew I would only appease them if I leaned into him for a juicy kiss. I decided, I would give them all a show, too.

I puckered my lips and tilted my head, leaning into Rich, I didn't have to go very far before feeling his wet, velvety lips crash into mine. He grabbed the back of my head and pulled me in closer, while using his tongue to part my seam. I nibbled on the tip of his tongue as it gained entrance into my mouth.

"Get a room!" I heard someone shout from a few rows behind us.

"Um, you guys! You do realize there is a small child sitting next to you watching, right?" This time it was the familiar voice of my best friend trying to break our lips apart.

I chuckled against Rich's mouth as he began pulling away leaving a trail of light kisses on my mouth, nose and forehead, before disengaging completely.

I looked up and saw my feverish complexion engulf the screen as the entire crowd went wild.

"We're celebs, sweets!" Rich exclaimed.

All I could do was break down in a fit of laughter as the kissing cam moved on to its next victim. Although in that moment, I didn't feel like much of a victim.

We finished all of the ballpark food that Rich bought at the concession stand before the game started and I felt my belly begin to rumble.

"Hey, baby, I know you want another Bud Light, right?" I asked with the sexiest, pouty face I could muster.

Rich laughed at me as he answered, "Yeah, I could use another one, but something tells me you want me to walk all the way to the concession stand instead of asking that beer vendor only five feet away from us?"

"Pretty, please. I'll make it up to you later, I promise," I said in my most seductive tone.

He quickly hopped to his feet, "Oh, you bet you will. What can I get you, sweets?"

"Two hot dogs with light mustard and lots of pickles, please," I replied.

At that, he furrowed his brows, "I didn't think you liked pickles. Remember you get the chili poppers and I get the pickles? What are you – pregnant?" Rich said, jokingly.

"Um, no, definitely not pregnant – I'm always careful," I reminded him. "Sorry, they just sound delicious, that's all. Now go get me my dogs."

As Rich walked away, I had to take a moment to think about the question he had just posed. *Pregnant? Could I be? No, I've been on the pill longer than I can remember. Definitely not pregnant – I just needed to file that thought away for another day.*

The seventh-inning stretch was upon us, and I looked over to see Rich staring at me intently.

"What's going on, baby? Looks like you're thinking about something mighty hard over there," I commented.

He cleared his throat before speaking … "I want baseball games to leave a happy memory for you, Brooke. I wish I could erase the past from your memory, but we both know that's not possible. Our past made us who we are today. … And, I happen to love us … together. We may not be able to rewrite our history, but our future is certainly still unwritten. I want us to be Tigers fans for life, together. But, always remember this – win or lose … I will always love you," Rich confessed, with emotion laced in his voice.

The next thing I knew, Rich dropped to one knee on the hard cement in front of our third baseline seats as everyone around us was singing "Take Me Out to the Ball Game." He removed a Tiffany-blue, ring box from the pocket of his '84 World Series, throwback sweatshirt and looked straight into my eyes. I swear I could see straight into his heart at that very moment … His teal eyes which seemed to match the color of the box in his hands had never looked so clear – or so in love. He opened the box and inside I saw the most beautiful and elegant marquise-cut, diamond ring with a band of seed diamonds encircling the center stone.

"Brooke Christine Anderson, please say that you'll share my byline and write our future with me. Say you'll be my wife. Will you marry me?"

In that moment, my world stopped. Just like Rich had so beautifully said … "Our past made us who we are today. …" I flashbacked nearly twelve years to the moment that I ran smack dab into the most beautiful man. … To the moment he brushed against me while walking to the campus' recreation center on that chilly October evening. … To the moment, in a mirror image, I ran smack dab into his firm chest once again. … And, lastly, to him showering me with roses and silly trinkets on Valentine's Day.

"Are you going to leave me hangin' here, sweets? Or, are you going to make me the happiest man alive right now? I'd rather not have to ask you twice, but I will if I have to …" he added with a smirk.

"Yes! Of course, I'll write my future with you, Rich. We'll write our future, together. Yes, I will be your wife!"

With that said, Rich popped back up from his kneeling position and slipped the ring on my left hand. "I hope you like it, Brooke. I had a little help from Cassidy. She let me know about the rings you always drooled over while you two window-shopped at Tiffany's."

"Seriously, Rich? It's amazing. I love that it's not huge. It's elegant and understated and I couldn't have picked out a more perfect ring for myself. Oh wait, I guess I did pick it out, didn't I?" I added, as I lightly elbowed him in the side.

Putting his hands on the back of my head, Rich pulled me in for a passionate, yet chaste kiss. After all, we were in the midst of forty thousand other people, who with the exception of a handful of clapping fans around us, seemed to be oblivious to what I thought was the most beautiful proposal of all time. I could tell by the fervent look in Rich's eyes though, that he intended on making it up to me later.

Just then, we were both bombarded by my two favorite girls. "Eeeeeeeep, you said, 'yes!' Can I plan your wedding. Ahhhhhhh, we're planning your wedding. I can't wait. You know we're starting tomorrow, right. You seriously need to extend your vacation at least for a few more days. We have to find your dress!" Cassidy gushed.

"Whoa, chillax, baby dinosaur! He just proposed, we just got engaged. We haven't even set a date. I don't need to buy a dress tomorrow. But, yes, of course you can help plan my wedding. I wouldn't dream of anyone else at my side during this process."

In that moment, I got a little sad thinking that my mom wouldn't be with me to find my perfect wedding dress, or hold my hand as the nervous jitters took over on the morning of my wedding. She wouldn't cry from the front pew as my dad gave her only baby away, or cheer us on as the pastor told Rich that he could kiss his bride. She wouldn't dance with her son-in-law, or tenderly kiss me on the forehead as Rich and I escaped on our honeymoon.

Rich must have sensed my mood change to brief sadness and he reached out for my hand, making sure to run his thumb over my newly placed diamond.

"Hey, she'll still be with us," he whispered in my ear so only I could hear. "Dad, too, they'll both be watching over us; cheering us on."

I didn't know how he did it, but he always sensed when I was thinking about her and he always knew exactly what to say to ease my pain.

"So, did I still surprise you?" he asked, attempting to change the subject.

"Of course, what do you mean?"

"Don't act all innocent, Brooke. I heard you sneak away when you thought your dad and I had finished our conversation earlier this week. I had originally planned to propose to you during the fireworks, but you ruined that one. I had to come up with this one on the fly – with the help of Cass over there. I knew you would never expect me to propose at a baseball game of all places. Just so you know, though, I would've still gotten down on my knee – win or lose."

I thought it seemed fitting that the Tigers actually lost nine to eight that day to the Yankees. They tried rallying in the ninth inning, but fell a run short. Kaitlyn even turned the pink cap that Rich bought for her inside out, just like he showed her. The crowd came to life in that ninth inning singing, Journey's "Don't Stop Believin'." They erupted when the band sang the lyrics about "South Detroit." Being a Michigander, I never did quite understand that part. Where exactly is South Detroit? And, why have I never been there, or seen it on a map?

As we were leaving the stadium, I contemplated the team's loss. It didn't matter. Rich was right ... he wanted us to be Tigers fans for life and win or lose, he would always love me. And, I would always love him.

"I love you, Rich Michael Davis. Thank you for rewriting my memories of baseball, and for making me the happiest woman alive today," I told him, as we walked with our hands entwined back to his car.

"Oh, Brooke, you just think you're happy now. Wait until I get you back to our room ... I'll have you screaming with ecstasy."

His promise for later excited me so much that I let go of his hand and took off running for the car, leaving him in the dust, or so I thought. Moments later, I felt him grab me around my waist and hoist me over his shoulder, slapping my ass in the process.

"In a hurry, are you, my Future Mrs. Davis?"

"Y ...e...s," I managed to squeak out through my giggles. "Rich, put me down. We look ridiculous."

"Hold still, Brooke. We both know that I'm much faster on my feet than you, even if you do look adorable, trying to beat me in a race."

He bolted to the car as his hand began to make its way up the leg of my khaki shorts and onto my ass.

"Oh, only a thong for me today, huh?" Rich likey."

"Oh. em. gee. You didn't actually just say that! You are such a dork, baby," I remarked while rolling my eyes.

After a few short strides, Rich made it to the little red, Chevy Malibu he had rented for our weekend back home. It wasn't as luxurious as he was used to, but we were in Michigan so it seemed important to support the state's auto industry.

He opened my door with one hand, while the other remained firmly planted on my right butt cheek. He let go of my ass and my body slowly slid down the entire, firm length of him. He gave me a much too chaste kiss on the lips as we heard Cassidy and Kaitlyn giggling behind us. The two hopped in the back seat as Rich walked around to his side and dropped into the car.

Chapter Twenty-one

Cassidy decided to fly back with us for a few days after our vacation in Michigan. She was determined to find me the perfect wedding dress and since Rich wasn't able to take any more time off, she was forced to travel back with us. Cass left Kaitlyn with her mom, saying that she needed a few days of "adult time."

I was looking forward to the Washington D.C. Annual Firemen's Gala to which Rich had been invited because of his frequent donations to the department. I was also ecstatic that my fashionista of a best friend would be in the city to help me pick out the perfect dress for the occasion. Maybe if I let her help me pick out the perfect gown for the gala, she'd back off the wedding dress talk, at least, for the time being.

Rich insisted that I take a few extra days off work; he also wanted me to use his credit card while dress shopping. I suppose that since he was both my boss and fiancé now, I really wouldn't win any arguments and because I was shopping on his dime, if we'd been shopping on Rodeo Drive instead of downtown D.C., I would be playing the part of Julia Roberts in *Pretty Woman.*

I tried on several dresses before I finally found it. I remembered that day so many years ago when I'd found that perfect, purple gown for my sorority's formal. Rich was my date all those years ago and this time he was so much more than just my date – he was my fiancé. *My fiancé. I was still having trouble wrapping my mind around that thought.*

"Hey Brookie, are you going to come out of that fitting room and show me, or are you just going to keep giggling like a school girl? I swear you're worse than Kaitlyn."

I walked out and I knew it was a winner when Cassidy's eyes and mouth opened wide.

"You're gorgeous, Brooke. That's the one."

She was right, it was the one. The Badgley Mischka sequin, tulle, combo dress in emerald hung perfectly on my curvy body. The sleeveless bodice accentuated my toned arms – perfectly. I had been spending a few extra hours in my apartment's gym each week and it was actually starting to pay off. I knew I could complete the look with the teardrop earrings that Rich had given me on my birthday and a simple, yet timeless, pair of black heels.

I was pulling my debit card out of my purse to pay for my purchase when I heard a text message come through on my phone.

> *Rich: You better use my credit card, and spend an insane amount of money, or you will be getting a spanking later.*
>
> *Yes, boss …errr, fiancé.*

Rich: You might get a spanking, anyways. You know what they say. A spanking is just a round of applause for a magnificent ass and trust me that ass of yours is MAGNIFICENT!

I rolled my eyes and chuckled to myself as I stuffed my phone back into my purse. I almost wanted to defy him just to see if he would actually follow through with his threats. Honestly, the thought of him spanking me into submission was something I was willing to explore.

I purchased the gown, with Rich's credit card, as instructed, and Cassidy and I went to the same deli that Rich took me to on my first afternoon in D.C. I usually loved the aroma of the freshly baked breads, pies and homemade soups, but today for some reason the scent was causing my stomach to turn in every direction.

"Are you OK, Brookie? You look a little pale."

"Yeah, I'm fine. I'm just feeling a little nauseous all of a sudden. Remember, I was under the weather last week, probably just not a hundred percent yet. I'll just drink some water. I should be fine."

"Weren't you craving pickles the other day, too?"

"Yeah, what does that have to do with anything?"

"Seriously? You don't know why I'm asking? Are you pregnant?" Cassidy blurted out.

"Why does everyone keep asking me that? Of course I'm not pregnant. Rich and I have always been careful."

"Um, you know nothing is one-hundred-percent effective, right?"

My mind began spinning ... When was my last period? Now that I think about it, I don't really remember. Am I late? Rich and I just got engaged. We've only been together for a few months. We don't even live together. I assume we will move in together before the wedding, but we hadn't really discussed it yet. What if Rich doesn't even want kids? We haven't talked about that yet, either. This can't be happening. Not yet, anyways.

"Brooke, are you OK in there?"

Tears were beginning to stream down my face, "I just can't be pregnant now, Cass. This isn't a good time."

"Oh, Brookie, it's never a good time. But, once you see those two lines on that test it will seem like the perfect time. Trust me, I know. Now, let's get you a bottle of water and get out of here. We need to make a stop at the drugstore before we go home, though."

I was leaning against the vanity in my bathroom as the cold tile against my bare feet sent a shiver up my spine. I had read the directions on the back of the pregnancy tests four times. *Yes, I said tests. I bought four different brands ... You know, just to be sure.* I heard a knock on the other side of the bathroom door as I was reading the third test for a fifth time.

"Need some help in there?" Cass questioned.

"Um, no, I think I got it. Pee on the stick, right? How hard can it be?"

"Shut up, Brookie. You know what I meant. Do you need me to come hold your hand while you wait for the results?"

"No, let me do my business and I'll be right out. You can hold my hand then."

Just a few minutes later, after I had peed on three different sticks, I came out to wait the allotted time with Cassidy at my side.

"Thanks for being here with me. I don't know what I would do right now without you." I told her.

"Well, you know I wouldn't be anyplace else. You were with me through it all with Kaitlyn. But, the difference between you and me, babe, is that you have Rich. He won't leave you like the jackass left me. He will love you and your baby, whether you have one in nine months, or nine years."

"Nine years seems a bit drastic," I laughed. "By some standards, I'd be over the hill by then!"

My cell phone beeped, alerting us that the necessary amount of time had passed.

"Do you want me to look for you?" Cass asked.

"No ... yes ... no ... I don't know," Before I had time to make a decision, Cass was back in the bedroom with the stick in her hand.

"Well ..." I asked.

Please be yes, please be yes ... Wait, did I really want this baby? Wasn't this a bad time? Yes, it may not be perfect timing, but I wanted a positive test result.

"You're going to be a Mommy! And, I'm going to be an Auntie!" she said, practically screaming.

The tears that I'd been holding back came out in full force.

"Oh, Brookie, don't cry. This will be a good thing, you'll see."

"These ... these are ... happy ... happy tears ... I ... promise," I said between sobs. "I'm going to be a little person's Mommy," I added while looking up at my best friend with what, I assume, was a grin wider than the moon.

We both started dancing around the room. All my previous fears had vanished, and I couldn't wait to tell my fiancé that he was going to be a daddy.

I decided that I would keep my little secret from Rich for just a few days and since the Firemen's Gala was the day before his thirty-second birthday, I would surprise him with my gift when the clock struck midnight.

I'd been feeling pretty well aside from a few bouts of morning sickness that I'd been able to hide from Rich. Because Cass was still in town, I was able to use her as my excuse for not staying with Rich at his apartment.

I took Cass to the airport on the morning of the gala. I would say that I'd become much more emotional since I found out I was pregnant. Saying goodbye to my best friend would be harder this time around, I knew.

We said our tearful goodbyes and I promised her I would be back in Michigan soon to talk about the wedding. She had grandiose dreams of a summertime beach wedding, while I was thinking of a much simpler winter affair. I told her I would think about her ideas, before squeezing her tightly and watching her walk through the airport's revolving doors.

After dropping off Cass, I decided to spend the day pampering myself at a nearby salon. I splurged and got the "exclusive package" which included a prenatal massage, pedicure, manicure, facial, up-do and makeup. When I looked in the mirror, I hardly recognized myself. I looked refreshing – glowing even. I always thought it was strange when people said that pregnant women had a "glow" about them, but maybe it was actually true.

When I returned home, I had just enough time to slip into my Badgley Mischka gown. I admired my figure in the mirror. I wouldn't keep my toned figure much longer, but standing there I placed my hands on my barely-there baby bump and smiled at the thought of a much rounder, fuller belly. I even welcomed a stretch mark or two. *After all, it was a rite of passage*, I mused to myself.

Rich had sent me a text message on my way home and said he was running late and would send the driver to pick me up. He had to run home and change into his tux and would meet me at the gala. I heard a knock on my door, and opened it to find Roger on the other side.

"Miss Anderson, your limo is waiting downstairs. I just came up to escort you down."

"Thank you, Roger. I just need to grab my purse."

I walked to the counter and picked up my clutch, making sure that Rich's birthday gift was tucked inside.

"All set," I told Roger, as I wrapped my arm through his.

I first saw my handsome fiancé, standing by the entrance of the St. Regis. He was leaning against the old-brick with one leg propped up behind him. His Armani tuxedo hung on his body perfectly. He really knew how to wear a tux.

I sat in the limo, for several minutes watching him, as we waited our turn in line. I had to chuckle at the number of women he turned away. I couldn't blame them for trying, he really was the epitome of perfection. He was smart, sophisticated, gorgeous – and, to top it off, a pure gentleman. Well, he is now, anyways, I chuckled to myself; I really had struck the jackpot this time.

We finally made it to the entrance, and my chauffeur came around to escort me to my breathtaking man. Rich's eyes brightened and his movie star smile appeared the moment he saw me.

"Hello, stranger. Waiting for someone, or would you care to have a dance with me inside?" I asked slyly.

"Well, hello, pretty lady," he said in his best southern twang, "I am waiting for my beautiful fiancée, but I don't think she'd mind if I danced with someone as ravishingly gorgeous as yourself. That dress is stunning on you. It really brings out the color of your eyes."

"Thank you, kind sir, but if I didn't know any better, I'd think you were hitting on me. I hope your fiancée isn't the jealous type."

"She knows I only have eyes for her."

With that, Rich escorted me into the gala and straight for the dance floor. We waltzed around the stage for several minutes, until the band finally played a song I recognized. Rich grinned as he pulled me closer to him, and twirled me around. We had danced to the Hunter Hayes song in our living room before, but now we had an audience. Rich began softly singing so only my ears could hear his sultry voice.

"Cause I wanna wrap you up. Wanna kiss your lips. I wanna make you feel wanted. And I wanna call you mine. Wanna hold your hand forever."

We danced around the ballroom floor just as we had in Rich's living room, like we were the only two people in the world. When the song finished, Rich escorted me back to our table and we enjoyed a fabulous catered meal of prime rib, garlic mashed potatoes and a seasonal vegetable medley. I didn't want to tip Rich off before my big birthday surprise, so I slowly nursed a glass of champagne before privately asking our waiter to refill my glass with sparkling, white grape juice. I was also relieved that Aubrey Sullivan didn't show up to this event and ruin my night.

Rich and I took to the dance floor a few more times before the gala began to wind down. It was just before midnight as Rich escorted me back to the limousine. The timing couldn't have been any more perfect. We were sitting hand in hand when I caught the time on Rich's Rolex. *Damn these pregnancy hormones were something else ... How was it even possible that his wrist alone made a watch look sexy?* Midnight. Showtime.

I loosened my hand from Rich's grasp and opened my clutch to pull out his gift.

"It's midnight, baby. Happy Birthday! I have a little surprise gift for you. I hope you love it as much as I do."

"I'll love anything you have to give me, Brooke. I'm sure it's just perfect."

I gave Rich the teeny-tiny box that I had meticulously wrapped in silver foil paper. He unwrapped it and unfolded the piece of paper that I had placed inside.

Redeemable for one baby
— Available February 2013

Rich just stared at it – tears forming in his eyes. "Does this mean ... does this mean that you're pregnant ... we're having a baby?"

"Yes, Rich. I'm pregnant and having your baby."

He pulled me into his chest and began kissing me all over – starting with the top of my head to the tip of my nose and finally on my lips. They weren't his typical, heated kisses, but passionate and sensual, nonetheless.

"I didn't think it was possible to love you any more than I did, Brooke. But, I do. You've just made me the happiest man on this Earth. Thank you for finally agreeing to let me into your life, for agreeing to be my wife and for allowing a part of me to grow in your body. I love you more than words can ever express. You are My Everything, Brooke Christine Anderson. My one and only; my always and forever."

Chapter Twenty-two

Early September 2012

I woke up to the sound of a loud thud, followed by harsh cursing, and noticed the time on my bedside clock read shortly after six. I stretched out and didn't feel Rich next to me in our bed. *It was still unbelievable to think that the two of us finally shared a bed and an apartment. It had taken us nearly thirteen years, but we were finally where we belonged ... together.* I snapped out of my daydream as I heard more cursing coming from our huge walk-in closet. I slipped out of bed and padded my way to the closet to see what kind of trouble my fiancé was causing.

"You all right in there, baby? It kind of sounds like our closet is beating your ass."

"Yeah, something like that, sweets. Put it on the scoreboard ... Rich –zero; closet –one. I can't find the damn green tie I want to wear to the rally. One of your bins of shoes just fell on my toe. Do you really think eight hundred pairs of shoes are necessary?

Come to think of it ... it's more like, Rich-zero; closet-two. Sorry, I woke you up though," he said, as he grabbed me for a long and drawn out kiss.

"Well, good morning to you too, Mr. Davis. And, I think you're being just a little dramatic. I probably only have six hundred pairs," I refuted with a wink. "I'll go make you some coffee while you continue to duke it out with our closet ... just don't let any of my shoes get hurt in your dispute. Oh, and baby, let me know if you need help packing."

He smacked my ass which was barely covered in a pair of cotton, boy shorts which read "Kiss it" right over my bum.

I heard him yell, "I plan on it," as I sashayed out of the bedroom.

Rich had kindly agreed, or more like insisted, to cover my assignment in New York City this weekend. There was a political rally scheduled for an upcoming tax bill and all the political bigwigs who sponsored the bill were supposed to be in attendance. Since it was an election year, it was important for the *Washington Post* to cover the rally.

I was originally intending to cover it since my recent promotion to government editor, but ever since we found out I was pregnant, Rich had become overly protective of me and our baby. I can't say I was disappointed when he insisted on going because the thought of flying did not sound appealing right now.

Even though I was still very early on in my pregnancy, I didn't want to risk anything, either. I wish someone besides Rich could go in my place, but this really was an assignment for a seasoned journalist and everyone else with the necessary skills was already booked for the weekend.

Rich sauntered out of the bedroom with his suitcase rolling behind. He looked ravishing with his navy Polo shirt which hugged his biceps perfectly, and his dark wash jeans which hung low on his hips. His hair was still damp from his shower and just the sight of him along with my raging pregnancy hormones had me about ready to pounce.

"Brooke, you need to put your tongue back in your mouth. You're about to drool all over your chin," he said, comically.

"Shut up, I was not drooling. You just look mighty fine this morning, Mr. Davis. ... It didn't take you long to pack. Are you sure you remembered everything?"

"Yes, sweets. I don't need twelve bags like someone else I know. It's just for two nights. ... And, I think I have some time before I need to leave for the airport. Why don't we try and satisfy your salacious appetite before I head out, Miss Anderson."

Suddenly, Rich grabbed my ass and hoisted me onto our kitchen island. He took my hands in his and brought each one to his mouth where he placed a gentle kiss on each before lifting my arms above my head and instructing me to keep them in that position. He gently gripped the hem of my tank top before pulling it up and allowing it to graze over my naval and my plump breasts. I quivered as the soft cotton flicked over the tips of my overly sensitive nipples.

After Rich removed my top, I couldn't keep my hands off his body any longer. I grabbed onto his muscular shoulders and pulled him closer so I could nuzzle into his neck. He smelled of the same scent that I had longed for during the previous thirteen years. I began frantically nipping the area between his ear and chin and would swear I heard him growl.

"Oh, sweetheart, you're being a naughty, naughty girl. Lay back. ... We need to remove these panties so I can properly kiss that ass of yours."

Again, I followed his instructions and laid my bare backside on the cold granite countertop. He ran just one of his fingers from my lips down my entire body, stopping to play with each nipple a bit more before continuing down the path to my panties. I lifted my ass ever so slightly so he could easily remove the small piece of cotton that got in his way of pleasuring me completely. I felt my panties slide down my bare legs and finally ending at my feet and toes before I heard them lightly fall to the floor. I already felt my sex oozing with pleasure even before I felt his mouth, without warning, latch onto my clit. I gasped at the sudden gratification.

"I love how your body responds to me. You are so fuckin' beautiful, my love," he said between nips. I began to quiver and felt my orgasm coming on - unabated.

"Don't let go yet, Brooke. I need to be inside when you ... when we ... release together."

Before I could even take another breath, Rich removed his mouth from my pussy and I heard him unbuckle his belt. Within seconds, I felt the head of his already fully erect cock brush against the spot his tongue had just abandoned. I felt a shiver of anticipation course through my body.

"I'm going to fuck you hard, sweets. I need this to last me for days."

UNWRITTEN

With that, Rich slammed into my ready and juicy pussy as I wrapped my legs around his waist and my backside remained planted against the cold granite countertop. He slammed into me several times and leaned forward just enough to flick and pinch my alert tits.

"Rich ... I love you. I'm going to come, baby. Please. let. me. come," I begged.

At my request, he began banging into me with carnal force and I knew he was going to come apart in a matter of seconds. Feeling my own release, I heard him scream my name. I was seeing the colors of the rainbow and convulsing with pleasure, as I felt Rich come unhinged inside me.

"Oh. my. god. You make me feel like such a man, Brooke. I love you so damn much," gasped Rich.

He fell against me on the counter for a moment before gently kissing my lips as his warm, swollen dick remained nestled in my body. Placing one last kiss on my cheek, he eased out of me.

"I need to clean myself up so I can catch my flight," he said, with a hint of exhaustion in his voice. "I would ask you to join me, but I'd surely be late."

"Next time, baby. There will always be next time," I reassured him.

With that, Rich ran to the bathroom to clean up before heading to the airport. I found my shirt half in the sink and threw it back over my shoulders before Rich returned to the kitchen with a frown on his face.

"Babe, you covered Hugs and Kisses," he said, using the pet names he had given my boobs.

"Yes, I did," I said, rolling my eyes. "You need to get going and I need to get myself showered and ready for work, Handsome. We don't have time for another rendezvous this morning, but you better be ready when you get back. This pregnant fiancée of yours is constantly in need of you and that sexilicious body of you--."

He cut me off as his lips met mine in a heated kiss. After our lips parted, he leaned down and kissed my belly.

"Bye my little Roly Poly. Daddy loves you. Be good for Mommy,"' he cooed.

I nearly melted each time I heard Rich refer to our baby as his "Roly Poly." He dubbed the fetus during our first ultrasound when the little squirt wouldn't stop moving. It was during that moment that we decided not to determine the sex of our "Roly Poly" until birth. After all, he or she probably wouldn't cooperate, anyways.

I watched from our penthouse window as Rich tossed his bags into the trunk of our new Cadillac Escalade. He insisted on buying a bigger and "safer" vehicle ever since we learned about the new addition to our family. Rich walked to the driver's side and hopped into the SUV before pulling away from the curb and into traffic.

We hadn't been apart for more than a day since he showed up at my doorstep on Valentine's Day. So much had happened in the last year. A smile crept across my face as I padded to the bathroom to wash our morning sex off my body and get ready for a typical day at the offices of the *Post* – if you could really call any day "typical" in the news industry.

Chapter Twenty-three

I was in the middle of transcribing an interview with the district's representative for a story I was working on, when the phone chimed on my desk. That's something else that Rich immediately changed after I finally agreed to our relationship. Although he still wouldn't fully admit to giving me fluff pieces as punishment for my stubbornness, I found it rather ironic that I'd received nothing but the elite assignments since Valentine's Day.

> *Rich: Flight just landed ... heading to the hotel before I'm due at the Rally in a little over an hour. Miss you, sweets. XX*
>
> *Glad you made it safely. I hope you weren't stuck next to any funky peacocks on your flight. Miss you and I'll talk to you tonight. XX*

I had to laugh a little to myself with my "funky peacock" reference. He had mentioned a person whom he'd seen once on a flight, who was dressed in very bold 1980s colors and patterns, and with crazy hair. Rich referred to this particular passenger as a "funky peacock" and the image he painted causes hysterical fits of laughter to come over me even to this day.

> *Rich: No, didn't come across any funky peacocks today. Thank God. I just had grandma sitting next to me showing me pictures of her grandkids the entire flight. They were adorable and I'm not gonna lie, I might have gushed about my Roly Poly just a tad. Now your boss says to get back to work! ;) XX*
>
> *Yes, boss ... Anything else, boss? ;)*
>
> *Rich: Behave ...*

While shaking my head at my mischievous fiancé, I set my phone back down and continued with my article. Before I knew it another hour had passed and my growling stomach alerted me that I had worked right through my usual lunch hour. As if right on cue, Caroline lightly knocked on my door before letting herself in.

"Did you forget to eat again?" she asked.

"Let me guess ... your boss making you check up on me?" I questioned with a raised brow.

"Well, maybe, but I need to eat too and we have some catching up to do. Want to hit Duffy's for a burger and fries? They shouldn't be too busy since it's past the noon lunch rush.

"Sure, I'm starving and a burger and fries sounds like just what the doctor ordered ... or, maybe in my case, what this baby ordered. I swear this thing is going to turn ME into the Roly Poly in the next nine months."

We decided to walk to Duffy's, a traditional Irish pub, which was located only two blocks from the office. Caroline was right – the lunch traffic had ceased and we were able to get an open booth in the back. A few guys were sitting at the bar indulging in some early Friday afternoon Guinness. I suppose some people really take the phrase, "It's five o'clock somewhere," to heart.

My eyes were suddenly drawn to the brightly colored, neon sign hanging in the restaurant's window. It was a green shamrock with a red flashing Duffy's in the center. I couldn't help but think the flashing red center resembled that of the light bar of a police car ... or, an ambulance. With the thought of an ambulance, a chill ran right up my spine and straight though my body. I couldn't help sink the bad thoughts that traveled to my brain ... Rich ... ambulance ...

I lunged for my purse, not even noticing the vivacious waitress that had come to our booth to collect our drink orders.

"Brooke, are you OK?" Caroline asked. She turned to tell our waitress that we needed a few additional moments, so she wouldn't be a witness to my sudden and apparent mental collapse.

"Brooke, seriously, you are scaring me. What the hell is wrong with you? Is it the baby?"

When I ignored her and continued to frantically rummage through my overly large, shoulder bag ... she must have become frustrated with me.

"Brooke, answer me, already! What's wrong with you? You look like you just saw a ghost."

I finally found my phone and checked the time before answering Caroline. It was nearly three o'clock. Rich should be at the rally by now.

"I don't know, Caroline. I just got this feeling. I don't know how to explain it. I need to get a hold of Rich. Can you just order us some burgers to go, please?"

Caroline didn't ask any further questions as she called for the waitress to order our lunch to-go.

At that point, I quickly typed out a quick text to Rich.

> *Hey baby, I'm guessing you should be at the rally by now. I hope I'm not missing anything too exciting. I'm sure you're just thrilled to death, lol. ... I know how much you love all of that political propaganda as you've called it since as long as I've known you. Anyways, just thinking about you. Please text me back so I know you made it safely ... please. XX*

I kept looking down at my phone while we waited for our to-go orders. I still hadn't heard back from Rich. I knew he was probably busy, but it wasn't like him to not respond with at least a "XX." We had chosen that as our sign for busy, but thinking of you.

I was growing impatient with each passing minute. My pregnant and empty stomach was not taking the sudden stress very well and I literally thought that I was going to begin dry heaving right then and there.

I excused myself and made my way to the ladies' room where I broke into hysterical sobs and began pleading with my phone to signal with a text from Rich. *What the hell was wrong with me? Was the pregnancy causing me to lose my fucking mind? I really need to consider seeing a shrink.*

As I leaned against the wall near the hand dryers and scooted my butt toward the floor, I shot Rich a second text.

Baby, you really need to text me. Please ... 911.

After several minutes and still nothing from Rich, Caroline stormed into the restroom and found me sunken on the bathroom floor with tears and mascara running from my eyes onto my cheeks. She gathered me into a hug and helped pick me up off the dirty and freezing, tile floor.

"Come on, Brooke. Our waitress has our food ready. Let's get you back to the office. Take a few, deep breaths. You need to relax ... for the baby's sake."

We grabbed our food and Caroline practically had to drag me back to the office. As we walked through the doors and into the newsroom, I knew immediately something big was happening, somewhere across the nation. Usually, when you walked into the newsroom, it's relatively quiet with just a few TV monitors playing the world news in the background, the tapping of computer keys and the buzzing from the police scanner.

This afternoon, however, every reporter was either running around in a mad frenzy, or talking frantically into their phones. Once I took in the scene around me, I focused my attention on the television which was playing live breaking news from New York City. I read the news ticker located at the bottom of the screen:

**BREAKING NEWS:
SHOTS FIRED, BY SEVERAL MASKED GUNMEN,
AT POLITICAL TAX RALLY IN NYC. THIRTEEN
CONFIRMED DEAD AND SEVERAL HUNDRED
INJURED.**

My mind swirled and my legs shook. All I remember before crashing down to the floor was a loud scream which I believe to have been my own. That's all I remember until I woke up in what looked like a hospital room with a pounding headache. I was shocked to see Cassidy and my dad both hovering over me.

"Why are you two here? How ... how long have I been out?" I moaned, as the bright hospital lights glared over me.

"Shhhh, Brooke, you've been out for over twenty-four hours. We've been so worried about you," my dad said, as he looked over toward Cassidy.

I recognized that look in my dad's eyes. It was a look of concern mixed with sadness. It had been the same look I'd seen when the nurse told us that my mother hadn't made it. And, Cassidy already had tear tracks running down her normally rosy cheeks.

"Oh God, something is wrong, isn't it? Wait, Rich should be here with you two," I started to panic and bile formed in my throat. "Rich ... where's, Rich?" I managed to squeak out before uncontrollable sobs rocked my body as I remembered the ticker I had read the day before – *Thirteen confirmed dead ...*

UNWRITTEN

The continuation of *Unwritten* will be available in *Unscripted,* coming in 2015.

Acknowledgements

First and foremost, I want to thank my husband for his support throughout this wild ride. Without his constant jokes about *Unwritten* remaining "unwritten," I'm not sure I would have actually finished. My inspiration and guiding force was to tell him that *Unwritten* was in fact "written!" To, Megan, my BBOPOF - yes, it's true - we really did create the texting language long before texting was even a real thing. You've been my sounding board throughout this entire process. You've been with Rich and Brooke since the beginning and I couldn't have done it without you. Seriously, I'm pretty sure *Unwritten* would only have a beginning and an end. Love you!

To my dad - there really aren't any words - you've been the best dad a girl could ask for and I wouldn't be the woman I am today without you. Thank you!

To, Angie, my real-life, "Cassidy" - you've been by my side for more years than I care to publically admit. Thank you for still talking to me even though you knew I was constantly taking notes for my book! Just wait until there is just a book about you! I love you to the moon and back!

To my beta readers, especially Aubrea and Jill – I couldn't have done it without you ladies! Thank you for taking the time to help me, give me suggestions, advice and answer my unending questions!

To my PA, Melissa – thank you for your support and pimping! My Facebook page would be sad without you!

To my WBW: MB, Cali and Sauce – I may have found you ladies later in the game, but I am so glad I have you girls now! Your support, ideas and friendship mean the world to me! I am so proud to call each of you my friend!

To Lisa and Jesey at Truly Schmexy Promotions – thank you for helping this newbie author out with the behind-the-scenes work! You have no idea how much your support means to me.

To all of the amazing ladies that worked to beautify *Unwritten*: my fabulous cover designer, Kari Ayasha at Cover to Cover Designs, for designing such a beautiful cover; Mandy Hollis of MHPhotography for the beautiful cover photography; and Christine Borgford of Perfectly Publishable for the stunning inside formatting – thank you!

To the indie authors I've met along the way who've been willing to offer advice and friendship, especially: Annica Rossi, Riley Mackenzie, Corinne Michaels, Gia Riley and Beth Ehemann – there aren't enough words to express my appreciation.

To the bloggers that have shared in the cover reveal, reviewed and promoted *Unwritten* – none of this would be possible without your constant hard work and dedication. An especially, big heartfelt thank you to Jesey, Trish, Jennifer and Amy at Schmexy Girl Book Blog, Stacia at Three Girls and a Book Obsession, Sharon at Sassy Savvy Fabulous Book Blog and Christina at The Book Vamps.

To all of my Schmexy ladies – you know who you are – I started on this reading (and eventually writing) journey because of you. Over the last year, I've made some of the best friendships that I could ever have imagined. One day, we will all be in the same room; we will clear all of the booze from behind the bar and dance on some tables!

To my readers – since you've made it this far, I can only assume you have finished. I hope you've come to love Rich and Brooke as much as I do. There are so many wonderful books to choose from and I am truly honored that you took the time to read my story! Thank you from the bottom of my heart!

Please feel free to join my Facebook group to talk about *Unwritten*. Plus keep up with news regarding the sequel, *Unscripted*.